JUST ROOM-MATES

USA TODAY BESTSELLING AUTHOR

CHARITY FERRELL

www.charityferrell.com

Cover Designer: Charity Ferrell

Cover Photo Photographer: Lindee Robinson Photography

Cover Photo Model: AC Parker

Editor: Jovana Shirley, Unforeseen Editing, www.unforeseenediting.com

CHAPTER ONE

Sierra

Age Eighteen

"SHOW ME YOUR ID."

I'm startled by the edgy voice, and my path is blocked when a powerful body stands in front of me.

Oh shit.

On my What Could Go Wrong list, this is at the top.

I shift to the right, planning to make a run for it, but he cuts me off.

Please don't be him.

If it's him, I'll die of embarrassment right here at his feet. At least the last person I'll see before meeting death is good eye candy.

My heartbeat rages out of control while I nervously lift my gaze. I gulp when my eyes set on a face darkened with frustration.

If this is a dream, it's not how I imagined one starring him would go.

It was more along the lines of me seducing him. Kissing. Us naked.

We've never crossed paths, but I know who *he* is.

Maliki Bridges, the owner of the Down Home Pub, the bar my eighteen-year-old ass snuck into.

A wave of light-headedness hits me—not from the liquor, but his presence.

I'm going to kill Ellie.

This was all her genius idea.

"We'll totally be fine, chicken," she insisted while we sipped wine coolers in her parents' basement. "Leo said as long as we stay in the corner with his friends, we're as good as gold."

There wasn't much else to do in our small town of Blue Beech, Iowa, so I stupidly changed clothes, tugged on a black baseball cap, and put on a fresh coat of red lipstick—all attempts at looking old enough to hang out in a bar.

Our plan was running smoothly. The guys ordered our drinks from the bar and carried them to us. It was all fun and games until I needed a restroom break.

And that's what brought me here—scrunched in a narrow, dimly lit hallway with a hot and very pissed off man.

Maliki crosses his arms and taps his foot. "I'm waiting."

I start to respond but shut my mouth at the realization that I'm holding a drink.

"Shit," I hiss under my breath—although it comes out louder than what I intended.

I shove the glass behind my back, and his glare hardens, as if I were a child.

Okay, or the teenager I am.

The clamor of other bar patrons fades away, and my heart races as I give myself an internal pep talk. I blow out a long breath and give him my signature *I'm innocent* smile—my *get out of jail* smirk, as Ellie calls it. It carries a high success rate of my parents' cluelessness to me doing shit like this.

I dramatically gasp, my open hand flying to my chest. "Oh my God! I must've forgotten it. I swear, with the four kiddos at home, I always forget something."

The irritation on his face doesn't falter.

I'm a terrible fucking liar.

Four kids? Really?

I should've gone with one … one and a half.

"ID," he demands again, his tone destroying any playfulness in mine.

Get out of jail smirk *crashed and burned.*

I reluctantly unzip my bag and retrieve what he wants, knowing damn well it'll make my circumstances worse. If I don't give him *something,* I'm definitely getting thrown out. My smile stays intact when I hand it to him.

"You could've at least given me a fake, Princess," he says, unimpressed.

Yeah, well, I don't own one, jackass. Otherwise, I would've.

I hold back the urge to roll my eyes. "I'm …" I stutter for the right words. "I'm waiting for my *of age* ID to arrive in the mail. You see, there was an error with this one. They mailed out a new one, but my postman broke his leg … and his knee was reconstructed … so he can't walk and deliver anything to our mailbox."

Dear God.

I'm rambling.

A rambler is always guilty.

Maliki cuts me off, "Spare me the lies. Everyone in this town knows who you are." He jerks his head toward the same door I strolled through earlier, huddled between Leo's friends. "Now, let's get you back to your pink bedroom covered with posters of boy-band heartthrobs." He moves his hand in a shooing motion as if I were a bug.

Okay, seriously rude.

"You suck," I grumble but then perk up as something hits me. "I'm a paying customer." *Well, Leo's friends are paying customers.* If he knows he'll make money off me, he might let me stay.

"Tough shit," he fires back. "I can't have teenyboppers sneaking into my bar."

I twirl a finger in his direction. "You wait until I'm twenty-one. I'll be here *every day* to annoy you."

He smirks and pats my head over my hat. "I'll appreciate the business in the future, little one." He gestures to the door again. "See your legal ass in a few years. You can exit the same way you snuck in."

I'm holding it together but close to losing my shit. Not only am I nervous about getting in trouble, but this is also *Maliki Bridges.*

He's the town's bartending heartbreaker—a man no woman has tamed, no matter how hard they've tried to hold him down. Rumor is, three women have dropped to their knees and proposed *to him.* A single, attractive man in this town is rare. It's *his* choice not to settle down.

I've heard plenty of gossip about him. He's funny—which so far, I've yet to agree with—and he always offers a helping hand to anyone in need.

"Whoa! Wait!" I shriek. My drink comes into view when I dart my hands out to stop him from leading me to the door. Him seeing my strawberry daiquiri is now the least of my worries. I'm stunned when he pauses and waits for me to explain. "You can't kick me out yet!"

"*And* that's where you're wrong, Princess."

"I have no ride home."

"Isn't your Barbie Jeep waiting for you outside?"

I throw him a death stare. "The battery is dead actually." My attention drifts to Leo's friends and the empty stool I safely sat in until my bladder turned on me. "I rode with a friend."

He takes a quick glance at the guys before looking back at me. "You came with *those* little assholes?"

I chew at my bottom lip. "Just a friendly tip: you might not want to refer to your customers as *little assholes* if you want to stay in business."

He yanks the daiquiri from my hand and points to my bag with it. "Call your parents."

"Absolutely under no circumstances is that happening. I'd rather you pour that drink over my head." I lower my tone. "Do you know who my father is?"

"Sure as fuck do, *Sierra Lane.*"

"Then, you know he'll kill me if I call, asking for a ride home from *a bar.*" I swallow. "*And* given he's the mayor of this town, there's no doubt he'll make it his mission to create problems for you. He'll want this place shut down, so the innocent children of Blue Beech can't sneak into your big, bad bar."

His jaw clenches. He knows I'm right. "Call your brother then."

"He's out of town."

He rubs the back of his neck, now appearing stressed. "A friend."

I groan. "*Fine.* I'll call someone, but it'll take them time to get here." I motion toward Leo's friends. "I'll hang out over there until they do."

Ten minutes ago, Leo received a call, needing to run a quick errand. Ellie joined him, and instead of tagging along, his friends offered to keep me company.

Maliki shoves my ID into his back pocket and catches my elbow in his fist. "Nice try, Miss Teen Blue Beech. You can wait in my office until they get here. I'll grab you a coloring book to pass the time." His grip is firm as he pulls me out of the hallway and to the edge of the crowd, hiding me the same way Leo's friends did.

"Won't you taking me to your office look worse than allowing me to enjoy a few drinks?" I ask behind him, struggling to not stumble in my heels.

His gaze flashes back to me. "You're too young to be in a bar, Sierra, not too young to fuck."

I slam my mouth shut.

Fair point.

I lick my lips, hoping I don't mess up my lipstick. Unfortunately, he looks as interested in fucking me as he does in serving me drinks.

He leads me through swinging double doors and down another hallway, and then he pushes me into a cramped office. A black desk with a computer and a tattered chair are the only furniture. The door slamming shut startles me, and Maliki strides around the desk.

He opens a drawer, drags out a sheet of paper and pen, and slaps them onto the desk. "I promised coloring books, but this is all I have."

I study him up close. I've admired him from afar—once at the grocery store and another time when he was running shirtless in Town Square before I rear-ended the minivan in front of me, unable to take my eyes off him—but he's more attractive in person. Captivating. Defined muscles are underneath his black tee that has the bar's logo on the right side of his chest. Dark stubble shadows his jaw, and his face is hard and handsome. His skin is tan—somewhat natural but also a result of being out in the sun. A backward black baseball cap covers his dark hair.

Hat twinning.

He could give any Instagram model a run for their money.

I wave off his lame offer. "Don't worry about me being entertained. I plan on snooping through your stuff as soon as you leave." I shrug with no shame.

"There are cameras in here, Pageant Queen."

"And?"

"And keep your hands off my shit."

We're interrupted by a knock on the door, and a loud

voice follows on the other side. “Ki! Man, we’re slammed! I need you out here!”

Maliki gestures to my phone. “Call every contact in your phone if you have to.”

I release an exaggerated sigh.

He opens the door, throws me one last irritated look, and leaves.

I snatch the pen and write *Screw you, asshole* across the paper while grinning, and my snooping party starts.

Fifteen minutes later, Ellie texts, saying she’s in the parking lot. Maliki says nothing as I leave, but when I peek back to the bar on my way out, he’s watching me.

I add an extra skip to my step and flip him off over my shoulder.

CHAPTER TWO

Sierra

Age Twenty

"ID."

Here we go again.

Like last time, I told Ellie sneaking in was a horrible idea, and also like last time, she persuaded me otherwise.

"We're home from college, and there's jack shit to do," is what she said, speaking the truth.

Leo swore on his grandmother's grave that Maliki was out of town and not playing ID regulator. No longer am I taking Leo's word on anything. I should've known the guy was trouble when he said he wasn't a dog person.

Two years have passed since my last attempt to sneak in. Maliki might think I'm old enough to drink now.

I dramatically sigh and slap the ID into his waiting hand.

Well, it's not exactly my ID.

He snorts while inspecting it. "Oh, your name is Ellie Ross now, huh?" He moves the ID from his view to gain a better look at me. "The strangest thing just happened. Minutes ago, I served a woman at the bar with the same name. That *Ellie* resembles the photo on the ID *way* more than you."

Ellie celebrated her twenty-first two months ago and got a copy of her ID, which went to yours truly. I normally have no issues using it. At the bars on campus, if you're cute, you're in. Not so much at this jackass's pub.

I shrug. "I filed a name change. It was no fun, sharing it with a beverage ending in Mist."

He holds the ID back up and studies it further, a grin twitching on his lips. "You changed not only your name, but also the color of your hair?"

"I went through a bad breakup. You can't get over a man until you change your hair."

He nods, eating up my responses. "I'll escort you out."

"I'd prefer you be a gentleman instead and *escort* me to the bar. Maybe buy me a cocktail?" I don't bother hiding my drink this time. "If I recall correctly, you told me I could've at least given you a fake last time. I followed your exact instructions."

"You took that out of context."

A flirtatious smile dances on my lips. "Let's talk compromise, shall we? How about this—we walk away from each other, pretend this chitchat didn't happen, and that you never saw me? I'll act invisible and swear not to cause any problems." I thrust my hand out, bringing up my pinkie, but drop it seconds later when he ignores it.

Maliki snatches the drink from me. "Did you drive?"

"No, Ellie did."

"Ellie, your friend, or Ellie, your alter ego?"

"I hate you," I bite out, narrowing my eyes at him.

"And I hate annoying teenagers."

"I'm not a teenager."

"I hate annoying *young women*. Is that better for your underage ass?"

"I hate annoying *old* men."

Technically, Maliki isn't that old. I don't know his exact age, but I'd guess around thirty. Ten years older than me isn't ancient, but dude was learning multiplication when I was pulled from the womb.

He smirks, now looking more humored. "How much have you had to drink to give you enough balls to talk shit to me in my own bar?"

Crap. I internally forehead-slap myself. *Play nice.* "Only a few. I'm not planning to get wasted and dance on the bar." I point to my glass in his hand. "I'll make this my last. I promise."

"And who the fuck served you?"

"Ellie Ross."

I should've done a one-eighty and hightailed it when I spotted Maliki behind the bar. Instead, I made Ellie play waitress and deliver my drinks to our table. Like last time, I sat in the corner. And also like last time, I had to abandon my spot for a restroom break. I shouldn't be punished for being a few months shy of turning twenty-one. It's not like I'm asking Sir Checks-ID-a-Lot to fill my sippy cup to the brim with vodka.

He takes off his hat and runs his fingers through his thick hair. "Jesus. You need to stop thinking you're a grown-up."

"I *am* a grown-up." I count down my reasons of argument on my fingers. "I'm legally old enough to play the lottery, buy cigarettes, and hell, even do porn."

He cocks his head to the side. "Interesting. I'd love to witness your father's face if the last one ever happens."

"So, deal?" I hold my hand out once more, this time for him to shake.

Again, he ignores it.

It falls slack to my side.

"As I explained before, you might be old enough to place bets and fuck, but you're too young to drink, Pageant Queen."

I yank the ID from him. "I've changed my mind. You won't be blessed with my business when I turn twenty-one. My money will be spent elsewhere."

"Perfect." He pinches the bridge of his nose. "Now, this is the part where you call someone to pick you up. You know the drill."

"Kyle motherfucking Lane!"

I gasp, and my chest tightens at the sound of the name yelled.

"Jesus fucking Christ," Maliki mutters under his breath, scrubbing a hand over his stressed face.

I see Kyle—my overprotective, older, police-officer brother—strolling through the bar with a cocky smile.

Kyle is cool but not cool enough to be okay with my being here. And even though Maliki wasn't the one serving me booze, he'll be held responsible. It's *his* bar.

My gaze swings back to the pissed off, broad-shouldered man, and his expression confirms we share the concern. He grips my hand and rushes us to his office. The door shuts, and I spin around, scowling at him.

"Call the person who picked you up last time you were a pain in my ass. You have an hour, Princess, or I'm ratting you out to your brother."

"You wouldn't dare," I hiss.

Maliki can easily snitch on me. He owes me nothing. And my money is on Kyle believing him.

He stares at me in challenge. "Care to find out?" His voice drips with an authority that causes me to shiver.

I gulp, turning quiet while figuring out my next move.

"Call someone, Sierra. Don't make me cause problems and tell your brother what you do in your spare time when he orders a beer from me in five minutes."

He starts to leave, but I stop him.

"The person who picked me up last time was *Ellie Ross.* The real Ellie Ross," I explain in exasperation. "And she's the person I rode with tonight. She's hammered, so I need another plan."

There's no Uber here, and my mom is friends with the only taxi driver in town.

"You have no other friends?"

"Not one willing to leave because I'm getting booted."

He grabs a remote from the desk, seeming to accept my answer, and tosses it to me.

The only changes to the office since my last visit are the TV on a wall and a wide sofa lining another.

I play with the remote in my hands, taking his gesture as a surrender in not tattling on me. "I see you glammed the place up."

"I don't know what the fuck that means, but sure." Tension rides his face. He has a crowded bar and has to deal with me *again.*

I fall heavily onto the chair and prop my feet on the desk. "How's your Netflix watch list?"

"I don't know. I don't watch TV."

Who doesn't watch TV?

I point to the TV with the remote. "You have a smart TV."

"When I'm in here, I work."

"Why did you buy it?"

He blows out an annoyed breath. Answering my questions is the last thing he wants to do, but I don't want to lose his company. I enjoy pushing his buttons, and hanging out in an office alone isn't much of a party.

"My sister works here and occasionally brings my cartoon-loving niece." With that, he whips around, cursing under his breath, and leaves.

I open Netflix, select *That '70s Show*, and take off my leather jacket before shuffling to the couch. When I drag my phone from my bag, it's dead.

Shit.

I yawn.

I'll watch one episode and then rummage through his drawers for a charger.

My eyes slowly shut as I relax.

A TAP on my shoulder startles me awake.

My head shoots up and connects with something hard. That something hard is someone's chin. The strong chin-holder and I simultaneously groan. I massage my head when he pulls away. When I peek up from the couch, I expect to find Maliki at maximum annoyance.

Instead, he looks drained. His bar tee is wrinkled and drink-stained.

"All right, Princess. Time for you to go home," he says.

I comb my fingers through my ratty couch-head hair, and my stomach drops. "My phone died. I'll call someone and wait outside until they get here."

Hopefully, there's someone sober with Ellie.

He extends his hand, helping me up, and retreats a step to give me room to walk around him. I snatch my jacket from the chair, yank it over my shoulders, and shove one arm in, stopping when he speaks.

"I'll take you home."

I gape at him, and my jacket falls loose on my uncovered arm. "Is that smart for me to get in the car with someone I don't know? Stranger danger and all?"

Who am I kidding? I've allowed him to force me into an office in the back of a bar twice. I've long surpassed smart decisions with him.

He shrugs. "You can walk, but I'd rather you not. Your choice."

"All right, but I'd make a terrible hostage. My dad would tell you to keep me, and I'm very demanding. You'd be forced to bring me hot wings and a hair straightener and provide plenty of company."

He snorts. "Me kidnapping you is nothing you'll ever need to worry about, Jailbait."

"Jailbait? I'm *so* not jailbait."

"You are jailbait. And trouble. The trouble of rich parents making a guy's life a living hell for talking to their precious daughter."

He's not wrong. My father would flip his shit.

"Come on. I'm wiped."

I follow him out of the office to a door with a bright Exit light shining above it. The silence tells me the bar is closed.

"What time is it?" I ask when he holds the creaky door open for me.

We step out into an ill-lit, vacant back lot of the bar. I'm a twenty-year-old woman catching a ride with a stranger after a night of drinking, but I'm not alarmed. Call me twisted for being thrilled to spend time with this man even if it risks dying.

Okay, I doubt he's a serial killer, but I live for dramatics.

"A little after two," he answers.

Good thing I'm staying at Ellie's tonight. My mother would have the police—aka my brother—searching for me.

Speaking of Ellie …

Did she not realize her best friend was nowhere to be seen?

I tighten my jacket around myself, my heeled boots crunching against the gravel, and follow him the short distance to a running car, the chilly breeze smashing into me.

"Do you have a phone charger?" I ask behind him.

He nods but doesn't glance back at me. "In the car."

He opens the driver's door to the black Camaro, and I do the same with the passenger side. We slide into our seats at the same time. I run my hands over my arms, grateful he heated the car.

I wait quietly when he opens the glove compartment, grabs a charger, and gives it to me. "Thank you."

He shifts the car into reverse but doesn't move from the parking spot. "You going to give me your address?"

"God, no," I rush out. "Do you want me sent to an all-girls' college?"

"I don't know much about being sent to one, but it sounds like an overdramatic sorority girl like you wouldn't like it." He shakes his head and smiles. "I'm amazed your parents haven't already shipped you off somewhere. I wouldn't have predicted their daughter dearest to be such a rebel."

"Trust me, neither did they."

He reverses out of the parking spot, his arm settling at the top of my seat. "Is it an act of rebellion? Desire for attention?"

"Neither. It's me being me."

I'm half-tempted to shine my phone in his direction to see the expression on his face.

Which reminds me …

I clumsily plug my phone into the charger. As soon as it powers on, I text Ellie.

Me: What the hell? I know you always forget shit, but I was hoping that stopped at your best friend!

My phone beeps seconds later.

Ellie: Calm down, drama queen. I watched you follow the hot bartender you have a thing for to the back.

Me: I do not have a thing for him!

Ellie: Yeah, okay. I'll make you a doctor's appointment for pretendinitis tomorrow.

Me: That doesn't clarify why you left me! YOU NEVER LEAVE A MAN BEHIND!

Ellie: Chill out. He let me check on you twice, and you were snoozing. Your brother and Leo hung out all night. When I tried figuring out an escape plan,

Maliki offered to take you. I've been waiting up for you to call, so I can let you in.

Me: He could've severed my head off!

Ellie: My sister used to bang him. He's not into that kinky shit.

Me: I hate you. We're broken up.

Ellie: I'll make you waffles in the morning and buy you a new candle.

Me: Two candles, and you'd better have Nutella.

Ellie: Fine, two candles, and duh. Do I still need to wait up, or are you staying the night with him?

Me: I'm on my way. He doesn't have a kink for chicks who can't legally drink either.

Ellie: What a shame.

"You going to tell me where we're headed?" Maliki asks, breaking me away from texting.

I drop my phone into my lap. "Ellie's."

"And where does Ellie live?"

"You should know since you've banged her sister."

"It's weird you're assuming and entertained with my sexual history, Jailbait."

I bite the inside of my cheek. "That's what Ellie said."

"If Ellie said it, it must be true."

I shift in my seat to face him and cross my arms. "Are you saying it's not true?"

He leaves the parking lot, not answering my question, and drives toward Ellie's house—confirming the sister-screwing. I've never been a fan of Ellie's older sister. Chick once spit gum in my hair. The fact that she slept with Maliki makes me hate her more.

"You know, I found condoms when I searched through your office last time."

He taps his fingers against the steering wheel and keeps his eyes on the road. "I know."

My mouth falls open. "You watched the cameras?" I rack

my brain over everything I did that night, praying it wasn't anything embarrassing. I talked plenty of shit about him to Ellie. If there was audio, there's no doubt he heard me.

"I wanted to make sure you didn't rob me."

"Sadly, I didn't find any money."

"Good. That means my hiding places are legit."

"Your condom hiding places are trash."

"Not wanting to stash them in places I have to search out to find." He chuckles. "I also saw you stole a few for yourself."

"Just in case."

He finally glances over at me. "You're trouble, Jailbait—a pageant princess with a crooked crown and leather jacket."

I grin. "I'm surprised you're just figuring that out."

CHAPTER THREE

Sierra

Age Twenty-One

I WALK into Down Home Pub, a smile filled with confidence and determination on my face.

It feels almost like home—a home I've never exactly been welcomed in.

Call me the unwanted stepchild of Down Home Pub.

Except, now, this rejected stepchild has the upper hand.

A group of sorority girls who aren't excited to spend their night in a hole-in-the-wall bar are behind me. Not only is the pub an hour from the city, but there's also no expensive DJ, VIP section, or bottle service.

I laugh to myself while picturing the look on Maliki's face if someone requested a VIP section. He'd probably throw them out faster than he tried me.

I pause to give the bar a once-over. It's the first time I've had the chance to look around since I always ducked and hid before. There's a long wood bar with beer taps at the rear of the room. Behind the bar is a shelved brick wall. Liquor bottles fill the top shelf, and glasses of various sizes line the bottom. People are huddled around pub tables cluttered with food and drinks. The small space looks near capacity.

Finally.

I'm the winner in this game.

No booting me tonight.

I'm ready for an evening loaded with drinking and smugly throwing my age in Maliki's face.

The best fucking birthday ever.

I find the pain-in-my-ass bartender in seconds and beeline toward the side of the bar he's manning, excitement shooting through me. There's a crowd waiting to be served around him. I ignore the dirty looks I receive when cutting my way to the front of the line.

I mutter, "Birthday girl," a few times, but their glares don't lessen.

I need a stiff drink after listening to my friends whine about coming here. I tuned them out, wondering what he'd do when he saw me.

No doubt he'll ask for my ID. I plan to throw it at him and prove I'm a big girl now. No more *Jailbait, Pageant Queen, Teenager* mocking.

I admire the sight of him before he notices me, and if I saw myself in the mirror, there'd be lust flickering in my green eyes. I lick my lips. His hair has grown out since I saw him last, and the expanse of his chest looks wider. His olive skin is still as smooth, and I'm tempted to ask him for his skincare routine. A backward baseball hat covers his hair, he's wearing his signature bar tee, and his cheeks are still sporting light stubble.

He blinks a few times when his attention cuts to me and meanders my way in no rush.

Huh. I expected him to bombard me with an ID demand.

"I'll have a vodka tonic, please," I order when he reaches me.

His mood is unreadable. "Sorry, did you say an organic

juice box?"

"*Fine,* give me an organic juice *with* a shot of vodka."

"I'll need to see a *legit* ID for that. A *real* one."

I crack a smile on my matte red lips and raise my arm, holding the ID between two fingers.

He raises an eyebrow, his lips tilting into a sliver of a smirk, and takes it from me. That smirk grows as he inspects it. "Motherfucking finally."

Pride rocks through me. I open my mouth to answer but am shoved into the bar.

"Hot bartender!" Louise, a sorority sister, yells, interrupting us. "I need shots and then more shots after that. You ever heard of Buttery Nipples?"

I stifle a laugh and shoot Louise a dirty look. *This is so not a Buttery Nipple place, Louise.*

"Heard of them? Yes. Made them? Fuck no," Maliki replies.

"Body shots then?" Louise fires back with a pout of her lower lip. "I promise to let you do one off me."

Hell no. Not on my watch.

Chick isn't coming anywhere near *my* Maliki.

I shove Louise's shoulder. "Go away. You're embarrassing yourself."

"What?" she draws out in a whiny voice. "Dude is hot." She clicks her tongue and points to him while backing away. "Buttery Nipples!"

Maliki shakes his head, clearly not offended. He's probably used to attention like this.

He sweeps his gaze over me, inching forward and settling his palms on the bar in front of me. "What can I get you, birthday girl?"

"Surprise me, *but* don't make it a Buttery Nipple."

"I'll make you something better than that or anything you've ever had." He smirks, pushes himself back, and turns on his heel.

"Seriously—I'll say it louder for the sorority girls in the back—you two have a thing for each other," Ellie says next to me.

I didn't even notice her presence. Call it the Maliki Effect. Everything around me fades away when he's around.

"Whatever," I mutter, rolling my eyes.

She clips her black strands behind her ear. "Ask him to take you to the office you've hung out in so many times. Tell him how excited you've been to see him like you've told me *all fucking month* long."

"I was excited to turn twenty-one and finally show him up."

"Yeah, okay," she replies sarcastically, bumping her hip against mine. "I won't interrupt your flirt-fest, and if any of these sorority girls try to sink their claws in him, I'll trip a bitch. Get your flirt on, girlfriend."

With that, she walks away.

Ellie attends Iowa State with me but called me batshit crazy when I suggested she join my sorority. Joining was a requirement for me. Luckily for her, her parents are more easy going than mine and not obsessed with their image.

I glance back to Maliki.

He pops a black straw into a glass, adds an orange slice garnish, and drops it in front of me. "Legal looks good on you, Princess."

The short red dress and strappy nude heels I'm wearing don't fit into the relaxed atmosphere, but I don't care. I wanted to look sexy tonight … *for him.*

I tap my nails against the beat-up bar. "I warned you I'd come on my twenty-first. It was necessary for me to fulfill that promise *and* throw it in your face."

"I thought you'd come back to rob me of condoms again." He tilts his head to the side and studies me. "We've never shared a conversation this calm here."

I laugh. "I know! I might find out you're as fun as people say."

He stands taller and slightly parts his lips. "Oh, trust me, I'm plenty of fun."

"Nothing I've received from you screams fun, so that needs to be proven to me." I stir my drink, take a sip, and moan when pulling away. "Holy shit. This is delicious. What's in it?"

He raises his chin. "None of your business."

"You can't *not* tell me what's in my drink. Isn't that against bartender code of conduct?"

"Alcohol. There's alcohol in it."

"You're one of *those* bartenders." I take another drink and swish it around in my mouth. "Whiskey." Another sip. "Southern Comfort?"

He stares at me, unblinking.

"Seriously?" I curl my lips around the straw, our eye contact steady, and take another sip. "Definitely SoCo and orange juice."

He slightly nods while grinning. "A girl knows her whiskey."

"A girl knows her whiskey." I take another drink and raise a brow. "Gin?"

"Possibly."

"Definitely gin. What else am I missing?"

"If I told you, I'd have to kill you."

"Oh God, never say that around me again. Your age is showing. My *father* says that."

He throws out his arms. "Hey, everyone fucking says that!"

I hold my glass in the air. "Keep these bad boys coming, bartender. By the end of the night, I'll figure out the entire ingredient list. Maybe I'll even throw in some tips to make it better."

The bar is packed, but he's not taking orders from anyone. He holds up a finger when they call his name, his eyes drinking me in as if I were his cocktail. Satisfaction hits me, and my cheeks blush. I'm the one who's holding his attention.

"Consider yourself special because I made you that drink. That's normally not my style." He rubs his hands together. "Now, I'd love to continue this guessing game, but customers are waiting. Go drink and enjoy your night."

I frown, not wanting to leave him. I grab my drink, but he stops me from turning around.

"One more thing, Jailbait."

My knees weaken when he comes closer. Mere inches separate us. I inhale his scent—cinnamon and spice—and nearly die when he drops his head, his lips brushing my ear.

"Tell me, birthday girl," he whispers.

I gulp. *Do not fall on your ass. Breathe.* "What?" I stammer.

"Who is the dude at the table behind you, shooting me a murderous glare? Does he know you came here for me?"

My nails dig into the bar, ruining my fresh manicure, and I shiver as something rushes through me that shouldn't—desire.

I was so hooked on Maliki that I forgot about Devin. I hate that I lose our contact when I peek back at Devin. His jaw is clenched, and his eyes are fixed on us.

Shit.

He invited himself tonight. We're each other's exclusive booty calls—not hooking up with other people yet not sharing love devotions.

I shrug, glancing back to Maliki. "He's kinda, sorta my boyfriend."

"Kinda, sorta?" he questions. "How the fuck is someone kinda, sorta your boyfriend?"

"I mean … we haven't made anything official."

"Some words of advice, Sierra: a man who wants you will never let you say he's kinda, sorta your boyfriend." He catches my chin and swipes his thumb over my lower lip. "This is on me, Jailbait. Go dump your kinda, sorta boyfriend and have yourself a great fucking birthday."

CHAPTER FOUR

Sierra

Age Twenty-Two

I STRIDE into Down Home Pub, and per usual, I head straight to Maliki. It's early evening, and the night crowd hasn't hit the place yet. That gives me plenty of time to annoy him before customers arrive with drink demands.

I drop onto a stool and watch him pour a beer for a brooding customer. He nods when the man pays him, and then his eyes meet mine. We share a smile—mine no doubt loaded with goofiness. He snags a cleaning towel, takes the few steps separating us, and stops in front of me. He leans back on his heels and waits for me to speak.

I shift my weight in the stool. "Guess what."

He dries his hands on the towel. "Who knows with you, Jailbait?"

"I moved home!"

He chuckles. "Oh boy, that's fucking trouble. We should alert the authorities."

"Don't act like you're not secretly thrilled I'll be able to annoy you more," I say with more dignity than someone borderline stalking him should.

I snatch a peanut from the chrome bucket on the bar, crack open the shell, and pop the nut into my mouth.

When I came home on breaks, I always headed straight to the pub to see him. I ordered all my drinks from him, ditched my friends to hang out at the bar with him, and spent more time here than at home.

Unfortunately, that doesn't mean we've shared in-depth discussions. The bar stays busy, and most locals order from him rather than the other bartenders. We make small conversation until he's called away again.

"Oh, princess, I can't wait." He inches closer, provoking my breathing to hitch, and softens his tone. "What made you come home?" His smile widens. "You want to see me every day, don't you? I love that you find me irresistible."

Thank God the bar hides the view of me clenching my thighs underneath my maxi dress. This is Maliki's game. He loves fucking with my head. He'll get closer, whisper in my ear, and then back away to serve a customer, a shit-eating grin on his face. The ass knows I'm attracted to him.

I roll my eyes and toss a shell at him. "You're so arrogant. Gee, I don't know, maybe I moved home because"—I hold a finger to the corner of my lips—"my family lives here. That's a mighty ego you wield there, bartender. You should drink some of it off."

"Your family *and me*," he corrects with a smirk.

Am I that transparent?

For as long as I can remember, I swore I'd never live in Blue Beech as an adult. My hometown was too small, too stuffy, but that plan changed a month ago. I graduated from college a semester early, and instead of apartment-searching in the city, I packed my stuff and came home. After being gone for four years, a girl needed some familiarity.

I straighten my back and clear my throat. "I've experienced the party life, and now, I'm ready to get a job and act like an actual adult."

He chuckles. "It's weird, seeing you mature, Jailbait. It seems like only yesterday you were in here, all doe-eyed and innocent with your strawberry daiquiri."

"Hey, I'm very mature, thank you very much. Just yesterday, I scheduled my own dentist appointment."

"Oh shit, look at you, all grown-up and changing the world by assuring you're cavity-free. Maybe next week, you'll advance to grocery shopping." He pauses, holds up a finger, and winks. "Hold up. I bet you're back for my drinks. They don't make them like me in the city, do they? I've ruined you for all other bartenders."

"I hate to pop your drink-making ego, but the booze selection in the city is *much larger.*" I smirk. "I'll give you some pointers."

Down Home Pub doesn't boast an expansive drink list—beer by the bottle and draft, mixed drinks, shots, and a few select wines. Nothing too fancy. There aren't any special house cocktails, but there's also no demand for it.

He shakes his head. "Eh, not interested. You can keep testing what I give you though."

Sometimes, Maliki gives me drinks to taste-test. I've never had one I didn't like.

I roll my eyes. "God, you're boring."

"For someone who claims I'm boring, you sure seem to enjoy yourself around me."

"I love drinking your *boring* drinks." I shrug. "'Tis all."

"You love my company, babe," he talks while starting a drink. "There are two sides of the bar. Mikey is free, and I guarantee he won't have a problem serving you. He's more your age and always up for a good time. Hell, he's probably more entertaining than I am. Why don't you go bug him?"

I scrunch up my nose. "*Ew.* Mikey sleeps with any woman who can count to ten."

He chuckles. "It's eleven now."

"Aw, I'm glad he's upped his standards."

Maliki drops my favorite drink in front of me, a playful grin on his face, and turns to help another customer.

I hate this part. The part where I share him with them.

He returns when he's finished serving their needy asses.

"You moving back in with your parents?" he asks.

"Unfortunately, yes. That's something I'm not looking forward to. I plan to find an apartment, but everyone knows there aren't many open rentals in this town."

"And the boyfriend?"

I lower my head and take a long sip of my drink. "It's, uh …" I gulp it down and sigh before clarifying, "Still complicated."

He nods.

Devin begged me to stay with him until he graduated. When I didn't, we agreed to spend time away from each other—physically, that is. We still talk, and he mentioned he was searching for apartments between Blue Beech and the town he had grown up in. I told him he was nuts, thinking we could move in together. My parents would cut me if I moved in with a man before marriage.

When I peek back up at Maliki, his attention is on me. Mine is on him. He's wearing his signature Down Home Pub tee and a backward baseball cap.

He raises a brow. "Sierra is single then?"

I shrug. "Kinda, sorta."

"What did I tell you about the kinda, sorta shit?" he asks in a scold-like manner.

Instead of making me another drink containing alcohol, I'm given a glass of water.

I play with the straw, jabbing a piece of ice. "We're taking a break."

I can't stop myself from admiring his arms when he crosses them. Infatuation barrels through my blood. It's absurd how drawn I am to him.

"I'm no expert, but couples taking *breaks* from each other isn't a sign of a healthy relationship, Jailbait."

"Exactly. I'm *jailbait.* We're young."

"Twenty-two isn't young, princess."

"How old were you when you acquired the bar?"

"Twenty-nine."

"Were you ready to settle down at my age?"

"Fuck no."

"Exactly! Why does everyone like to give out advice but never take their own?"

"I also wouldn't string you along if I didn't know what I wanted. I'd be straight up and ask you to be straight up in return."

We're interrupted by my phone beeping with a text.

"Ugh, it's my mother," I say, reading it.

He strokes his face stubble. "Why's that an issue? You love your mom."

"She's throwing a welcome-home party for me." I grimace. "All the folks of Blue Beech can't wait to see me and ask three thousand questions." I get up with a huff and rub my brow to ward off the impending headache. "Most of them ask why I'm still single, just as you did."

He holds his hands up. "Hey, babe, I'm not telling you to get hitched to some frat boy just to please people."

My phone beeps again, my mother asking if I've picked out what I'm wearing. I hold up the phone to show him the text. "See! She already wants to know what I'm wearing!"

"What will you be wearing?" he asks suggestively with a smirk.

"Clothes." I click my tongue against the roof of my mouth. "Maybe a dress with no panties." I grin when his eyes widen and his jaw flexes. "You'll probs see me later when I come to drink the party away." I wiggle my fingers in a wave. "Bug you later, bestie."

"I SWEAR TO MOTHERFUCKING GOD, I'd better not see your ass on *Dateline*," Ellie says. "I refuse to do an interview, talking about the girl you were before becoming obsessed with that man behind the bar."

I press my hand to my chest and fake offense. "What are you talking about?" I bump my shoulder against hers. "You'd better never go on *Dateline* and tell my secrets."

"Never. I'm referring to my friend being annoying on *my* birthday because she's daydreaming about the bartender dicking up her vagina." She shoots me a grin of amusement.

"*Or* this friend is staring at the bar, debating on what her next drink will be."

This isn't the first time we've had this discussion. I've lost count of the number of times she's told me to ask Maliki out. I question if she's started smoking crack. Maliki would turn me down, and I'd never step foot into the pub again.

That can't happen, and not to mention, a relationship would never work with us. We're too different. So, I'll admire him from afar like he's a handbag in a store I can't afford.

She tugs her hair into a tight ponytail. "Honey, you spend more time here than your own home *and* with your boyfriend. Do your parents know this?"

"Nope. They think I'm working crazy hours, *which is true* with my new job."

"Does Devin know about your favorite pastime and why you keep pushing him away?"

"Hey, I don't push him away," I lie.

She snorts. "Dude has brought up marriage to you like ninety thousand times, and you brush him off. If that's not pushing someone away, I don't know what is."

"We're too young to get married." I chug my drink. "Are *you* ready to get married?"

"That's a big *hell no*."

Tamara, our waitress, returns to our table with another round of drinks. "Maliki asked me to drop these off."

She throws me a wary look identical to the ones the other bar employees give me. The waitresses and Maliki's sister, Liz, aren't my biggest fans.

I signal to them. "Oh no, we didn't order these."

Ellie shoves my shoulder, giving me a dirty look. "Of course we did." She side-eyes me when Tamara shrugs and walks away. "What is wrong with you? You never turn down free drinks. Living with your parents again fucks with your head." A quick smile spreads across her lips as if something hits her. "I mean, we know you'll only take free drinks from the bartender though because you're in love with him."

I roll my eyes, a pain forming in my throat. "You've lost your mind."

---

4 Months Later

"ANY PLANS LATER?" Maliki asks.

"Nope," I answer. "Unless you count hanging out here."

Instead of replying, Maliki focuses his attention on something behind me. When his eyes narrow, I shift in my chair to find what's suddenly pissed him off.

I wince.

What the hell?

Maliki tenses when Devin meets us at the bar.

My kinda, sorta boyfriend slings an arm over my shoulders and kisses my cheek. "Hey, babe."

Devin looks like he came straight from the office—sporting khaki slacks, a white button-up shirt, and chestnut-colored

Sperry slide-ons. Ever since he graduated and moved home, he comes around more.

The two men I'm attracted to couldn't be more opposite.

I cringe and force a smile. Devin's kiss isn't what has upset me. It's *why* he kissed me, acting as if I were his possession. It's a reminder to Maliki that I'm not his.

Last night, Devin emailed links of possible condos to look at, and his father offered me an interior design position at his building firm, to which I accepted.

My breathing accelerates, and I grow more flustered by the second.

How rude would it be to shrug him off?

"What are you doing here?" I ask.

He tugs me closer, giving me a tight squeeze, and feigns ignorance that Maliki is here. "Corbin said you and Ellie were here. I had a break in my schedule and wanted to surprise you." His hand creeps to my waist. "I've missed you, and I needed to see your gorgeous face. *Plus*, I found a condo you'll love."

This is when I jerk away from him. He knows I can't move in with him, but again, *Maliki.*

After my twenty-first, Devin questioned me about Maliki for weeks—asking how I knew him, if I had a thing for him, if we'd ever hooked up, if I was into older men. He accused me of flirting with Maliki, but I never entertained the conversation. Devin and I weren't in a committed relationship then.

I grind my teeth and twist in my stool. "We've had this discussion."

Maliki snatches my half-empty glass from the bar and walks away, shaking his head in irritation.

Devin grins at the loss of Maliki. "Sorry, I needed to clear the air, so we could enjoy our night."

"I wasn't aware Ellie invited you," I mutter.

"She invited Corbin, who then called me." He shoots me an accusatory look for my lack of invite to him.

Corbin is Devin's cousin and Ellie's new boyfriend. I fixed them up after she broke up with Leo.

Devin captures my hand, and I hop off the stool, allowing him to lead me to Ellie and Louis's table, wishing I could return to my stool and stay with Maliki.

Maliki is glaring at us when I turn around, and me mouthing, *I'm sorry*, to him further pisses him off.

He turns his back to me, wanders over to a woman, and talks to her for the rest of the night. He doesn't look at me again the entire night, and it infuriates me.

I fake interest in conversations but have no clue what anyone has said. The drink Devin brought me earlier—one he'd ordered from Maliki and complained he was an asshole to him while doing so—is half-full and watered down. For the first time, I'm relieved when Devin asks if I'm ready to leave Down Home Pub.

Devin walks me outside and kisses me good night, and we walk to our cars. Instead of leaving as he does, I slump down in my seat.

I'll stick around and reflect for a moment.

Settle down from the anxiety of the night.

Screw Devin for pulling a power move like that.

It's nearing last call, and I question my sanity as I watch each minute tick by. When the time hits one fifty-five and I notice people leaving, I wander back into the bar, fear surging through me.

Stupid, stupid girl.

Maliki sets down the bottle in his hand and stares at me in question. "Did you forget something?"

As I hoped, the place is almost empty with the few lingering people gathering up their belongings and heading toward the door.

I shake my head, and a brief silence passes over us while

he waits for me to explain why I'm here. "I thought you might need help cleaning up."

"You thought I might need help cleaning up?" he slowly repeats. "How much did you drink?"

"Not enough." I move further into the bar, praying he won't kick me out—something he's never had an issue with. "Even if you don't want me to clean, can we hang out?" I hop onto the bar and swing my legs back and forth in an attempt to prevent them from shaking.

He shrugs, circles around the bar, and starts placing stools on pub tables. "I'm always up for pleasant company."

He considers my company pleasant.

Yay!

I jump off to help him, and when I can't take the silence any longer, I blurt out the last question I should, "You don't like Devin, do you?"

He practically throws the next stool onto the table, and it slides forward. "You won't like my answer to that."

I grab a stool, but my lifting skills are nowhere near as graceful as his. Things are heavy. "Why not?" *Why am I asking this when I already know the answer?*

He collects dirty glasses, deposits them onto the bar, and snatches a rag to wipe a table down. "I don't see you with him long-term. He's a wet blanket that'll drain the light inside you. I fucking dread that happening."

I understand his reasoning. My brothers disclosed the same worry, wording it differently. They don't know Devin like I do. He's a different person around me.

We met at a function my sorority threw with his fraternity. I was so frustrated that day. The guys stood around while us girls did the work but not Devin. He grabbed the ribbons I was hanging, stepped onto the ladder, and helped me. He was goofy, sweet, and funny in his own way, and he spoiled me with attention. We shared a few classes and had regular study sessions that led to hook-ups.

The problem is, the more Devin hangs around his father and frat friends, the more he takes shape to them. He's now judgmental and less understanding. He prefers spending time at his parents' country club while I prefer spending time here.

I halt at the table I'm at and play with the back of the ripped stool, unsure of how to respond.

"Do *you* like your kinda, sorta boyfriend, Sierra?" he fires back.

"Of course I do."

His eyes darken. "Why are you here with me instead of with him then?"

His question almost knocks me on my ass.

"He has an early morning tomorrow."

He comes closer, his focus on me growing stronger. "Again, why are you here and not in bed with him?"

Even though I want to, even though I *need* to, I don't break our eye contact. I wish the pub weren't so underlit. I want a better view of him, want to observe everything that's him. I don't have an answer to his question. Not an honest one.

I run my sweaty hands down my jeans. "I wanted to hang out with a friend. With our history, we should consider ourselves friends."

He laughs, not buying my answer. "Yes, we're such excellent *friends.*"

CHAPTER FIVE

Sierra

"YOU'RE QUIET TONIGHT," Maliki says, restocking beers into the cooler.

Me helping him close is now a regular routine.

I relax on the bar, crossing my ankles and holding them out in front of me while watching him work.

"How many women have you slept with?" the abrupt question rushes out of my mouth before I can stop myself.

Tonight, I don't have a care in the world. Devin and I argued earlier, and all my fucks left with the last drink Maliki poured me.

For years, I've wondered but never had the guts to ask. There's no missing the women who look him up and down like he's a snack they can't wait to devour. They flirt with him, write their numbers on bar napkins, and touch him in ways I wish I could. My fantasies are appalling, provided I'm in a relationship, but that doesn't stop me from resenting them.

Maliki pauses, sets the beer in his hand on the bar, and roams his eyes over me. "What?"

Oh, he heard me.

"How many women have you had sex with?"

He shrugs and returns to the cooler. "I don't know."

"You don't know how many women you've slept with?" I slowly say, unhappy with his answer.

Maliki blowing off my question isn't surprising. He never ventures into personal territory. We make small talk, like what we did during the day or movies, and he shares crazy customer stories with me.

"Nope," he bites out, crouching down to get the last crate.

I scrunch up my face. "That's weird."

Exhaustion fills his eyes as he casts them on me. "How's that weird? I don't keep a fucking tally, Sierra." Irritation burns along with his words.

"It's a lot then, huh?"

He shuts the cooler with extra force. "I'm not clear what your definition of *a lot* is."

"A lot …" I waver, struggling to strike the perfect words. "I don't think I've slept with *that* many guys. It's most likely a smaller number than yours. It's—"

He shoots his hand up and interrupts me, his voice cold, "I don't care how many men you've slept with." He shakes his head, turns away, and opens the register. He jams cash into it and slams it shut. "Why are we having this talk?"

"I was hoping we could get to know each other better." *I'm also jealous, insecure, and confused with my life.*

He leans against the wall and scowls at me. "Sierra, I know your favorite color, favorite food, favorite fucking movie. I don't need your sex list or care to know your goddamn favorite sex position."

I cross my arms. "What if I want to know yours?"

"Is there a reason you're asking me this tonight?"

I tug at the top of my shirt, the room heating up. "I just … I don't know … I don't know if I'm good in bed."

"Good in bed?"

I nod and drum my fingers against the bar. *Stop talking. Stop talking. Do not pass go and spill your guts to him.*

I stupidly pass go and tell him, "Devin." I clear my throat. "We used to have sex all the time. I mean, *all the time*."

I'm stopped by Maliki talking over me, "Okay, got that fucking point across."

I gulp. "It seems like he's always too busy to … *you know*." My voice weakens. "I don't want to be that needy, annoying girlfriend, but it's weird."

I've already had this chat with Ellie, who insisted Devin is busy with work. I need a man's perspective, and God knows, I can't ask my brothers.

He grinds his teeth. "I've said countless times, he's a dumb shit. I don't get what you see in him."

"I bet you're awesome at sex." I slap my hand over my mouth. *Oh my God. I did not say that.*

Maliki grimacing confirms I definitely said that. "I'm not talking about sex with you."

"Why?" I blurt out. "Maybe I need some tips." I cover my mouth again. *That wasn't supposed to pass go either.*

"The only tips I have are given to me after serving someone a drink."

"I'm serious, Maliki. There has to be something wrong with me."

He stares at me for a moment, looking almost disgusted. "Tell your boyfriend to pay me a visit, and I'll give him some tips. Number one: stop being a fucking dumbass."

My ponytail falls loose when I throw my head back, my blonde strands cascading down my shoulders. "Let's forget how much you hate him for a minute, okay? Devin and I have dated off and on since college, *but* he hooked up with other women when we were on our breaks." I lose Maliki's gaze as tears prick at my eyes. "Maybe I'm not as satisfying as those other women were. We had an argument tonight, and he demanded to know how many men I'd slept with while we were separated. I told him the truth—*zero*. He refused to answer when I asked him the same. We fought more, and he confessed to sleeping with six women while we had been broken up."

"Allegedly broken up," he cuts in, his tone sharp. "What's the point of this story, Sierra? That your boyfriend is fucking trash? News flash: we already knew that."

"I'm over that. We weren't together then. I'm worried that I'm boring *now* and that those women were better at sex than I am."

He scoffs. "Doubt that, princess."

"What about the women you've slept with? What do they do during sex? What do you do to them?"

Let's be honest. My question is more than wanting reassurance that I don't suck in the sack. I crave to know more about Maliki, to find out what he's giving other women that I'll never have.

"Find another man to have this conversation with because it won't be me."

I perk myself up, my voice turning fake cheerful. "Come on. We're ole buddies, ole pals. Tell me."

"No," he snaps.

"*Please,*" I sing out, unsure of why I'm so desperate for his answer.

I gasp when he erases the distance between us and rests his palms on the bar on each side of my waist.

"What do you want me to tell you, Sierra?" He smells of lime and mint as he stares down at me in impatience. "Do you want to know how a woman writhes underneath me while I finger her until she comes?" He half-whispers, half-hisses, "Do you need me to brag about how hard I fuck women or love to eat pussy? Is that what the fuck you're asking for? *Why*?"

I swallow as tears burn my eyes. My breathing matches my racing heartbeat.

"I sure as fuck don't want to hear about you fucking another man." He pushes off the bar when I don't explain myself and remains in front of me, a wild look in his eyes.

He told me to stop pushing, and I didn't.

I'm not giving up now either.

"Why not? Why don't you want to talk about this with me?"

"It's not the relationship we have. You want to talk sex? Call one of your sorority sisters."

My chest tightens, and I solemnly look at him. "But …" *No, don't pull away. Don't.*

"Quit pushing it, Sierra."

I open my mouth to continue this argument … or whatever it is, but I shut it when my phone rings. We both look down at it resting on the counter next to me. He curses at the same time I tense. Devin's name along with a selfie of us flash across my screen.

Maliki shakes his head while stepping away from me. "I'm drained, and I have an early delivery tomorrow. Go ask your boyfriend why he's slept with so many women, break or no fucking break, and why you're seeking out this conversation with another man about how you don't feel stacked up to those women. Do you need a ride home, or do you want to call him?"

I shake my head. "I'll call Ellie."

He doesn't wait for me to answer while stalking across the bar. I text Ellie, and thankfully, she can be here in five minutes. I'm fighting tears as he walks to the other side of the bar and fake focuses on paperwork.

He looks at me with sharp eyes when I tell him Ellie is here and holds his palm to the base of my back while silently walking me outside. He nods hello to Ellie, helps me into the car, and slams the door without a word. I watch him as she pulls away.

His arms are flexed, his face is red, and his knuckles are balled into fists. He shakes his head, releases his fists, and walks inside.

I don't know if I'm crying over my fight with Devin or

over my fight with Maliki.

Maliki. Most definitely Maliki.

MALIKI HAS BEEN AVOIDING me since our argument.

When I order drinks, he gives them to me and walks away, saying as little as possible. He has, however, made it clear that another bartender is helping him close from now on, hinting that my company isn't needed … isn't wanted. I was wrong for pushing the conversation, and I'm now paying for it with the cost of our friendship.

That's changing tonight.

I need him.

For reasons unknown, he's who I run to. I trust him, and trust isn't easily given out by me. I don't trust people I've known my entire life, and tonight, my family was betrayed.

Devin wouldn't understand. His family is structured and clean cut. Scandals and secrets don't supply their closets.

The bar closed twenty minutes ago, and the parking lot is empty. It's a weeknight and raining, so the night was probably slow. I jerk my hoodie over my head, wipe away the tears I cried on the ride here, and jump out of my car. Hard downpour smacks into me as I rush to the door of Down Home.

It's locked.

I knock.

No answer.

I pound harder and call out his name.

I stumble forward when the door shoots open, and Maliki catches me in his arms to stop me from falling. He swiftly locks the door behind us and shoves my head into his shoulder as I break down. He rubs my back, walking us further into the bar. Instead of dropping me onto a stool, he carries me to the back, up a flight of stairs, and into an apartment.

He kicks the door shut with his foot and carefully settles me on a black leather sofa. I peek up at him standing above me, knowing my eyes are puffy and black mascara is matted to my face, aware I'm the picture of a hot mess.

I wipe my cheeks with shaking hands.

I'm pissed. I'm hurt. I want to kill a man I love.

"My dad," I whisper before raising my voice. "He's …"

"I know. I was going to call you after I finished closing." He sinks to his knees and stares up at me, pushing soaked strands of hair away from my face. His shirt is wet from my tears. "Have you talked to him?"

I shake my head. "I waited in his office for hours, but it was useless. He's not dumb enough to come home until this scandal passes. I gave up and drove here." *Came to you.*

He wipes away my mascara smudges. "Come on. Let's get you changed into dry clothes, and then we can talk."

I nod, my body relaxing. I run my eyes over the room that no doubt belongs to him when he leaves. It's tidy and simple, only a few pieces of furniture. It's clear he doesn't spend much time here.

Seconds later, Maliki returns with clothes in his arms.

He gives them to me and points to an open door. "Bathroom is there."

Yawning, I change into a tall, baggy bar tee and an extra-large pair of black sweatpants that sag, even after tying them tight around my waist. I don't glance in the mirror or attempt to fix myself up. It'll only make me feel uglier.

He's on the couch when I come out. I settle next to him and spill every secret I've learned about my father tonight, stumbling over my own words every so often.

My father had an affair resulting in an illegitimate child. That illegitimate child is my brother's girlfriend's nephew.

I sob while explaining how heartbroken my mother is, and my lips quiver when I grit out how I can never look at my father the same. I never want to see him again after he damaged our family.

When I'm done, a weight is lifted from my shoulders. Maliki sat and listened, not interrupting or advising me on how to feel. He stands, walks to the kitchen, and pours me a glass of water.

I take the glass from him. "You've been dodging me."

"I've been busy," he says.

"Bullshit." I'm dealing with lies from my dad. I won't accept them from him, too. "Ever since that stupid sex conversation, you've hardly spoken to me."

"That night proved a friendship between us wasn't a wise idea. We're too different, Sierra, and you have your own relationship issues to work out."

Us being friends is necessary for my sanity, for my heart. No words from anyone I've spoken to tonight were as comforting as being with Maliki. It's been hell, not seeing him.

"I swear, no more sex or relationship talk. I'll even sweep the floors, and we'll act like it never took place."

He smirks. "You enjoy my company, don't you? Your boyfriend is so fucking stale that you'd rather be around me."

I roll my eyes. "Oh my God, someone needs to make himself a humble drink."

"SIERRA, listen to me. Do not go inside," Ellie urges over the phone.

"What? Why?" I ask.

"The news about your engagement has spread all over town. Your mother told everyone at the benefit breakfast this morning. There's no way it hasn't hit Down Home—that it hasn't hit Maliki—and from how well I know you, I'm sure you haven't told him."

I twist the diamond ring on my finger and bow my head. He should've known before any random person.

Devin proposed ten days ago, and since then, I've been terrified of seeing Maliki. I've also been miserable, not seeing him. He should've found out from me, face-to-face.

I couldn't do it though.

I knew what he'd do.

He'd grill me about my saying yes. Give me shit. He'd see straight through me and rip out every uncertainty I possessed about marrying Devin, throwing them at me.

That's what Maliki does. He makes me tackle my truths, which fucking terrifies me.

My voice cracks, my stomach rolling as a chill hits me. "I should've told him myself."

"Trust me, he doesn't want to see you. Babe, I hate to tell you this, but it's in your best interest to put your closing nights with Maliki to rest if you marry Devin."

I force a laugh. "Oh my God! Maliki won't care. We're *friends.* He's made that clear from day one." *Lies.*

In the pit of my stomach, heart of my soul, I know Maliki will most definitely care.

Ellie releases a worried sigh. "Tell me then, what would you feel if Maliki got engaged?"

I swallow down the curses ready to fly out of my mouth. "I mean, I wouldn't like it." *I'd fucking riot.*

"Bullshit." Her tone turns sharp. "I'm ordering you right now to turn around, leave that parking lot, and arrive early to your cake-testing appointment with your mother."

My mother has started wedding planning. Hell, she might've started the day Devin asked my parents for permission to marry me. Devin proposed in front of our families, making it hard for me to say anything but yes.

I planned to wait a few years until our nuptials, but then I saw my mother's face and heard the excitement in her voice while she talked about locations, flowers, and dresses. I didn't have the heart to tell her to relax and give me time. I missed her smile too much.

It's not that I don't care about Devin. I don't doubt my future with Devin or his feelings. Even with our relationship issues, I don't see Devin breaking my heart.

Maliki? He's never had a stable relationship.

Hell, he's never shown interest in having one with me or anyone.

We're friends. Period.

I need to accept that.

Moving on will help me.

"I'm going in," I tell Ellie.

"No! Do not make me drive up there and drag you out as if I were your mother! I won't allow you to make an ass of yourself."

"Good-bye, bestie."

She's still threatening me when I hang up.

Eyes are pinned to me when I walk into the pub, and I focus on bringing one foot in front of the other, fearful of tripping. I'm light-headed before even reaching Maliki.

I should be happy.

I'm engaged!

"Well, well, look who it is," Maliki deadpans, meeting me at the front of the bar as if he's been waiting for me. "The future Mrs. Kinda Sorta."

"Not funny," I grumble, dropping onto a stool.

"You know what else isn't funny? Marrying someone you don't love." His lips curl back in disgust. "But hey, what do I know about love? I've never had a healthy relationship like you where I break up with a person a few dozen times." His response is precisely how I imagined.

I sigh, my shoulders rolling forward. "It's complicated."

"Complicated?" His eyes widen. "He proposed. You said yes. And, now, you're wearing a diamond on your finger. That isn't complicated, Sierra."

I can't stop myself from drifting my hand upward and admiring the ring. Devin did a fantastic job. The view of Maliki's bitter smile when I look back at him erases all the happiness of my new accessory.

"In fact, why don't I make you a celebratory drink? What about The Heartbreaker? That's the future of your joke of a marriage."

My eyes burn, and a tear slips from the corner of my eye. My hair conceals that side of my face, so I don't bother wiping it. He can't know he's not the only one doubting this marriage.

"Don't, okay?" I muster out.

He lifts his arms and snarls. "Don't what? Tell you you're stupid for saying yes? I don't fucking lie, Sierra." He stops and drops his voice when he notices people are staring. "If you want someone to believe in your sham of a relationship, it won't be me." He slams his hand down on the bar and backs away. "When's the big day? According to what I've heard, you're putting something together quick."

I nod and level my eyes on him. "It'll be a short engagement."

He cringes and comes closer. "Holy shit, you're pregnant. You're pregnant, and your parents are forcing you to marry him."

"What?" I shriek. "No!" I hold my hand out and control my breathing. "Look, my mother hasn't been this happy in years. *Years*, Maliki."

"Buy her a fucking puppy. Don't marry someone to make her happy. That's the dumbest shit I've ever heard."

"Maliki," I breathe out.

"I have a job to get back to. Enjoy the married life."

MALIKI ISN'T HERE TONIGHT.

That's odd.

He always works Friday nights.

Mikey is running one side of the bar, and Liz is working the other. Liz has made it clear she doesn't support my closing parties with Maliki. Well, my *past* closing parties with Maliki, given we haven't talked in weeks.

I'm ready to move to Mikey's side and ask where Maliki is, but I'm stopped by Liz.

"He's not here tonight," she states, irritated.

She doesn't bother asking if I need a drink. She knows why I'm here.

Liz has the same dark hair as Maliki but with softer features and kinder eyes. Well, kinder when they're directed at anyone but me. She's older than Maliki, and according to him, she moved into the mother role when theirs left.

"Stay away from my brother."

"What?" I stutter out in surprise.

"You sent him an invite to your stupid wedding." She gives me a frigid stare. "That was pretty fucking shitty, you know."

This is what I was scared of.

She's right.

I wavered on inviting Maliki to the wedding. Would it piss him off to invite him … or *not* invite him? I was unsure but finally mailed the invite. Maliki ignoring my text, asking if I could stop by the bar, gave me my answer. He's pissed.

I muster up the courage to defend myself even though I feel like an absolute ass, like Ellie said. Guilt consumes me.

"It'd have been shitty not to invite him."

"You're so clueless."

"Excuse me?"

"You're marrying another man, but you come here to hang out with one you're *not* marrying. Is that not a warning that, *I don't know*, you shouldn't get married?" She taps her temple.

She's right, but the wedding is paid for, family member flights are booked, and my mother is over the moon.

"Can you tell him I stopped by?"

"Nope."

All righty then. I clench my fingers around my phone. It's been in my hand all night while I've waited for a reply from him.

"No offense, but you're a selfish brat," she continues without allowing me a chance to speak. "Grow up. You can't have your cake and eat it, too." She gives me a tight-lipped smile. "Have a good night, and leave my brother the hell alone."

I HAVE COLD FEET.

Not ones I can fix with tugging on a pair of comfy UGGs.

Cold feet about marrying Devin.

The night before our wedding.

The closer it gets, the more nervous I get.

Devin is nice. Sensible. Secure.

Maliki is wild. My future with him would be a mystery.

That's *if* he'd even want anything more than just friendship.

When we used to close together, he made it clear that we were staying in the friend zone.

But I can't marry Devin when my heart isn't one hundred percent with him and wants someone else.

I texted Maliki an hour ago, but he hasn't replied. He's turned into a master of avoiding me. Every night I went to the bar, Liz said he was gone.

Until now.

Earlier, as my stalker ass had done for the past week, I drove past the bar's back lot. Tonight, Maliki's car is parked in his spot.

He's back.

It's a sign, and him being home is all I can think about. When I went over last-minute arrangements with my wedding planner, I merely nodded, not paying attention to what changes she'd made. I canceled the bridesmaid sleepover at my house, claiming I wasn't feeling well, and told my mother I needed alone time.

I need to see him. I'm about to turn my life upside down.

I unlock the door to the pub and walk in. Maliki gave me a key pre-engagement. Sometimes, I would come to the bar after closing and let myself in.

The jukebox is statically playing a song I don't know, and I don't see Maliki.

Weird.

He usually turns off the music promptly at closing, in need of peace.

What's also weird is, the bar isn't cleaned. Trash litters the tables and floor, the stools are randomly thrown around the room, and the bar top isn't wiped down. I slip the keys into my purse and head toward his office, hoping to find him there.

I freeze when I hear it.

"Yes! Harder!"

It's a woman's voice. A woman's *breathless* voice.

Nausea rises up my throat, but I talk myself down. Whoever is in the office is fucking, but it can be anyone—Mikey, Liz, or hell, even a cook.

I'm praying for any of those alternatives to Maliki as I stupidly migrate closer to the office.

"Oh my God, Maliki!" she cries out. "Your dick is amazing!"

Well, there goes that hope.

"Fuck," a man groans out. *Maliki* groans out.

My heart splinters into shattered fragments, and I can barely breathe as I push myself to continue in their direction.

The echo of smacking skin is screaming at me in warning to run, but I can't.

I have to see.

I cover my mouth, in fear of vomiting and making a noise. The office door is cracked open, and my weirdo self peeks through the narrow crack.

A dark-haired woman is spread naked on the desk. Maliki is standing between her long, tan legs, just as exposed. Their moans continue, and I can't walk away.

Then, my attention shifts to only him. His chest is beautifully sculpted with muscles, and sweat glistens his abdomen. I can detect his cock pumping in and out of her, but the desk cuts off my view from eyeing anything lower.

The desk moves with each thrust as he wildly fucks her. He reaches forward to skim his palms up her chest and squeezes her breasts—breasts that are fuller than mine.

I'm comparing every inch of myself to this woman.

"Shit, I've missed you," she moans. "I love you so damn much."

She lifts herself up on an elbow, reaching for him, and he leans down, smashing his mouth to hers, devouring her.

Tears hit my eyes. I've never experienced hurt so hard. I taste bile and anger and hate toward Maliki and this mystery bitch for taking what I crave to be mine.

You can't be mad.

He doesn't belong to you.

You did this.

I was stupid and played games.

I should've told him how I felt. It's too late now. He's having sex with a woman, kissing her, and she told him she loved him. There is a connection between the two. They've had sex before. That's why he's been avoiding me—not for the invitation, but because he has a girlfriend.

Even though I can be arrested for watching them, even though it's ripping me apart, I can't turn away.

That changes when my phone rings, the ringtone blaring.

Everyone stops.

Oh. My. Fucking. God.

This is not happening right now.

I jump backward as I shakily tug my phone from my pocket, careful not to drop it, and silence the stupid thing. I don't look back while sprinting out of the bar as if Michael Myers were chasing me.

If Maliki pulls up the camera footage to find who was creeping on him, I'm moving out of Blue Beech for good.

CHAPTER SIX

Sierra

Three Months Later

LOUD KNOCKING on my front door wakes me up.

I yawn and check the time on my alarm clock.

Five a.m.?

No, thank you.

They can wait until regular waking hours.

Whoever's banging on the door doesn't agree with the waiting game and only pounds harder. I push off my blanket, expletives falling from my lips, and stomp into the living room.

"Chillax!" I yell. "I'm coming!"

I grip the doorknob but withdraw a step when my name is called on the other side.

Hell to the no.

This isn't going down at five in the fucking morning.

I attempt to calm my breathing—failing miserably—and the knocking persists.

I'm hallucinating.

This is a dream.

Only one way for me to find out. I stand on my tiptoes and check the peephole.

Nope. Not dreaming.

It's him.

Shit!

This can't happen now.

I need time to prepare myself before facing him—words need fine-tuned, an outfit chosen, and a minimum of three hours of meditation done.

Maybe if I don't answer, he'll give up.

I count to twenty, and the knocking doesn't cease. He gives me no choice but to answer unless I want my neighbors to call the cops on him. They're assholes like that. It's no biggie for them to have wild sex all night, but it's a crime for me to jam to Britney in the morning.

I swing open the door, air knocking from my lungs, and cover my mouth in fear of vomiting. Maliki is standing in front of me, and even though it's been months, he looks the same. Well, except he's now wearing clothes and not sticking his penis in another woman. I shudder, my stomach knotting at the memory of seeing him and her.

Our eyes meet, and he doesn't look happy to see me.

Why is he here then?

My hand drops from my mouth, and I rest against the doorframe, hoping it makes me look collected when, in actuality, it's so I don't fall on my ass. I wait for him to explain his unexpected wake-up call.

"You've been avoiding me," he states.

No shit, Sherlock.

"You know why." I'm shocked at my honesty, surprised I didn't throw out excuses like I've been working late or I had to wash my hair.

After my wedding, Maliki texted me with a simple, *Congrats*. I didn't have the guts to reply. He sent another text after I returned from my honeymoon, and I wanted to throw my phone as I read it. He'd watched the camera footage and seen me watching them that night. An apology was added in his text, but he didn't fail to add a jab after it, claiming I had no right to be angry with him because I was climbing into another man's bed at night.

That time, I didn't reply out of anger.

Our friendship is over.

There's no moving past my marriage and his office-screwing.

He scoffs, "Because I was with another woman?"

He had a brief fling with the woman he'd screwed that night, according to Ellie. She had been appointed my Maliki informant. Just because I refused to step foot into Down Home or reply to his texts didn't mean I couldn't keep tabs on him. Two weeks ago, she told me the chick was no longer coming around.

"Yep," I clip out.

"You're pissed at me for sleeping with another woman. Meanwhile, Sierra dearest, you were fucking *engaged* to another man."

"And, now, I'm *married* to that man." *Why did I find it necessary to define that?* It was a blow to compete with his asshole attitude.

"Wrong. You *were* married to him."

I wince. "Excuse me?"

He motions toward the inside of my condo. "Get dressed. We're leaving."

This is when I realize I didn't change before answering, not that he gave me a chance to. I'm wearing the pub shirt he gave me the night I came to him after the news broke about my father's affair and short strawberry-patterned boy shorts. I don't know why I'm wearing the shirt, given our fallout, but I'm blaming it on the comfort of it.

I cross my arms to cover the shirt. "I'm not going anywhere with you."

He juts out his chin. "Get fucking dressed, Sierra."

"What's going on? I work in three hours."

"I'll return you in time."

I sigh. "You're not taking no for an answer, are you?"

"Nope."

I wave him inside. "*Fine.* Give me ten to brush my teeth and change clothes."

"Nice shirt, by the way," he remarks as I head toward my bedroom.

My back stiffens, and I don't bother looking back at him. "I'm behind on laundry."

"Liar."

What is happening?

Confusion crackles inside me as I get dressed in leggings and a baggy sweatshirt, tug my hair into a messy bun, and slide on flip-flops. I'm worried his visit has something to do with Devin. Swear to God, my husband had better not have done anything stupid enough for me to castrate him for.

Maliki is holding a gold-framed photo when I return to the living room. My wedding photo.

I clap my hands. "We need to make this quick."

He gives the picture one last glare and sets it facedown onto the table. "After you."

I hop down each step and spot Maliki's Camaro as soon as we hit the parking lot. I inhale a deep breath when I get in, attempting to pick up the scent of a woman as if I were a golden retriever. All I detect is the rich amber of Maliki's cologne.

Maliki doesn't say a word, and I tug my phone from my purse. There's a text from Ellie, a voice mail from my mother, and nothing from Devin. I talked to him before I went to bed last night.

I respond to Ellie's text and drop my phone in my lap. As much as I want to call Devin, I can't. Not yet. When I peek up, I notice we're driving out of Blue Beech.

"Whoa, where are we going?"

Maliki keeps his eyes on the road and doesn't say a word.

That only pisses me off further. "I want goddamn answers, Maliki, or I'm jumping out of this car."

His fingers clench around the steering wheel, and he still stares ahead, as if he were waiting for something to run out in front of us. "Trust me on this. No matter what's happened between us, you know damn well you can trust me."

"Are you kidnapping me?"

"Negative. If I recall, you once told me you'd make the worst hostage—something about hot wings and hair shit. Not dealing with those problems."

I can't help but smile at the memory.

He scrubs a hand over the stubble of his cheek. "Do you love him?"

I stare blankly in his direction, his question taking me aback. "Who? Devin?"

"No, the other man you're married to."

I punch his arm. "I forgot how irritating you are."

He rubs the spot I hit, and relief hits me when he finally glances my way. "You love how irritating I am. Just like I love how fucking irritating you are."

Momentarily, in my mind, our situation dissipates, and I shut my eyes, savoring his compliment.

Then, I remember I'm married.

I adjust my ring and fix my eyes on the solitary princess cut diamond.

"Seriously," I say. "What is this about?"

"Answer my question." Aggravation is in his voice again. "Do you love him?"

"Obviously. I wouldn't have married someone I didn't love."

"Do you love him or the idea of him?"

"This is ridiculous. Take me home. I have better things to do than defend my marriage."

"You'd better not defend it after today."

"Please, stop talking in code … or circles … or whatever

the hell you're doing. I'm getting pretty dizzy over here. Did I tell you about my motion sickness? Blue Beech Fair 1999, the Tilt-A-Whirl had me puking up pink cotton candy all night."

"You want straight up?" he grinds out in a raised voice. "Your husband was partying last night at a bar. I saw him there."

His response doesn't bother me and isn't what I expected.

"I'm well aware he was at a bachelor party," I deadpan.

His irritation grows. "Are you also *well aware* he was fucking another woman at that bachelor party?"

Disbelief rushes through me. I struggle to breathe, struggle to think … hell, I even struggle to remember my own name.

No way. I open my mouth to protest, but fear constricts me from speaking.

Our relationship isn't perfect, but since our wedding, Devin has been the model husband. I've never doubted my trust in him. There have been no signs of an affair—no whispering in the other room or a passcode on his phone, none of the signs my friends have busted their husbands with.

"You're lying," I accuse when I manage to gather words.

He isn't.

Maliki wouldn't drag me through this torture if it wasn't true, no matter how tattered our friendship is.

He winces in frustration, appearing almost pained at me doubting him. "Do you think I'd do this for shits and giggles? I was there last night and witnessed it."

I shake my head as a tear trickles down my cheek. "No."

"Good, but I want you to see it for yourself, so the little cocksucker can't lie his way out of it."

"What do you mean, see it?" I gape at him, horrified. "Jesus, please tell me there's not a sex tape or something like that, and that's how you know about this."

"A sex tape? I hope the fuck not." His face twists into a line of disgust. "Do I have proof without seeing his weasel dick? Affirmative."

I'm so lost.

My stomach tightens at his failure to elaborate, and I'm afraid to ask for details. I snatch my phone with sweaty hands, unlock it, and scroll to my husband's name. Him not coming home last night didn't worry me. He'd rented a hotel room for him and his friends the night of his party. I'd expected it. Hell, I'd *helped* him pack his overnight bag.

I shake my head, powering off my phone, and toss it into my bag. I'll ask his side of the story after seeing this *evidence.*

We don't speak the rest of the ride, and twenty minutes later, Maliki pulls into the parking lot of the Twisted Fox Bar. It's a newer establishment in the surrounding county and tends to drag in the younger crowd. Devin comes here to hang out with friends … and this is where the bachelor party was last night.

Maliki picks up his phone from a cupholder and calls someone. "Hey, man. We're here." He nods a few times and ends the call.

We step out of the car, and he leads me to the entrance of the building. The door is unlocked. A man behind the bar is the only person here. He looks around the same age as Maliki and was here the few times I came with Devin.

He circles the bar and comes our way. He has light-brown hair, and even though he's on the slimmer side, he's hot.

Maliki lifts his chin. "Yo, Cohen." He jerks his head toward me. "This is Sierra."

I politely wave at Cohen, and he responds with a sympathetic smile before telling us to follow him.

He takes us through the kitchen until we reach an office with a desk covered with two large computer monitors. Reality strikes me when Cohen sits in the chair by the desk.

Cohen is showing me the evidence of Devin cheating.

I'm not prepared for this.

I stay in the doorway, watching Cohen punch a few

buttons on the keyboard and turn to Maliki, a curious look on his face.

"You sure she wants to see this?" he asks.

"She needs to," Maliki replies.

I hold up my hand. "Uh, *she* is standing right here."

Cohen only nods and puts his attention back to the computer.

Maliki curls his arm over my shoulders and steers me to stand behind Cohen. I gulp and resist the urge to shut my eyes.

This has to happen.

When Cohen pulls up the bar's camera footage, I immediately spot Devin. My belly knots with panic while I watch him take shots with friends. Then, he's talking to a woman at the bar, and he buys her a drink. My hands curl and press against my stomach. I recite two quick prayers—the first that I'm not about to see my husband cheat and the other that I don't vomit on Cohen's head.

I grip the back of the chair and tense when Devin turns stupid.

Oh, this motherfucker.

He grabs the woman's hand and takes her to the restroom. Even though Cohen speeds up the time, I'm aware of how much has passed. Fifteen minutes later, I watch my husband exit the restroom, buckling his pants, with the woman lagging behind him.

"That motherfucking asshole," I bite out. "And that two-faced tramp."

Cohen drops his head back to look at me. "You know her?"

"She was a sorority sister. Louise." My attention shifts to Maliki. "The bitch who asked you for Buttery Nipples on my birthday."

"Never trust a chick who drinks Buttery Nipples," Cohen comments.

I never got along with Louise. One night, Devin drunkenly confessed she'd slid into his DMs during one of our *breaks* but swore he'd ignored it. I doubt that now.

I bury my face in my hands. "Well, if this isn't humiliating."

"For him," Maliki says, gently squeezing my shoulders. "Not you."

I twist out of his hold to face him. "Why?" My voice shakes. "Why did you show me this?"

I move when Cohen wheels his chair away from the desk and springs to his feet.

"I'll leave you two to do whatever," he says.

I wait until Cohen disappears through the doorway before speaking.

My chin trembles.

Don't cry.

Don't you dare cry.

"Why?" I ask again, fighting to keep my voice calm.

Maliki raises his hands next to his head in a mind-blown motion. "Are you shitting me? What did you expect me to do? Sit back in my chair at the back of the bar and let him fuck around on you?"

I stammer for the right words.

"Do whatever you want with the information, but you needed to know. Whether you stay with the cheating bastard is your call." He stops me when I turn around to leave. "Oh, and don't be surprised if he has a black eye when you see him."

CHAPTER SEVEN

Sierra

I'M PACING the living room, wiping tears away as they fall, while waiting for my cheating bastard of a husband to come home.

My life will change when he walks in.

I'll be divorced before reaching my thirties.

Hell, I'll be divorced before making it to our first anniversary.

The video of him and Louise has consumed my every thought. I had two glasses of wine for breakfast after Maliki dropped me off at home—attempts to erase the memory of the video, but it didn't help.

Maliki asked if I needed help packing or if I wanted him to give Devin another black eye.

Do I stay or go?

I stop when the front door opens.

This is it.

There's never been a longer silence in my life as I wait for Devin to come into the living room. I clutch my stomach, nausea creeping in, and suck in a life-changing breath. Suddenly, I'm struggling to find the words I prepared, the words I held back from calling and screaming at him over the phone.

My lip trembles when he comes into view in what seems like slow motion.

"Hey, babe," he greets, gripping his overnight bag.

My plan to handle this rationally flies out the window, and I grab our wedding photo, hurling it toward him. His eyes bulge, and he shuffles back a step, barely dodging it.

"Shit," he rasps, looking from the frame to me. "Is it that time of the month?"

There's no regret on his face. Had Maliki not told me, I would've never suspected him cheating. His hair is combed over in the same style he's worn since college, his clothes are wrinkle-free, and he shows no symptoms of a hangover. There is a slight discoloration beneath his eye—a bruise that wasn't there yesterday. The black eye Maliki mentioned.

"You cheated on me?" I scream, my hands shaking. "You cheated on me with Louise?"

His face pales, and he drops his bag to the floor. "What the fuck? Who told you that?"

"Maliki. His friend works at the Twisted Fox." I make a sweeping gesture toward his face. "The man who gave you the black eye."

His hand lifts to his eye. "That fucker hates me and hit me for no reason." He sneers, an attempt to cover his lies, but his shoulders droop. "I'm insulted you'd believe him over me. I've never made you doubt my love for you."

"There are cameras there." My voice raises. "I saw you with her!"

"I swear, it's not what it looked like."

"Oh, come on! I'm *insulted* you'd think I'd believe that lie."

He extends his arms out and steps closer. "I'm sorry! I was drunk." He focuses his eyes on me and expels an audible breath. "It's eating me alive that I hurt you."

"I can see it's really *eating you alive.*"

"It was a bachelor party. It's not the first time a man has accidentally hooked up with a woman at one."

Oh, that's his argument?

I grab another frame, and he dodges it flying toward him again.

"That's supposed to make me feel better?"

He takes another step toward me.

I take one back.

"*Please,* baby," he pleads. "We've had so many years. Don't let this fuckup—my *only* fuckup—tear us apart. It won't happen again. I swear it."

"No, you tore us apart." Fear and hurt spiral through me, and I pick up my bag from the couch. "I can't even look at you."

He catches my arm, turning me to face him, and guilt surfaces on his features. I swallow, hurting while watching his face contort in pain, and it torments me not to console him.

I mean, he is my husband.

I care about him.

Not enough to stay though.

I jerk out of his hold.

"Please," he whispers. "I made a mistake."

I remove my wedding ring and allow it to fall to the floor. "And I made a mistake in marrying you."

He calls my name when I walk out.

"TELL me you left his sorry ass."

I didn't know where to go.

My mom would know something was wrong. My brothers would want to kick Devin's ass. Not that he doesn't deserve an ass-kicking, but today, all I want to do is clear my mind of my husband cheating. I don't want them to know yet. I need time to process it myself before hearing their relationship advice.

Stay with him.

Leave him.

Kill him.

I drop my purse onto the bar and fall down on a stool.

"I left his sorry ass." I fight to keep my voice steady and confident even though I'm near losing it.

Being back at Down Home seems surreal. It looks the same, smells the same, *feels* the same, like I never stopped coming.

Maliki beams with pride while standing behind the bar. "Where do you go from here?"

"No idea. Not only did we live together, but I also work for his father. I'm now homeless, possibly unemployed, and husbandless. *Yay.*"

Moving in with my parents is a *hell no*. They're working to move on from my father's infidelities. Ellie lives with Corbin. No doubt Devin would show up there, wanting to talk.

I press my forehead against the bar and groan. "I'm so screwed."

"I can help you in the housing and employment department. As for the husband position, you'll have to seek help elsewhere," Maliki says.

I lift my head to see the seriousness on his face. "Trust me, I don't even want to sweat about a husband."

He nods. "Good girl. You need to get rid of the one you have now." He rubs his hands together before ducking down and grabbing me a bottle of water. "The guest bedroom in my apartment is open, and you can work here."

Whoa. Definitely wasn't expecting that.

"That's …" I unscrew the bottle cap and take a drink. "That's …"

"An offer, Sierra. Take it or leave it." He's not insulted by my response. "I'm helping a friend."

Friend.

I raise a brow. "Is that what we are? Friends again?"

"We've always been friends … after you quit being annoying and sneaking into my bar."

I sigh. "I appreciate the offer but don't know if it's a stellar idea."

"If you change your mind, let me know."

"I SWEAR on my shoe collection, that asshole isn't stepping foot in my apartment," Ellie says after I decline her offer to stay at her apartment. "You won't need to worry about seeing him because I'll kick his ass before he makes it through the front door."

I called an hour ago and asked her to meet me at our favorite taco joint outside of town. She was as stunned as I was when I broke the news about Devin and Louise's restroom field trip. I'd been nervous about going out in public, in fear of a breakdown, but I've stayed strong.

Each time I almost cry, I take a tequila shot instead.

It's working perfectly.

"While I appreciate your loyalty, kicking his ass will only lead to problems with you and Corbin," I tell her.

She lifts her margarita. "Corbin will be lucky if I allow him to hang out with a man who has no issues with banging tramps in restrooms."

"I'll figure something out. If worse comes to worse, I'll be at your doorstep."

Do I tell her about Maliki's offer?

Nope.

She'll go into full freak-out mode. It wouldn't surprise me if she suggested I screw Maliki, tape it, and then send the video to Devin. Ellie loves a good revenge.

"You swear?"

I nod. "I swear."

"What are your options then? Moving home?"

"Not if I can help it. Hopefully, I can find a rental."

"Good luck with that in Blue Beech. Finding a rental there is like snagging a golden ticket to Wonka's factory. The people never leave their homes. They pass them down through generations like bad genetics."

I press my palms to my temples. "Ugh, I know."

"Where are you crashing tonight? The offer is open for my place even if it's only temporary."

I chew on my lower lip, tasting the lingering tequila. "Undecided. Can you drop me off at Down Home? I told Maliki I'd help him close and then ask Kyle if I can crash at his place."

She grins. "She runs to her prince in bartending armor."

I throw a chip at her. "Shut up. I'm not running to anyone."

"You are *so* running to him. And no judgments over here, babe. Maliki is hot and will have no problem fucking every thought of Devin the Douche Bag out of you."

I gulp down the rest of my margarita. "There will be no sex with him. We're friends. I'm comfortable talking to him."

"Gee, thanks, *best friend.* I'm all for you running to him for sex, *but* I'm the one you're supposed to feel the most comfortable talking to."

"Trust me, you know way more about me than he does. It's just …" I pause, struggling to define my relationship with Maliki. "We have this weird friendship."

"Turn it into a fuckship, and I won't be offended by you going to him and not me."

"God, I love yet also hate you."

She pushes her shoulders up and smirks. "You love me." She motions for our waiter. "Now, let's get you good and drunk before you go to your future fuck buddy."

I lower my voice. "I'm not even divorced yet!"

She shakes her head. "Devin set the marriage bar when he stuck his pencil dick into a sorority tramp."

The waiter comes, and she orders us another round of margaritas.

And two shots of tequila.

"YOUR CLOSING PARTNER HAS ARRIVED," Ellie announces while helping me walk—no, *stumble* into Down Home.

I had four margaritas and lost count of how many shots I downed during dinner. My purse swings from my shoulder while I dangle off Ellie's. I can walk. It's just easier to do it with help.

What a way to celebrate your husband cheating.

A few loners are settled around the bar, vacant stools between them, and my vision is too fuzzy to make out who they are. Chances are they know me though.

Everyone knows me in this godforsaken town.

They'll hear about Devin's restroom scandal. It'll become the scandal of the year—right behind my father's.

Keepin' it classy in the Lane family.

"And she's wasted," Maliki says, rounding the bar to meet us.

"Wasted and asking for you," Ellie clarifies. "I trust you'll take care of her?"

"Always." Maliki wraps his arms around my shoulders, relieving Ellie of my weight, and pulls me into him.

"Perfect!" Ellie kisses my cheek. "You two kids have fun."

She leaves and heads to the parking lot where Corbin is waiting. I'd reluctantly let him pick us up from the restaurant. At first, I was afraid he'd tell Devin my business, but Ellie swore on her firstborn—my future godchild—that he wouldn't.

Maliki guides me to the corner of the bar and assists me

onto a stool. "I'm insulted you drank somewhere else. What's wrong with my liquor?"

"I needed to get away from Blue Beech," I answer.

"I get that."

"And I'm not drunk. I'm tipsy. I can say my ABCs and recite every word of 'Toxic.' " My words are slurred, but I trust Maliki can understand me. He's regularly around wasted people. Drunken gibberish is his second language.

He chuckles. "I'm happy tipsy you remembers her Britney Spears songs."

"Damn straight. And I'm impressed, Bridges. Im-freaking-pressed."

He raises a brow in question.

"You know who sings 'Toxic.' It makes me like you more."

He laughs. "Nice to know." He squeezes my arm and steps away. "I'll grab you a water and food to sober you up."

I gulp, realizing how dry my mouth is. "Water—yes, please. Food—God, no. I devoured enough chips and queso to feed a small country."

I rub my forehead and drag my phone from my purse. I turned it off hours ago after Devin wouldn't stop calling and texting. You can only hit the *fuck you* button so many times before you lose your mind.

I glare at it for a moment and then slide it away from me, up the bar. When I turn it on, no doubt dozens of texts from Devin will pop up. I'll make Ellie delete them later.

"Drink this." Maliki passes me a water. "And eat this." A basket of fries comes my way next.

I pick up the water and chug it. Luckily, Mikey is working with Maliki tonight and is helping the few customers here. In an hour, the crowd will grow, and Maliki won't be able to give me his full attention like this.

He leans back on his heels. "It's nice, seeing you back here. It'd better become a regular sight again, princess."

Don't say it. Don't say it.

"That depends."

I said it.

"Depends on what?"

The alcohol makes me brave. "If you're screwing women on desks."

He winces, surprised at my response, but quickly recovers. "I promise, no other women when you're here."

"And what if I'm not here with you?" I capture an ice cube from my water, bite into it, and chew it before sucking it into my mouth. Water drips down my chin.

Maliki's smile drops, and he tilts his head to the side, as if he's studying me. I grab another cube and do the same thing. The aroma of his cologne wafts through my nostrils, and I gasp when he comes forward, his large hand cupping my chin. His finger sweeps across my skin, smoothing away the water, and every muscle in my body tenses.

My lips quiver, and me gasping breaks him away from touching me. He pulls back, placing distance between us, as if he'd temporary slipped faking that we were only friends.

He clears his throat. "Did you decide where you'll stay?"

"Nope." I snatch a fry and shove it into my mouth, wondering if I made a mistake in coming here.

The home I grew up in wasn't happy—still isn't. And now, thanks to my brother's new girlfriend, the entire town knows our business. They talk in hushed whispers about my father cheating on my mother and how his mistress is now incarcerated. Thank God I dodged the cheating husband bullet before Devin knocked up another woman.

"Where do you plan to sleep then?" Maliki asks, annoyance clear in his tone.

"In my car," I answer with a shrug and chomp on another fry.

"The fuck you are."

I don't actually plan to sleep in my car. The backseat of

my Lexus is roomy, but I can't park somewhere and not expect to be murdered.

I had multiple motives in coming here tonight.

"Calm down, killer," I say, growing flustered. "Is your, uh …"

"Spit it out," Maliki demands even though I can tell he's aware of what I'm about to ask.

"Is your roomie offer still open?"

"For you? Absolutely. For anyone else? Fuck no."

I run my tongue over my lips, blushing and feeling special that it's only open *for me.* I play with the splintered wood of the bar, now feeling shy. "Thank you. I need to get my stuff from Devin's."

"I can do that for you."

"Horrible idea. He hates you."

"And I hate the little asshole. If we didn't share a common interest, I wouldn't give a shit about him."

I snort. "And what common interest could you two possibly share?"

"You." The word slips from his lips in seconds—confident and strong.

My eyes shoot to his face, our contact locking, and I swear to God, I almost fall off my stool as he stares at me with hooded eyes.

"Oh …" I frown when our eye contact slips, him doing the pulling away—*again.* "Ellie offered to help, but I'm not sure if that's a smart idea. She's also on the list of people who want to kick Devin's ass."

"That's probably a pretty fucking long list."

Mikey turns up the volume on the TV when a boxing match starts, and I look around the bar, noticing how busy it is now. It's always packed on fight nights.

Maliki flashes a smile. "Come on. I'll help you upstairs, and you can make yourself at home."

I yawn, shaking my head. "No. I promised to help you tonight."

"You'll be no help, trust me. We can resume our closing parties tomorrow."

He helps me off the stool and claims my hand in his. Dizziness rushes through me as he walks me upstairs to his apartment. It smells of fresh lemon cleaning products and him—a delectable scent. It's clean, like last time. He doesn't drop my hand until he shuts the door behind us.

He strolls down a hall, opens a door, and does a ta-da gesture. "This is your new bedroom."

It's smaller than what I'm used to, and the bed is only a full, but it's either this or sleeping in my car. The biggest benefit of staying here is Maliki's company. That compensates for the lack of space.

I point to the bed that's complete with a blue plaid comforter and matching pillows. "That thing had better be comfortable," I joke.

"Babe, anything is more comfortable than sleeping next to cheating slime."

Truth.

He moves to the side, allowing me entry into the room. "I'll grab you something to sleep in."

I look down when he leaves the room and pull at the hem of my silk blouse that I paired with black leather-like leggings and studded gold sandals. I collapse onto the bed and kick off my shoes, exhausted. I need a decent night's sleep, so I can figure out where I'm going from here.

Maliki returns with a change of clothes, but I've already slipped underneath the blankets.

"I'm too lazy to change," I say around a yawn.

He chuckles, taking a seat on the edge of the bed. "That's the best kind of drunk. I'll be downstairs if you need anything. Call. Text. Come down."

I nod, giving him a shy smile. "Thank you."

My breath knocks against my lungs when he reaches forward, clips a fallen strand of hair away from my face, and tilts his head to the side. “I don’t get it.”

I blink, shuddering at his touch. “Get what?”

“How a man could cheat on you.”

CHAPTER EIGHT

Maliki

I'M A DUMBASS.

That's the only excuse I have for inviting her to be my new roommate.

Sierra Lane is an itch I've been struggling to scratch for years.

The first time the barely legal eighteen-year-old snuck into my bar, I owned it less than a year. I had been stressed about pouring all my savings into a business I wasn't sure would survive. On top of that, an employee pulled a no-call, no-show. I was headed to my office to find a replacement, and there she was.

I knew her. Everyone did. Her parents showed her off at every town event.

The first thought when I saw her shouldn't have been how gorgeous she was while I followed her path. I wasn't sure of her age, but I knew it wasn't old enough to be in a bar. When we got face-to-face, I took in her every feature. Her face was slightly sun-kissed, and the only hint of makeup she wore was red lipstick. A sprinkle of faint freckles scattered along her cheeks, and I loved that she didn't cover them up.

She stared at me with wide, innocent eyes. I knew she was used to getting her way as she tried to talk me out of not kicking her out. I'd wondered if I was the first person to tell her no—though technically, I hadn't done that either.

As much as our cat-and-mouse game pisses me off, it also entertains the fuck out of me. And since then, every time she's stepped into my bar, my heart speeds up. It's more than arousal that crashes through me when she plops her pretty ass onto a stool. She pushes my buttons and never fails to make me laugh, and nothing is more attractive than seeing her possessiveness come out when other women flirt with me. I hold myself back from telling her I don't want them, that I want *her.*

The issue is, I shouldn't.

She's too young for me, we come from different backgrounds, and it'd never work. We're infatuated with each other—and that's how it'll stay. We'll never pass that.

"Care to explain why Rebel Barbie is dragging an expensive-looking suitcase up to your apartment?" Liz asks, storming into my office.

There are two entrances into the apartment—an entrance on the other side of the building with stairs that lead straight to the apartment and another at the back of the bar. I'll remind Sierra to use the side entrance for more privacy.

Liz is scowling at me when I look up from my paperwork, prepared to hear her bitch my head off. For unknown reasons, she doesn't like Sierra. Liz said she doesn't want me to get hurt even though I've made it clear that my relationship with Sierra is strictly platonic.

I lean back in my chair and rest my arms behind my neck. "She left her husband, had nowhere to go, so I offered the guest bedroom until she figures it out."

"Have you lost your fucking mind?"

I shrug. *Yes. Yes, I have.*

"She has money, and her family is royalty here. She can find a rental in a day, *or* I'm sure she has friends or family who wouldn't mind her staying with them."

"*Her parents* have money, not her, and she doesn't want to stay with anyone else." I rub the back of my neck. "Why are you concerned? Do you plan on moving back in?"

We grew up in the apartment above the bar. Every childhood memory I have is there—good and bad. My dad moved to Florida after signing the bar over to me, and Liz and my niece left a year later. Now, it's just me—not that I'm complaining. I've declined all rental offers until Sierra. Hell, hers was an offer *from me.*

I was shocked when I threw out the invitation. I enjoy my space and privacy since I'm surrounded by people all the time. Customers love nothing more than coming to the bar and venting out their sad songs to the bartender. It's a motherfucking cliché.

"Negative," she answers. "My concern is *you.*"

"You have no reason to worry about me."

"I made it clear she was bad news when she played *Little Miss Helper*, and it's an even worse idea to play house with her. If she's too busy having brunch and manicures with her friends, I'll gladly look up rentals for her."

Shit. The wrath of my big sister has never been pretty.

"Be nice to her," I warn.

She pinches her lips together. "I'll *try* to, but I won't keep my mouth shut if it goes south."

"Nothing is going south." Except for my hand to my dick plenty of times while masturbating to the thought of Sierra in the other room.

"Yeah, yeah. Now, we have another order of business."

"What's up?"

"I'm visiting Dad."

Just the mention of him spikes my blood pressure. "What now?"

After my mother left years ago, my father has relied on his children too much, especially Liz. He moved to Florida after meeting a woman on Match.com, and they broke up a year later. Instead of coming home, he decided to stay there—a smart move. He doesn't do well in Blue Beech. There are too many memories of my mother.

"He has a new girlfriend, and things went south." She sighs. "Okay, maybe not another girlfriend."

"You're losing me."

"He got married."

"What?"

"He eloped without telling anyone."

"Let me guess; shit fell apart?"

"You know it."

"So, he needs help cleaning up the mess, and you're running to his rescue?"

"Yes."

"Nothing new there," I mutter.

Her face softens. Liz is protective and the biggest cheerleader of our family not falling apart. "He's a heartbroken man, Maliki."

"He's a grown-ass man who's been *heartbroken* for over a decade, and might I remind you, his *heartbreak* is from his bullshit actions. It's time for him to quit whining over the past. He doesn't deserve pity from anyone. He was a dick to Mom, chose his career over the family, and didn't realize his mistakes until after he lost her. Fuck, I take that back. He still doesn't own up to those mistakes."

"Give him a break, okay? Don't you care? He's *our father*."

"It's not that I don't care. We can't change him, and our only choice is to either continue to worry about it or move on." I stand up from the chair and head toward the door. "Me? I'm choosing to move on."

"It's not as easy to move on for some people as it is with you."

"Let me know if you need any advice on learning how to."

"You'll be the one asking *me* for advice when Blondie ruins you." She taps my shoulder. "Don't do anything stupid while I'm gone, and stay away from her the best you can. The chick was trouble back then and more trouble now."

"YOU'RE MAKING PROGRESS," I say.

Sierra smiles up at me with a shirt and a hanger in her hand. "I'm working on it. Ellie gave me a ride to the restaurant to get my car, so I at least have the clothes I took yesterday. I'll start rental-hunting tomorrow but will most likely have to search out of town."

I'm in no rush for her to leave, but that can change. I've spent time with her in the bar, but nothing more than that. She might be messy as fuck or do some weird shit.

"Oh!" She snaps her fingers. "How much is rent?"

I rest my back against the wall. "Zero dollars."

"I can't live here for *zero dollars.*"

"Sure, you can."

"Give me a number to write on a check."

"Zero dollars." I smile in amusement. "I wouldn't waste the paper, but if you want, I'll take that and that only."

"That's taking *nothing.*"

I push off the wall and tap her door with my knuckle. "Get settled. I work tonight, but if you need anything, call or come down. The kitchen, both here and in the bar, is open if you're hungry."

"I need to run more errands, and then I'll be back."

"Sounds good."

"I might come keep you company tonight."

"I have no problem with that."

Sierra doesn't show during my shift, and when I go

upstairs after closing, her bedroom door is open. She's lying horizontally on the bed, sleeping, and the TV is on. I hesitate, unsure if I should wake her. I don't. Instead, I snag the blanket off the couch and drape it over her.

CHAPTER NINE

Sierra

"I HOPE you don't mind. I'm a stress-cleaner."

That's what I tell Maliki when he strolls into the kitchen to find me scrubbing the counters. I've already organized the closet and cleaned the guest bedroom and bathroom, and I'm finishing the kitchen. If he hadn't been sleeping, I'd have already dragged the vacuum out.

Stress-cleaning is a gift passed down from my mother. She cleaned when she was worried—a constant occurrence—and my brothers would hardly pick up their dirty laundry, so I helped. Now, I get the same relief from a deep scrubbing.

I glance at the time. It's one in the afternoon, and Maliki is just waking up. That's not a shocker though, given his job requires him to stay up all night.

I drink in the sight of him standing in front of me, shirtless. He's wearing gray sweatshorts that hang low on his waist. His hair is a wild mess, and his eyes are still half-asleep.

"You'll get no complaints from me," he says.

"Although I'm disappointed there wasn't much to clean. I've never seen a guy's house so spotless."

He drags out a stool from under the island and sits. "One

of the waitresses likes the extra cash and cleans the place once a week."

I slowly nod, uncertain of how I feel about someone else up in my space.

"I'll tell her to steer clear of your bedroom."

"No," I rush out. "Totally unnecessary."

"Your face dropped at the mention of her. Either you don't want her around your shit or her in the apartment. Which one?"

"Both." I perk up. "How about this? I'll clean for the both of us. I'm not paying rent. It's the least I can do."

"All right, but let me know if you change your mind."

I jerk my thumb toward my chest. "Stress-cleaner, remember?"

He frowns. "I hope living here won't cause you any stress, *so* let me know if you change your mind."

"I will." *I won't.*

The three waitresses who work at the pub are gorgeous, and I've seen them flirt with my new roomie aplenty. I'm the only one allowed to do that in this apartment now.

At least, that's what I want.

Oh my God.

I'm jealous.

Jesus.

I can't be jealous. I'm *married.*

"You don't work today?" His question breaks me away from my thoughts.

"I quit my job." I called in the day I learned about Devin's affair and haven't returned.

He leans inward and clasps his hands together.

"I'm not irresponsible for not putting in my two weeks." I'm uncertain why I feel the need to defend myself. "I tried, but his mother rattled on about forgiveness. *Then*, she used my parents' situation as an example, which *totally* pissed me off." The only thing I'm forgiving is my heart for being so damn dumb, trusting him. "I'm also not fond of working with an ex."

It sucks, losing my job. His father's firm was reputable and had a notable client list, and the pay was great. It'll be difficult, finding something like that in Blue Beech, so I'll have to look in surrounding towns.

"Any other job prospects?"

"I've had a few," I answer with a frown.

"Why do you look unhappy about that?"

"None of them are jobs I want." All of them are part-time gigs that'll hardly pay my grocery bills. I have money in savings, but that's for finding a new place. "Not to mention, the pay sucks. The demand for an interior designer in this town is practically nonexistent." Some residents haven't updated their homes in decades.

"I'll hire you to renovate the pub."

My breathing catches. "What?"

"The pub hasn't been updated in fuck knows how long. Renovate it … work your magic."

Excitement ripples through me, causing me to grin, and I squeal, clapping my hands. "I would *love* that! I've already thought of ideas of how I'd change things if ever given the opportunity." I needed something to do to pass the time when Maliki left me to make someone a drink.

I suddenly remember the conversation I planned to have with him this morning. Even with his offer, one job won't exactly load my bank account. Plus, I can't charge him as much as Devin's dad did his clients.

"You know …" I pause. "I have my bartending license."

He stills. "What?"

"I have my bartending license. I bartended on campus my senior year for extra cash."

Even though my parents paid my tuition and a chunk of my bills, I worked two jobs. Most of that money went toward the down payment for the condo.

"Your parents were okay with that?" he asks skeptically, raising his brows.

"Hell no."

My father would've flipped his shit.

A grin twitches at his lips. "How'd you manage to hide that from them?"

"Told them I was tutoring." I hold up a finger. "Which, technically, wasn't a lie. I was tutoring. It just wasn't where most of my cash came from."

"What about now? If I hire you, there's no lying about tutoring. This is a small town, princess … and you're *you.*"

"Their opinions are the least of my worries. My father ruined our family name with his little affair, so I can't do any worse damage. Plus, a change would be nice." *I'll also be able to hang out with you.*

He taps the countertop. "Lucky for you, my sister is leaving for a few weeks. You can take her bartending shifts. When she comes back, I'll have to move you to waitressing."

Shit. I forgot about Liz.

He laughs, as if catching on to my thoughts. "Don't worry. I told her to be nice."

Ugh, I'm not three. You don't have to force someone to be nice to me. "So, I'm hired?"

A slight smile hits his lips. "Why not? Looks like you scored yourself two jobs today."

"When do I start?" I ask eagerly.

"Whenever you want. I planned to ask Mikey to cover her shift tonight if you're game?"

"That works." It'll take my mind away from the chaos of my life. I give him a wide grin and bounce on my tiptoes.

He laughs. "Look at you, Jailbait. You're redecorating the pub, slinging drinks, and cleaning like a boss. Is there anything you can't do?"

"Keep a man."

"No. A man can't keep you."

"ANY BRILLIANT IDEAS YET?" Maliki asks, stopping next to me.

I grin. "You have no idea how many I'll pitch to you. You might regret hiring me."

"As long as you don't remove the authenticity and create a replica of the club you worked in the city, I trust you."

"I'd never."

With the little clients I've had, I've never forced my styles onto them. They tell me what they're looking for, and I bounce ideas off that.

"It needs to keep that easygoing vibe. And brace yourself … there's shopping."

"Shopping?" He groans dramatically. "Don't I write you a check, and you do all the work?"

"We can do it that way, but I don't suggest it. This is your bar, your baby, Maliki. I prefer you have a voice in the changes. You're looking at it for the rest of your life, not me." I signal to the empty bar. "I promise, nothing crazy." I clap him on the back. "We'll look at paint, furniture, decor. It'll be fun."

"Oh fuck, I'm going to regret this, aren't I?"

"Hiring me is one of the smartest moves you've ever made."

I proceed around the room, jotting down ideas, for an hour. When I'm finished, Maliki gives me a tour of the bar and explains everything that happens behind the scenes. I'm shown where all the alcohol is stocked, he introduces me to the kitchen staff, and I ask him countless questions.

When we're finished, he curves an arm around my shoulders and drags me into his side. "Welcome to the Down Home Pub team, princess."

I WAS SMART, making my first night during the week. I'll have time to adapt before the weekend comes.

This is the only place in Blue Beech if you're looking for fun or seeking to drink away your sorrows. Like every bar, the pub has its heartbroken, drunks, and partiers.

The pub is nothing like the club I worked in. It's relaxed compared to crazy coeds who just turned old enough for their first shot of vodka. There was no relaxing at the club like it is at Down Home—no sharing a quiet, deep conversation.

The prying eyes come as soon as my shift starts. The pub is hosting a pool tournament tonight that usually brings in a decent crowd—meaning more people seeing me and the higher the chances my parents find out about my new job. I'm already dreading the phone call.

"You okay over there?" Maliki calls over from his side of the bar.

"I'd be better if someone ordered a drink from me," I answer with a sense of rejection.

Nearly every customer has ordered from Maliki, avoiding me as if I had the plague. Either they don't trust my drink-making skills—which is a joke, considering the drinks served here are basic as hell—or they're scared of my father finding out I served them. I've already spotted a few of his employees.

He nods in understanding. "Give it a few shifts. It was the same when I started working with my dad. They're comfortable with me."

I hold my hand up and cross my fingers. "Let's hope so. Otherwise, I'm coming over there and making their drinks without their permission."

"What the hell are you doing here?"

The glass I'm holding crashes to the floor when Liz steps into the bar area. Her hands are parked on her skinny hips, and her usual snarl toward me is darker. I lean down and scramble to pick up the pieces of glass.

Great. Already dropping shit on my first day.

Maliki comes up behind her, towering over her small frame, and his eyes set on me. "I gave her a job."

Liz backs away to face him and shakes her head. "Last time I checked, we weren't hiring."

"Someone needs to cover your shifts while you're in Florida," Maliki replies sharply.

I twist to grab a rag from a shelf to stop the glass from cutting me as I clean up and focus on their standoff.

"Have Mikey cover them," Liz says, raising her voice. "Not a girl who's probably never stepped foot behind a bar."

I rise and toss the shards of glass into the trash. "I worked in one of the busiest clubs in the state."

The glare shot in my direction tells me she either didn't expect that answer or for me to defend myself.

Her face tightens. "Of course you have, Barbie." She rolls her eyes, turning her back to me, and continues yelling at Maliki, "What happens when I come back?"

"She'll serve," Maliki bites out. His eyes drift to me in reassurance and then return to his sister. "Now, unless you have business to discuss other than my employees, I don't want to hear it."

"Whatever," Liz huffs out. "Fuck up our family business because you're thinking with your dick."

Maliki's jaw tightens in frustration. "It's *my* business, and I'll do with it as I fucking please."

"Wow," she draws out. "We're going there now, huh? I'll be back in a few weeks. Oh, and consider this my resignation."

She storms away, and Maliki is running his hand over the stubble of his jaw when his eyes snap to me.

I smooth down my tank top and rush out my words. "You can fire me. I don't want to cause friction between you and your sister."

He chuckles, the stress slowly fading from his face. "Appreciate it, but Liz *resigns* once a month."

He squats down to clean up the remnants of glass I

missed. I didn't exactly want to crawl around on the floor by their legs.

He tosses the pieces into the trash can, and a relaxed smile crosses his face. "Now, get to work before I write you up."

I salute him, and he drifts back to his side of the bar.

"Your brother is going to kick your ass, and I'll take a Bud Light, please."

I shift my attention from Maliki to Gage—Kyle's best friend since childhood. They're partners on the Blue Beech police force.

I groan. "Please tell me he's not coming."

"Last I heard, he was," he answers with a smirk.

"Perfect."

I was so concerned about my parents' reaction to my job that I didn't think about my brothers. Rex, my younger one, won't give two shits about it. He'll probably ask me to make him a drink. But Kyle, as the overprotective older brother, won't be happy.

"I take it, he doesn't know about this new gig of yours?" Gage asks.

"Nope, so I'd appreciate it if you kept your lips sealed and led him to Maliki's side of the bar … or better yet, inform him the bar has shut down for the night and he can stay home." I smile, reach into the cooler for his beer, and hand it to him. "Don't forget my generous tip."

He slaps cash onto the bar. "This is a shitshow I can't wait to see."

I nod. "Facts."

"Then, why do it?"

"I need money to, I don't know, not starve to death."

"Seems legit." He swipes his beer from the bar. "I'll make sure to order my drinks from you, so you can have a cheeseburger tomorrow."

I roll my eyes. "Very funny."

His phone beeps. He reads the screen, laughs, and shows it to me. "Oh, he's most definitely coming."

Kyle: Is my sister working there?

My mouth turns dry, and I pour myself a water while groaning. "Great. The masses have already started gossiping."

He slaps his palm against the bar. "Good luck, little one."

I chug the water and refill my glass. Just as I'm about to finish it off, Kyle bursts through the crowd.

"You. Me. Talking now." He shoots his thumb toward the kitchen area.

My gaze darts toward Maliki, who gives me a silent nod, as if he knew Kyle would show up. I slam down my water and circle around the bar. Kyle is talking behind me, but I ignore him and take us to the back office.

I slam the door shut when we make it there. "Seriously? You're going to get me fired!" I haven't finished one shift, and I'm already bringing drama into the workplace.

My brother looks nothing like me. His hair is darker, taking after my father. He's built, strong, but he has nothing on Maliki.

Sorry, big brother.

He folds his arms over his chest and places his glare on me. "A. Maliki won't fire you. B. What the fuck is going on? Since when are you a bartender?"

I swallow hard, tears approaching. "Devin cheated on me."

"That son of a bitch," he hisses, straightening his stance. "Good."

"Good? How the hell is my husband cheating on me *good*?"

"I can kick his ass now. He's always annoyed me."

"Seriously, Kyle, don't touch him."

His face tightens. "I should've known he was a joke when he wore loafers to a barbeque." He balls up his fist. "I'm going to kill him."

Even though he works in law enforcement, he'd have no problem roughing Devin up. Being the oldest, he's protective of our family, especially now with everything that happened. His relationship with a woman who carries serious baggage has made him more vigilant.

"You're not killing anyone," I say. "Last I heard, inmates don't like police officers in their block. Do you know how bored you'd be when they stuck you in solitary confinement?"

My joke eases some of the tension on his face, and he blows out a breath that calms him further.

"Thanks for the tip, little sister, but I won't go to prison for punching him a few times."

"I want it to be done and move on with my life."

"So, you found out your husband cheated, and instead of coming to your family, you ran to Maliki?"

That does sound crappy. It takes me a moment to reply to his question. "Yep," I finally croak out.

He's mentioned how much time I spend with Maliki several times, and I've always blown him off—the same as with everyone.

His shoulders loosen, and with each minute that passes, the more he eases. "You're in better hands with Maliki anyway."

"Me and Maliki … we're not—"

He cracks a smile. "Not yet."

I shove his chest. "Hey, I'm still married—only a few days separated."

"I'm not saying marry the dude. He's an awesome guy, a good friend to you, and from what I've heard, he's a wonderful fucking boss." He whistles and jerks his head toward the door. "Now, come on. Let's see how well you serve a beer."

I glance back at him. "With extra spit."

"KI, I'M OUT OF HERE!" Tamara calls out while scooping up her tips and shoving them into her purse. "What time do you want me to come over tomorrow?"

I drop my towel on the bar, and my blood turns colder than the beers chilling in the cooler behind me.

Excuse me?

Tamara is one of the gorgeous waitresses. Her boobs are bigger than mine, her curves are sexier, and I don't know anything about her. She's an outsider who lives in the next town over. She also has taken up flirting with Maliki as a second job.

My attention shoots to Maliki, who's on his side of the bar, ridding it of empty glasses and baskets of bar food.

He takes off his hat and scratches his head. "Tomorrow doesn't work. Let's try again later this week."

She nods, smiling brightly at him. "Just text me."

She uses three fingers to wave good-bye to me, and I turn the dirty look I'm giving her into a fake smile while doing the same wave. She doesn't deserve my animosity, but I can't stand watching her flirt with him.

Maliki walks her out and locks the bar when he comes back in. That's one thing I respect about him. He walks his female employees to their cars at night. He cares about the people who work for him.

"Why are you shooting murderous glares at my waitress?" he asks.

I pull in a breath and set my attention on cleaning the bar. "Do I need to find somewhere to go *later this week* when she comes over?"

"She cleans the apartment."

"Oh." The annoyed expression remains on my face. His answer still hasn't put me at ease.

"Why do you still look pissed, even after I explained that?"

"Does she do more than *clean your apartment*? Is there a

particular time I should steer clear of the apartment, so you and her can have privacy *to clean*?"

"All she does is *clean,* so there's no need for privacy. Is there a reason we're having this conversation?"

I shrug. "Just in case we have people over to—"

"Ahh," he cuts in. "In case I have someone over to fuck." He leans back against a pub table, crosses his arms, and releases a laughter filled with edge. "Are you going to have guys over to fuck? Do we need to set up schedules?"

"What? No." I stare at him, baffled.

"Then, why is this coming up?"

"*I'm* not planning on sleeping with anyone in your apartment."

"Appreciate that."

"I don't want to be a buzzkill for you and … your women."

"I won't bring a woman home while you're there, okay?"

"So, what?" I grimace. "You'll go to their house?"

"Why are you asking so many questions?"

"I told you, I'm curious."

"Do you not want someone to come over because you don't want me with anyone else other than you?" He tilts his head to the side.

Yes. "How would you feel if I was going to another man's house and sexing it up?" I mirror his head tilt.

"You can do whatever you want, Sierra." He shoots me a frustrated look. "You've done that for a while now."

CHAPTER TEN

Maliki

"NOW THAT YOU'VE slept on it, how was your first shift?" I ask Sierra, strolling into the kitchen. "Still want to work with me?"

She's wearing a tight, ribbed tank top with a sports bra underneath that shows just the right amount of cleavage and black leggings. Her blonde hair is swept back into a ponytail, and her face is makeup free—my favorite look on her.

The view of Sierra early in the morning is the best goddamn view ever.

Scratch that. Even though I'll never see it, I'm sure the best goddamn view of her is waking up next to her in bed.

Thank fuck she gave up on asking me irrelevant questions about Tamara and bringing other women home when we finished closing last night. I'd never pull that shit with her here. From what it seems, Sierra believes I've screwed every woman who's flirted with me at the bar. Little does she know, I've wanted to punch every man who looks at her with desire while ordering his drinks. As the night turned later, people grew more comfortable, heading to her side of the bar.

She cracks an egg into a skillet. "I liked it, so no quitting from this girl." She grabs a bottle of coconut water and takes a long swig. "Egg?"

"Sure."

She cracks another egg. "How do you like them?"

"However you want to make them. I'm not picky."

"What if I add pickles and mustard to them?"

I scrunch up my face. *The fuck?* "Do you add pickles and mustard to them?"

"No, but you didn't know that. That could have been how I liked my eggs, and then you'd be stuck with them for breakfast."

I chuckle. "You are the most random person I know."

She grins and holds up her spatula. "Over easy eggs coming right up."

"Sans pickles and mustard?"

"You shall see," she sings out.

I circle the island to start a cup of coffee in the Keurig. "How'd the chat with your brother go?" I talked to Kyle after his conversation with Sierra and assured him I'd look out for her.

"It surprised him, is all."

"And your parents?"

"I have three missed calls from my father and eight from my mom. They know something. Whether it's my new job or my leaving Devin, I have no idea."

"You'll have to tell them eventually."

"I know. I'm visiting them after this afternoon. Devin is out of town this weekend with his father for a work thing. I texted Kyle this morning and asked if he could help me move my things out." She stops. "Shoot, I forgot to ask for my schedule. Do I work tonight?"

I shake my head. "Nope. We have the night off."

"Oh, cool." She places the eggs on the two plates next to her and slides one along with a fork in front of me. "Do you have any plans?"

"I'm having beers with some friends."

She leans in, not bothering to touch her food, and places her elbows on the counter. "Do I know them?"

She doesn't realize it, but her stance is giving me an even better view of her cleavage. She doesn't have large boobs, but they're also not small. My hands wouldn't be full if I played with them.

I shove another bite into my mouth, hoping it distracts me from brainstorming about the things I could do to those breasts.

When I glance back to her face, she's waiting for me to answer. *Shit.* I forgot she'd asked me a question.

"My friend Cohen."

She flinches. "The guy from Twisted Fox?"

"Yes, that guy."

She nods back and bites into her lower lip, looking disappointed. "Ahh … well, have fun."

CHAPTER ELEVEN

Sierra

"I CAN'T BELIEVE Devin is so stupid," my mom says, squeezing a lemon into a pitcher of lemonade. Even though her face is twisted in disgust, you'd guess she was referring to a sunny day. She has the sweetest voice I've ever heard, and no matter how angry she gets, it never rises or changes. "What a little asshole."

I crack a smile. "Oh my God!" I smack her arm as I walk past her and snag a cookie. "Mom!"

"What?" she asks, wiping her hands down her flowered apron. "He hurt you."

She was waiting for answers as soon as I walked through the front door. She'd made my favorite cookies—cookies and cream cheesecake—and she was starting on the lemonade—also my favorite. She consoles through stomachs, claiming cookies and hot meals always make someone feel *a little* happier.

Nancy Lane is the sweetest woman you'll ever meet. If someone is sick, she's at their doorstep with chicken soup. If a family is in need of charity, she not only pulls out her checkbook, but she's also at the family's side, taking a list of anything they need.

I didn't bother taking my time to break the news. I blurted out, "Devin cheated," when I walked in.

She knew what to do—immediately wrapping me up in a hug as I cried for the ending of my marriage. Then, she told me she had cookies waiting for me.

She was right.

It did make me feel better.

Her calling Devin a little asshole puts a cherry on top.

Nancy Lane is not someone who curses on the regular.

She frowns. "I was so excited for you to get married. Maybe I pushed you too hard, and you should've waited. I should've known he was wrong for you." She sniffles. "Mothers are supposed to know these things."

I kiss her cheek. "Don't worry. I threw something at his head." I bite into a cookie and savor its yumminess. "Healthy communication at its finest."

She circles her fingers around the handle of the pitcher, grabbing a few glasses, and I snag the plate of cookies while following her to the kitchen table. We sit down where my sister, Cassidy, is texting on her phone. She's home from college—most likely so that my mom can do her laundry and send her back with food, so she doesn't starve.

"Did you ask him why he did it?" my mom asks.

"He slept with someone because he was thinking with the scrawny thing between his legs. That's the only explanation I have." I pour myself a glass of lemonade. "No, wait. He told me it wasn't so bad because it happened at a *bachelor party*."

Cassidy drops her phone. "Ew. That's really what happens at bachelor parties? I thought that was just in the movies." She shudders. "Devin seriously sucks."

"No, honey," my mom says. "That isn't what happens at all bachelor parties."

Cassidy and I took after our mom in the looks department—blonde hair, lighter eyes, somewhat on the short side.

Even for her age, my mom is beautiful. She's made it a

full-time job to run charities, help people, work in the kitchen, and keep up with her appearance. She wears makeup and dresses up more than I do.

"Never get married," I tell Cassidy, snatching another cookie. It seems leaving my husband has led me to turn to carbs, making Devin an even bigger bastard.

"Hey now, marriage is a beautiful thing," my mom argues. "It's just … sadly, some aren't respectful to their vows."

I reach out and capture her hand, lightly squeezing it, and see the compassion in her eyes. Right now, we're both suffering through infidelities, but I'd take on my mom's hurt over mine any day. Her heart is too big for this pain.

I cringe, wondering but too afraid to ask how she can look at dad, knowing what he did. I always saw her as this strong woman and was so proud when she threatened my father with a divorce. Then, I cried the day she told me she changed her mind and was taking him back. As much as I love my father, she didn't deserve that, and he doesn't deserve a woman as amazing as her.

"Now that I've decided I'm never getting married," Cassidy says, shooting her attention to me, "what's going on with you and the hot bartender? Eight people asked me about it at the gym this morning." She pours herself a glass of lemonade. "And let me put it out there that Maliki Bridges is so much hotter than Devin."

"Oh my God. People your age are talking about me?"

She shrugs. "You know it's a small town, and you're getting it on with the town's hottest bachelor. People will talk."

"Cassidy!" my mom shrieks, her tone having a sprinkle of warning in it.

"What?" she asks. "I bet he wouldn't cheat at a bachelor party."

I point to her bookbag on the floor. "Go study."

She shakes her head, pulls out her ponytail, and glides her

hand through her hair. "No, this conversation is so much juicier than Anatomy."

My mom's awareness slides back to me, her features loaded with concern. "Now that you've scared your sister out of marriage, we need to talk about your new job. Devin said you quit his father's company, and word is, you've not only switched jobs, but also moved in with Maliki?" She touches her face and pauses, as if she's thinking. "Now, honey, you know I don't judge, but we didn't spend thousands of dollars in education for you to end up working in a hole-in-the-wall bar. I don't look down on those in the service industry, but I never want my daughter around drunk people. I've read plenty of crime books. Most serial killers prey on women at bars."

"Yep! I just saw this Netflix documentary. That crap is *creepy*," Cassidy cuts in and shuts her mouth when my mom shoots her a disapproving look.

"Cassidy, go study, text, take selfies, something," she says.

She raises her hands high in surrender. "All right, I'll keep my mouth shut, but I'm staying. I love hearing lectures that aren't pointed in my direction."

"Mom, it's a transition period until I find another job," I say in my best voice of reassurance. "I'm using my degree and renovating the pub, so technically, that's my job. The bartending is for extra cash to get a new place."

"You can stay here. Your room is always open. Plus, you know your father and I will help you with any financial issues you're having."

"I'm a grown woman. I'm not moving in with my parents *or* taking money from you."

"Can I volunteer as tribute with the cash offer?" Cassidy interjects.

Instead of answering her, my mom keeps her focus on me. "Why not? I make amazing banana nut bread, you'll always have a hot breakfast, and I'm sure I keep a home cleaner than a bachelor."

"I'll let you know if I change my mind, okay? But right now, I need to do this on my own. It's time for me to figure out this new chapter in my life."

"You're not on your own if you're living with another man." Her words are gentle, but her blow is harsh. She's trying her hardest to sound sweet, but it's what she's feeling at the moment.

"We're friends."

"I know you, honey. You wouldn't just move in with someone like that."

"We have separate bedrooms. It's nothing different than when I lived in the dorms at college. I'm renting a room from him. That's it."

Cassidy snorts. "For now."

"You're right. I'm sure you weren't an angel in college." Mom wiggles her finger at me. "And you have fun explaining that to your father. Maliki's family doesn't have the best reputation in town."

"Right now, neither does our family. Maliki is a loyal man, and I trust him more than I did my own husband."

KYLE SCRUBS his hands together and surveys the living room of my condo—well, *old* condo. "Is that it?" He peeks over at me. "We're leaving everything else, right?"

"Yes. All I want is my personal stuff," I answer.

Rex groans and thrusts his arms out toward the living room. "Come on, sis. Take the TV. The couch. *Something.* That cheating bastard didn't pay for all this shit himself."

He's right. I paid for half of everything—the down payment, the furniture, the bills. When the divorce papers are drawn up, I'll insist we sell the condo and split the profit.

Easy-peasy.

Ending this divorce shouldn't be a challenge.

"I don't have anywhere to put it," I answer. Nor do I want the memories of shit I shared with Devin. I'd rather buy new furniture.

"You know," Rex sings, "I wouldn't mind storing that sixty-inch flat screen in my living room." He shrugs. "I'm that nice of a brother."

I roll my eyes. "*Fine,* you can have the *bedroom* TV."

"Hell yeah," Rex says. His gaze darts around the room again. "What about the fine china? I could use something classier than paper plates."

"*Oh my God,* you can have the dishes."

"And the fridge?"

"Jesus, you're not taking the fridge." I push his shoulder. "Come on. I'll treat you to pizza for being the muscles."

"Pizza sounds awesome," Rex says, snapping his fingers. "And speaking of pizza, you have to let your baby brother have that kick-ass pizza oven."

"What the hell?" Kyle says. "That was my wedding gift."

Rex slaps Kyle's stomach. "If I recall, you told her you had the same one and fucking loved it. Your ass doesn't need another."

"*Fine,* you can have the pizza oven too," I tell him.

"HOW'D you find out Devin cheated?" Rex asks, taking a bite of his pizza.

Fred's Pizzeria is the only pizza joint in town, but even if it wasn't, it's still where I'd always come. They have the best pizza, subs, and garlic bread. If you're looking to stuff yourself with carbs—which, apparently, is my new hobby—Fred's is the place to go.

I saw the eyes on us when we walked in. That, or I'm so

paranoid that I'm convinced anyone who looks in my direction knows what happened with Devin, as if a neon sign were shining above my head.

I take a drink before answering, "He was at a bachelor party and wasn't smart enough to know that people talk. He had a restroom break with another woman, and when they came out, it was obvious what had happened."

Rex smooths a hand over his mouth in an attempt to hide a smirk. "He could've been drunk and needed help finding his small dick."

I tear off a piece of crust and toss it at him, giving him the dirtiest look I can muster. "I hate you."

He holds up his hand. "Jesus, no more bread-throwing, crazy woman. You know I'm kidding." He leans back and relaxes in his booth. "I was never a Devin fan, so no love lost there. He was lame, and hopefully, your next boyfriend"—he stops to dramatically cough and covers his mouth—"Maliki"—another cough—"has somewhat of a sense of humor."

I chew on my bottom lip. "Hey, he wasn't that lame." I ignore the Maliki comment. Everyone is calling Devin lame, so what does that make me for marrying him? Lame, too?

Rex snags his drink and takes a sip. "You were complacent with him. He did what you wanted … had no balls."

"He had enough balls to cheat," I fire back.

"He hardly challenged you, and I know from growing up with your mean ass that you love being challenged. Sure, you liked him, but he was the easy way, not *love*, love."

Frustration rattles through me. Not at my brother, but at being so blind. Marrying Devin was a mistake.

I level my elbow on Kyle's shoulder, who's next to me in the booth, and narrow my eyes on Rex across from us. "Okay, Dr. Drew, how are you such an expert on relationships? You've never even had a serious girlfriend."

"Coaches don't play, sister." He shrugs and pops a pepperoni in his mouth.

I roll my eyes. "You're dying old and alone."

"No, I'll have my booty calls at my funeral, crying at my casket, sad that their favorite screw bit the big one."

I glance over at Kyle. "Swear to God, you're taking care of him when the nursing home kicks him out for bad behavior."

My arm falls when Kyle shifts to look at me. "Nope, dear sister. He'll shack up with you, considering you'll both be single."

"I hate you too," I grumble, pushing my hand over his hair, messing it up as he attempts to pull away.

"Where are we moving your shit, by the way?" Rex asks.

"You moved my stuff all day and never thought to ask that?" I reply.

Kyle chuckles, shaking his head. He borrowed Gage's truck, and after dinner, we're dropping off what I'm not taking to Maliki's at the storage unit I rented.

A wide grin spreads across Rex's face. "I was too busy staking out the residence for shit I wanted you to give me."

I roll my eyes.

"You still haven't answered my question," Rex continues. "Are you moving home? I have an extra bedroom at my place if you want to crash there."

"Hang out with your college buddies?" I ask. "I appreciate the offer, baby bro, but that's a hard no."

"You know the offer still stands to stay with me," Kyle says.

"Your place is full," I say. "Not to mention, you have so much happening with Chloe and Trey. It'll be uncomfortable for everyone there."

Chloe is Kyle's girlfriend, and Trey is her nephew. Trey is also our half-brother. Chloe never told Kyle that my dad was Trey's father, even after they started dating. Our family found out at the same time as everyone in town. All thanks to Chloe's sister, Monica's boyfriend shouting it out for everyone to hear. That was the night I went to Maliki. The night our family changed. Now, Trey comes around from time to time. Kyle and him are close, given they live together, and Rex bombarded himself into Trey's life, wanting a relationship with him. Rex felt bad for him, that he'd been handed such a shitty life, and wanted to change that. My brothers have taken him under their wing.

"So, Mom and Dad's it is," Rex says, sipping his Coke.

I shake my head.

His lips form a wide grin. "I know where this is headed. You're moving in with your side boy toy. I dig it." He dramatically waggles his eyebrows.

"Shut up. I don't have a side boy toy."

Rex snorts. "Who is Maliki to you then, huh? Even when you were with Devin, you had a thing for him."

"We'll be roommates for a minute. That's it," I answer.

"Holy shit, so you *are* moving in with him."

"It isn't like that," I argue.

"Keep your head straight, sis," Kyle says. "Maliki is cool, but as long as I've known him, he doesn't do committed relationships. You're already dealing with a broken heart, and I have a feeling a broken heart from him will be harder on you." He shakes his head. "Ki won't let it get that far though, so you shouldn't have anything to worry about."

Kyle's warning tugs at my heart. He's not only right about Maliki not doing a committed relationship, but he's also spot-on with how Maliki has the ability to pulverize my heart.

He did it that night I found him in his office.

It's a bad idea, moving in with him, but any opportunity I get to be around him, I'll take, consequences be damned.

"Not to mention, you'd be hooking up with your roommate and *boss*," Rex adds.

I groan. "Can we stop talking about my love life now and move on to someone else's?"

"Trust me, you don't want to talk about mine," Kyle says. "We'll be here all night."

I smile over at my big brother. "But you and Chloe are happy now, so that's all that matters." I clap his shoulder. "How are things with the adoption agency coming?"

He releases a stressed breath, gritting his teeth. "We're trying, but with her family's history, it's proving difficult." A grim expression falls across his face.

This isn't the place to discuss his relationship.

So, on to Rex.

"Looks like we're moving on to you, little brother."

Kyle snorts. "The only love life he has is the one with his hand."

"Lies," I sing out, tilting my head toward Rex. "He's going to marry Carolina."

Kyle snorts again. "Carolina is too smart to marry him."

"I'm right here, assholes," Rex chimes in, furrowing his brows. "And no, I'm not marrying Carolina."

"Kyle is right," I say. "She is too smart to marry you. You should've taken your chance in high school, but it's probs too late now."

"We never dated because we're best friends," Rex grits out.

Carolina is a touchy subject for him. They've been best friends since high school, and he's more protective of her than he is of his own sisters. I've never seen my brother care about someone so much. There's no doubt the love for each other is there between them, but Rex is scared to ruin their friendship.

"Best friends who secretly love each other." I angle my gaze toward him. "You just wait. I'm calling it right here, right now. You'll be with her before you hit your thirties."

"I don't know," Kyle says. "I think he ruined his chance."

"Both of you can fuck off," Rex grumbles.

CHAPTER TWELVE

Maliki

I COME to the Twisted Fox when I need a beer and peace away from my customers. You can't enjoy a relaxing drink in your own bar. Clients and employees are demanding even if you tell them you're off for the night.

That's why Cohen and I have a thing.

I come here when I need away from the chaos.

Down Home is his destination when he needs space from here.

It's like our bars are friends, too.

Tonight, neither one of us is working, so I sit down at a table. Cohen comes strolling through the bar, navigating around his customers, holding a beer in each hand. He slides one to me, twists his stool around, and straddles it backward, resting his arms on the back.

"How's everything at the bar?" is the first question he asks.

It's our version of, *What's up, man?*

"Busy as hell," I answer. "We're out of the red and pulling in a respectful revenue."

I finally started turning a decent profit two years ago. I'd managed a bar before this. The owner had given me complete control, and I doubled the revenue, reduced expenses, and raised his Yelp rating two stars. I worked myself to death at that bar for one goal: to own my own.

Everything changed when Liz called, crying.

She'd rooted through my father's mail, and what she discovered wasn't pretty. He had the bar in a financial mess, held countless loans and liens against it, and if he didn't write a hefty check to the bank in seven days, he'd lose it. It wasn't my issue, was what I told her. I didn't want the bar, didn't want to move back to Blue Beech, didn't want to clean up our father's goddamn mess.

Liz was determined to keep it in the family and decided she'd try to take over. She tried and struggled—struggled to secure loans with her less than average credit score and lack of funds. I love my sister and didn't want to see her kill herself to make the bar work, so I paid the debt and took over.

Pissed, I'd hardly spoken a word to my father when he sold it to me, but now, I'm glad I did it.

Cohen shifts in his stool, making himself comfortable. "Remember when we talked about launching a bar together?" He shuts his eyes in recollection. "Look at us now, owning our own and some might say in competition with each other."

"Shut the fuck up. You're not my competition," I say, kicking his foot with my Converse.

Cohen and our friend, Archer, asked me for the go-ahead prior to opening the bar. Some might be pissed if their friends opened a bar thirty minutes away from theirs, but I was happy for their success. Cohen and I had dreamed of having our own business, and here we are, fulfilling that goal. Plus, I get to hang out with my best friend all the time.

He shrugs. "We should revisit the idea sometime."

"It's poor timing right now. My hands are full, getting the place back up and running. Plus, I'm renovating and upgrading my shit."

Not only am I having Sierra redo the face of the bar, but I'm also purchasing new kegs, kitchen appliances, and upgrading my taps. I'm not the founding father of Down Home, but I can still make it mine. I've considered a remodel for a while, but hiring Sierra has gotten the ball rolling.

He nods slightly while grinning. "That's awesome, man. I'm fucking happy for you."

He raises his beer into a cheers motion, and I clank mine against his.

I met Cohen through a woman I dated. He dated her best friend. He worked at another bar in the city, a lame-ass one, and I hired him where I worked. That was eight years ago, and we've been friends since. If there's anyone who understands me, it's him. We grew up in bars, and now, we eat, sleep, and breathe our businesses.

He snaps his fingers a few times and grabs his beer. "Oh, I meant to ask you, what happened with the chick and cheating husband?" He takes a long swig of his drink.

Oh shit.

I didn't think of Cohen asking me about Sierra. I came here to clear my head and get a grip on the situation.

There goes that.

"She, uh … moved into my place."

He spits out the beer in his mouth, liquid spewing on his lap and the table. He snatches a few napkins and cleans the mess, laughing. "Are you shitting me?"

I shake my head.

"You've never let anyone move into your place. Your motherfucking ass wouldn't even let one of our best friends move in."

"Her losing her place of residence wasn't her choice. Finn, on the other hand, was kicked out as a result of banging his roommate's sister."

Finn is a friend and also works at Twisted Fox.

He rolls his eyes. "Yeah, yeah. Now, let's return to the fun subject of you and your hot new roomie. I'm sure you'll have no problem screwing the hurt from her cheating husband right out of her."

I reach forward to push his shoulder. "We're not fucking. We're simply roommates, and she's helping me renovate the bar."

He drags his hand through his hair. "You must know her pretty damn well to let her move in. You were also pissed enough that you beat the dude's ass like he'd just cheated on your little sister. Is she a friend's sister? Why do you care so much about her?"

I contemplate my next move and scratch my cheek while looking away from him. "Do you remember when I used to tell you about the teenage brat who kept sneaking into the bar?"

He smirks. "Holy shit! That's her?"

I nod. "That's her."

He smacks his knee. "Man, I told you that something would happen with her someday. She's not even your type."

I massage my neck, suddenly feeling tense. "I have a type?"

"You for sure have a type."

I raise a brow.

"Emotionally unavailable, like you, is your type. Women who are fine without wanting more from you. I don't get that vibe from her. Hell man, she's married."

"Soon-to-be divorced."

"You sure about that?"

I nod. "Positive."

I don't tell him how well I know Sierra—that I know how fucking strong she is and that she won't take Devin's punk ass back.

At least, I hope not.

I TOSS my keys onto the kitchen island and head into the living room where I hear the TV playing. I shove my hands into my pockets when I see Sierra slouched on the couch. Her legs are drawn to her chest, and she's staring at the screen as if it were the most fascinating thing in the world.

It's a fucking vacuum infomercial.

She peeks back at me over her shoulder, her eyes red and puffy.

Shit.

"You were out late," she deadpans.

I should've canceled my plans with Cohen and stayed with her, but damn, she seemed fine. It surprised me with how relaxed she's been the past few days, given her situation. I just found out Sierra is a closet crier. She waits until she's alone to expose her wounds.

I swallow a few times, guilt rising up my spine, and level my voice. "It's midnight. I'm normally not in bed until four in the morning. This is early for me."

That only grants me a sullen look. "Did you have fun with your friends?"

I'm sure I had more fun than her. She looks like someone ran over her dog.

I proceed further into the room to face her. "It ended up being only me and Cohen hanging out."

The initial plan was drinking in the city with our other friends, but I didn't want to leave Sierra alone all night. When I told Cohen I wanted something more chill, he stayed behind with me.

She repeatedly nods. It almost makes her look like she's rocking back and forth.

"What about you? Did you do anything?"

Her face falls more. "I talked to my mom, and then my brothers helped me move." She rubs at her tired eyes. "Other than having my entire life overturned, nothing."

She needs a friend, and I wonder why she didn't call Ellie. That chick seems to be the Robin to her Batman.

Looks like I'm her Robin tonight.

I crash on the other end of the couch, giving her plenty of space. "Did you get everything out of the condo?"

She chews on her lower lip to block it from trembling. "I did."

"And have you talked to him?"

"He's called a few times, but I've dodged his calls. He knows about me working at the bar and had the guts to accuse *me* of cheating on him with you." She drops her legs and snorts. "I didn't even bother replying. I hope he thinks I'm screwing your brains out, so he can feel as stupid as I do."

My head jerks back. "Screwing my brains out, huh?" My dick stirs. *Why does she have to say shit like that?*

"You know what I mean."

"It can be arranged, if you'd like."

Our eyes briefly meet until she breaks contact by rolling hers. "Whatever. I annoy you."

"True. You're right. I shouldn't screw an annoying woman's brains out."

"So, is that what you were doing tonight?"

"Screwing an annoying woman's brains out? Negative."

"What *were* you doing then?"

"Hanging out with Cohen."

She sucks in what sounds like an aggravated breath. "You already said that." She yawns. "I've had a long day. I'll see you later."

I capture her arm when she gets up, stopping her. "Don't bullshit me, Sierra."

She sinks back against the cushions. "What are you talking about?"

"I'm talking about your rounded-ass questions you ask in some code that I'm supposed to understand, and then you get pissed when I don't speak in code right back. I had drinks with a friend."

"So you told me."

"Why are you upset about that?"

"I'm not."

"Bullshit."

She throws her head back. "I don't know why I am, honestly." She shrugs, tears hitting her eyes.

"Again, speaking in code."

"I hoped maybe as roommates, we'd hang out or something." She shakes her head and slaps her forehead. "Oh my God, that sounds so stupid and immature."

I stand, walk to the kitchen, and grab two beers from the fridge. My next stop is the pantry where I snag a bag of kettle corn and chips. I reach into the freezer, pull out a container of ice cream, and open the drawer for two spoons.

"What are you doing?" she draws out, her attention bobbing from me and the snacks clutched in my hold when I return.

I plop back down on the couch, closer to her this time, and the chips fall between us. "If you want to hang out with me, just say it." I hand her a spoon and the tub of ice cream. "I bought this at the store earlier. Mint chocolate chip is still your favorite, right?"

She nods as a blush hits her cheeks.

"Good. Now, pick something to watch. I'm exhausted, and I can't promise to stay awake long, but I'm here. I'll always be here."

CHAPTER THIRTEEN

Sierra

TONIGHT IS my first weekend shift.

Maliki briefed me this morning on what to expect. A live band is performing, so no doubt we'll be busy. He answered my last-minute questions. We reviewed drinks and prices. I'd used a cheat sheet my first night, but I won't have time for that.

He'll change the ice and kegs—thank God. The last time I attempted to change a keg, it doused me, and I smelled like stale booze all night.

Maliki is on his side of the bar, prepping his area, when I get downstairs. Even though it's not that long of a bar, when working, it's almost like we're in two different worlds. I slip my bottle opener into my jean shorts pocket and start setting up my space.

The jukebox plays in the background as I slice my garnishes, restock my straws, and get all my supplies in place. Everything needs organized, so this shift slips by with ease. So many people have shown their doubt about me working here, and I need to prove I know what I'm doing.

People don't come to Down Home only for the drinks and kick-ass bar food. What brings them here is the live music, events, atmosphere, and of course, the old-fashioned dance floor. I've witnessed sad souls with downcast eyes walk onto that dance floor, and when they return, their smiles could light up the room.

The atmosphere unwinds you.

That's why I love it here so much.

Well, that, *and* Maliki.

I don't stress about fitting in here like I do at a benefit dinner with my parents or when hanging out with Devin at a country club. My hair can be messy, my clothes casual, and no one bats an eye.

There are a few customers already here, mainly on Maliki's side, and when a customer plops in front of me, I take his order.

Jack and Coke. Bacon cheeseburger and onion rings.

I yell his order to the kitchen and start his drink. After handing it to him, I return to cutting my lemons.

"You look fucking gorgeous tonight."

I get a whiff of his cologne when Maliki stands behind me. I love how he smells. It's clean but masculine. I focus on my task, frazzled, and don't glance back at him. Every muscle in my body convulses as his chest hits my back, and I shiver when his cold hand brushes my hair away from it, his fingers slightly running along my neck.

Oh my God. Oh my God.

I squeeze my thighs together, and my heart clunks against my ribs. If only I were brave enough to grind against him, but there are people around, and public rejection doesn't sound like a great time. I grip the knife in one hand and use the other to clutch the bar while struggling to control my breathing.

I don't know what to expect when I turn around to face him.

Maliki retreats a step, his eyes wide and focused on my fingers

I meet his gaze and realize I'm still holding the knife.

"Shit," I mutter, dropping it onto the bar. "Totally wasn't about to go all stabby on you." I sigh and run my hands down my shorts. "And thank you."

I'm wearing cutoff jean shorts that my mom would call inappropriate and have my bar shirt tied around my waist, revealing a hint of midriff. A shiny, new pair of pink Doc Martens are on my feet.

"I have to make those tips," I add.

He chuckles. "I see. You're trying to steal my cash because you're cute."

He doesn't seem anywhere as worked up as I am about our little encounter. Meanwhile, my heart is banging batshit crazy.

"Damn straight." How I'm speaking is beyond me.

I bite into my tongue, holding myself back from mentioning how hot he looks tonight with his hat, torn jeans, and boots. I don't because it'd make things awkward. Maliki knows how to play off his flirting. Me? I'm a disaster. It always comes out wrong. We're working together all night, so it's in my best interest to not make it weird.

But he isn't making it easy with the whispers in the ear and touching.

He levels his eyes on me, as if he's about to break news I don't want to hear. "There's a bachelor party tonight. I would've given you a heads-up, but I just found out. You cool with that?"

"Of course." I pat his chest a few times and fake a smile. I'm not *exactly* okay with it, but I'll deal. "I'm a professional, Maliki. I mean, I might kick a dude in the junk and kick him out if I see him cheating on his wife, but other than that, I'm peachy." I shrug, grab my knife, and slam it into the cutting board.

He laughs, smoothing his hand over his jaw. "Please don't kick anyone out. That's my job, remember?"

"I learned from the best."

Our attention flashes to the opening of the kitchen when someone calls his name.

"Let me know if you need anything," Maliki says. "I have all your stuff in your area, so you won't need to search for anything."

"Maliki, you don't have to do that. It's *my* job."

"And?"

"You don't help Mikey set up his space. People will think you're giving me preferential treatment."

"Sierra, if someone *doesn't* think I'm giving you preferential treatment, they're dumb and should be fired."

"I'm serious," I whine with frustration.

He smiles, showing off his bright white teeth. "Look, you're my friend, roommate, and … someone I like to look after." He glances to the ceiling, either searching for the right word or asking God for an answer. "Little sister?"

Oh, hell no.

He didn't just pull the little-sister card.

"Oh my God. Never refer to me as your little sister again."

"That's not how I meant it. What I'm saying is, it's obvious I help you as much as I can and watch over you." He shrugs. "That's it."

"While I appreciate that, I don't want other employees talking shit about me."

"They won't." He chuckles. "Not to your face."

I kick my boots against the floor. "I already know they hate me."

His voice lowers. "They thought it was weird." Irritation flashes along his features. "Just like I'm protective of you, so are my employees of me. Not as much, but they are."

I blink at him. "Protective of you for what?"

"Over me hanging out with a woman who has a boyfriend at home."

His face falls as if he remembers every time I left him and went to Devin. Shame crushes through me.

Why did I do that to him? Why did I do that to myself?

He clears his throat. "I need to get back to work. Holler if you need anything."

He walks away, his strides long, as if he wants to put as much distance between us as he can.

Guilt, so much fucking guilt, shatters through me.

I'VE ALREADY SPILLED a beer on myself and messed up three orders.

One waitress keeps shooting me death glares.

The other is giving Maliki all her orders after my screwup.

So much for proving myself tonight.

I'm blaming it on my conversation with Maliki. It completely threw me off my game.

I know when the bachelor party arrives. They come straight in my direction and are annoying as hell. With every shot, they have a stupid saying.

"Here's to losing your freedom!"

"To having your balls on a leash!"

"To having only one pussy for the rest of your life!"

I'm positive Satan invented bachelor parties.

I'm never getting married again.

CHAPTER FOURTEEN

Maliki

THE BAR IS SLAMMED TONIGHT.

Money is flowing.

People are enjoying themselves.

Normally, I wouldn't complain.

It's what you want in your business.

What I don't want is every motherfucking man flirting and drooling over my new bartender, roommate, my … whatever the fuck Sierra is to me.

Friend?

I shake my head, attempting to clear my thoughts, but it doesn't help.

Shit.

Now, I wish I hadn't started the *no drinking on the job* rule.

My night is a circle of actions.

Ask someone what they want. Look at Sierra. Make their drink. Look at Sierra. Give them their drink. Look at Sierra.

She's smiling, and the men love it. No doubt she's killing it with tips, but she isn't overly flirty or eating up the attention. What drives me insane is that they perceive her friendliness as interest.

Yeah, fucking right.

I've seen Sierra flirt.

I know what it looks like when she's interested in someone.

Because she does it with me.

She's flirted with me since her illegal ass sauntered into my bar. At first, it was almost comical. She couldn't flirt worth shit, and though I was drawn to her, I never planned on anything developing with us. She was legal and, even though she tried to hide it, innocent.

So damn innocent.

Some men love innocence.

Me? Not so much.

Innocence leads to confusion.

Innocence wants more from you than a simple fuck here and there.

Innocence gets their heart broken.

So, yeah, that's why I steer clear of innocent blondes.

Although, Sierra isn't exactly innocent anymore.

I've done a decent job of controlling myself until I see a guy take hold of her elbow. Sierra jerks away, and he grabs her again—this time with a creepy-ass smirk.

All I see is red as I drop the glass in my hand and charge over to them. I'm at her side in seconds, and I reach across the bar to shove him away.

"What the fuck, dude?" the guy yells, catching his balance.

I point to him. "Keep your filthy-ass hands off my employees."

He gets closer, and the booze on his breath reeks. "Dude, I was only talking to her."

I don't have time for this bullshit. "You order your drinks from me the rest of the night, do you hear me?"

The scrawny guy perks up his chest—an attempt to look intimidating, but it does the opposite. "How do you know she doesn't want me to touch her? She's been teasing me all night."

Sierra rolls her eyes, not bothering to look my way, and

grabs the guy another beer. “Here.” She hands it to him. “I’ll add it to your tab.”

“Thanks, gorgeous.” He winks at her and turns his attention to me. He tips his glass my way, swings around, and walks away.

Sierra smacks her arm into my stomach to block me from jumping across the bar and kicking his ass.

Her eyes are narrowed when she looks at me. “This is your bar, Maliki. You can’t pull that with customers.”

“I can if they’re making you uncomfortable,” I grind out.

“I can handle my own.” She blows out a noisy breath and crosses her arms.

“Doesn’t mean you have to or will under my watch.”

“Oh, really?” Anger burns across her face, which confuses the fuck out of me. “Maybe you shouldn’t be hanging out with a woman you’ve hooked up with *on my watch*.” She scoffs. “*Literally*.”

“What?”

She makes a sweeping gesture toward the woman parked in the corner on my side of the bar.

Oh fuck.

“I recognize her,” she hisses. “She might not be moaning your name while you’re banging her on your desk, but I saw her. That’s the woman you were screwing the night I came over.”

Oh, so she wants to talk about that night.

I’ve been dying to do this.

This is the wrong place, wrong time, but here goes.

“Why did you come here that night?” My tone is even, and I lower my arm to stop her from ducking underneath it and scurrying away. “We hadn’t talked in fuck knows how long. In fact, it was the night before *your wedding*.”

She clenches her slender jaw, and a blush rises up her cheeks. “It doesn’t matter.”

“If it doesn’t matter, then why don’t you tell me?”

"We have a crowd of people waiting. I have men to flirt with." Her lips curl. "And you have a woman you've fucked to serve." She smacks my shoulder. "Gotta run, boss."

I fasten my hand around her arm, stopping her again. "Why did you come to the bar?" I grit out, wanting the answer more than my next breath.

She came for a reason. A woman doesn't visit another man the night before her wedding for no goddamn reason.

"Tell me."

She wriggles free from my grasp and looks away from me. "I needed a drink."

"You needed a drink?" I snort. "Bull-fucking-shit. Your husband might have bought your lies, but I see right through you."

She shrugs, her voice almost sounding resentful. "Whatever. I need to get back to work and make some cash."

Reality slaps me, reminding me again this isn't the place. I shake my head and return to my customers. Penny grins and signals to her empty glass.

Penny works for one of my beer distributors. We clicked, went out a few times, and fucked a whole lot of times. That ran smooth for nearly a year. I'd made it clear I wasn't looking for a relationship, and everything was perfect until she developed feelings and hit me with the L-word. She'd said it numerous times during sex—those don't count—but never over a meal. So, I had to end things with her.

We didn't talk for months before the eve of Sierra's wedding. She randomly showed up, and I needed to clear my head—to forget about Sierra.

And because I kept needing to forget about Sierra, I used Penny as that buffer—until I realized it wasn't fair to her. I haven't seen her since the night I broke it off, though we both left in an understanding that we'd remain friends.

I didn't invite her tonight, haven't spoken to her in months, but I can't kick her out. She's done nothing wrong.

Friends don't ignore friends, but I've tried to stay clear of her the best I can tonight. It's difficult, considering she keeps ordering drinks and food.

I make her a vodka soda, and before I get the chance to walk away, she seizes my arm in her hand, her fingers dancing along my skin, and leans forward, her cleavage spilling out.

"Are you doing anything tonight?" she whispers.

"Working and then crashing," I answer, bored.

"You want some company?"

"Nope. I'm pretty tired."

"Oh, come on. You never turn me down when I'm in town, and we need to catch up. It's been a while."

I jerk away and take a step back. It's just my luck that when I glance to the other side of the bar, Sierra's attention is pinned to us. Her face is pinched together as she gives me a stony glare.

Of motherfucking course.

"I've been busy," I practically fume.

She narrows her brown eyes at me. "What's up with you?"

"Nothing."

She motions to Sierra. "Is there funny business going on with you and prep-academy girl over there?" She laughs. "Where did you find her? She looks like she belongs anywhere but here."

I grimace at the truth in her observation. She's right. Sierra doesn't belong in a run-down bar like this.

"I don't know what you're talking about," I say, feigning disinterest. "She's my employee, and I want to make sure she's okay." The last thing I need is Penny starting shit with Sierra.

Her eyes latch on to Sierra, who's turned our back to us, and her face turns guarded. "Liar. You've been undressing her all night, staring at her ass, slamming shit around anytime a man talks to her. I know what it looks like to want someone. You've given me those looks *plenty* of times."

The way I've looked at her will never match how I look at Sierra. Never.

"I'm busy, Penny," I say. "Enjoy your night."

She sighs loudly and doesn't speak until I shift on my heels to leave. "What a shame. A man like you falling for a woman like her."

I whip around. "The fuck is that supposed to mean?"

"I know who she is." She plays with a toothpick in her mouth and grins. "The mayor's daughter. She might fuck you, Maliki, but she'll never keep you."

"And you could never keep me, Penny."

Fuck this night.

I wish Liz or Mikey were here. I'd ask them to take over, so I could go upstairs, have a drink, throw something, run a mile.

Anything to forget Penny's words.

Anything to stop thinking about a woman I can't have.

"SIT YOUR CUTE ASS DOWN. You've had a long night."

The bar is closed, and it seems working the rest of the night has cooled off Sierra. And me. Neither one of us has mentioned Penny, and I have no issue with that.

Sierra snorts. "Uh, you did most of the work and were here earlier than me, meaning you've had a longer night."

My attention fixes on her, and I fight with myself on whether to say what I want to tell her. Against my better judgment, because I feel it needs to be said, I do. "You know, you don't have to work here. I'll loan you the money, help out, whatever to get you back on your feet. If you need an advance for the bar renovation, I can do that, too."

She winces. "Where is this coming from?" She's silent for a few moments. "Is this your way of telling me you don't want me working here? Did your spread-legged friend convince you

I don't belong here?" She tosses the rag she was cleaning the bar with down into the sink.

I love seeing pissed off, attitude-filled Sierra.

Not so much when it's thrown at me.

"Penny?" I shake my head. *Just when I hoped we could go without mentioning her.* "Penny has nothing to do with this. What I mean is, you can find something better for yourself … for your image."

"Fuck my image," she seethes. "And fuck you for letting your fuck buddy, *Penny*, change your mind about me. If I'm a burden to you, I'll move my needing-a-better-image ass out. If you don't want me around for whatever lame reason you're thinking, I'll quit." She shakes her head and sucks in a deep breath to keep her voice steady. "I mean, I don't understand why she's so bothered with my working here. I'm not stopping her from screwing you again. Call her over." She flicks her hand through the air and slides it over the middle of the bar. "Fuck her right here, right now if you want."

I've never seen Sierra so pissed off, and it's fucking hot as hell.

My cock jerks in my jeans. Not with the thought of fucking Penny there, but with the idea of seeing Sierra spread wide, allowing me to have my way with her. Sierra's back hits the bar when I crowd toward her.

"Is that what you want?" I say, out of patience. "For me to fuck her right here, right now, in front of you?"

Her eyes widen, my words startling her, and she chews on her lower lip. "Not particularly, but it's whatever. There's nothing between us, right?" She nudges my shoulder, but I stay firm in my spot, only inches away from her. "No, you'll screw every other woman in this town though."

A mix of emotions flashes across Sierra's gorgeous face—frustration, desire, hunger. I wouldn't be surprised if mine resembled the same.

I lean in, my lips touching her cheek. "What's up with your fascination with my sex life?"

She gasps when I cup my hands on the sides of her waist and prop her up onto the bar—exactly where she told me to fuck Penny. Her legs spread, producing the perfect amount of space for me as I shift between them. She shudders, goose bumps fluttering over her skin, when my hand settles on her thigh.

Her attention drifts to my hand, but I don't move it, and she fights to keep her voice steady. "I'm not *obsessed* with your sex life."

"Yes, you are."

"Call me crazy for being curious about the chick you boned in your office, which I'm sure wasn't the first time that happened. Hell, you've probably screwed her on this bar."

I remain silent.

It's the truth.

"Wow," she says. She shoves me back, drops off the bar, shudders, and scrapes her hand over her body. "Let me get the whore germs off me—both yours and hers."

I clench my hands. "Do I ask you if you've slept with anyone who comes in here?"

She flings her arms up, and she's so close that her hand almost smacks me. "I've hardly touched anyone in this godforsaken town!"

"Good."

"Unlike *you.*"

"Babe, you have no idea what I've done with who, so quit that imagination floating through your brain and stop assuming I'm fucking every woman who smiles at me." I draw out a breath. "You know, I'm a little confused on why you even care."

I move closer, and she backs into the bar again. She doesn't stop me from repeating my actions from earlier—

grabbing her waist, hoisting her onto the bar, and sliding my body between her toned legs.

I capture the back of her neck, dragging her closer to my face, and my fingers caress her skin. "Do you want to be one of those women, Sierra? Is that why you care so much?"

Her breaths come out in tiny pants. Her eyes flash down to mine and turn wild as they drink me in. She's turned on, and *fuck*, so am I.

I ease my hand down her neck, cupping her chin, and I tilt it away, giving me space to brush my lips along the curve of her jaw. Her skin is soft against my lips. I skim kisses up her neck, feeling her chest hitch against mine, and suck on the spot below her ear. I sink my fingers into her bare thighs and spread her legs wider, noticing a flash of her panties underneath her short shorts.

This is a bad fucking idea.

It's a line I swore I'd never cross with her.

I'm not the man for her. She needs a professional, nine-to-five man who wears fucking loafers. Not me, not a man destined to spend his life here and a man who can't give her the life her parents have all these years.

"Is that it?" I ask, my voice harsh as I whisper against her skin. I can feel my dick growing harder with every touch. "Is that why you're so pissed off?"

She trembles. "I work here. That's why."

"Bullshit." I pull back, my hands tightening on her thighs. "I can read you like my favorite book, Sierra. I see you—the real you—and as much as you fight to hide every thought running through that pretty little head from me, I see it. Let me give you an example: Right now, I see how pissed you are at me." I lower my tone. "I also see how much you want me."

She reaches down to dig her fingers into my hand resting on her thigh. "You're so full of yourself."

I raise a brow, staring up at her. "Am I lying?"

"Maybe I can see through you. Maybe you're the one who wants me."

"Trust me, you can't read me."

She laughs. "Oh, but I can. Do you think I don't notice your jealousy as much as mine? That I don't see how you have to snap yourself out of your feelings for me? You want me as much as I want you, Maliki. The problem is, you're too chickenshit to do anything about it."

"Too chickenshit?"

"Too fucking chickenshit."

My lips crash into hers.

Chickenshit, my ass.

We moan, and just as I start to taste her, just as my tongue enters her mouth, a loud banging blares through the room.

What the fuck?

My phone rings.

The bar phone rings.

Someone bangs on the bar door and is yelling behind it.

I make out something along the lines of, "Forgot my wallet!"

"Fucking hell," I grumble, pulling away from her.

The first time I've tasted her, and it gets interrupted like this.

Is this a sign we shouldn't cross this line?

We both catch our breaths, and I wipe my arm along my face while stalking to the door. I'm half-tempted to tell the person to fuck off, but they won't stop fucking knocking.

I unlock the door … and in walks Penny.

You've got to be shitting me.

I hear Sierra curse under her breath.

She hops off the bar and practically snarls in my direction. "It's been a long night. You should probably help her find her *wallet.*"

She glares while passing us on her way back to the apartment, and I pray it's not to pack her bags and leave.

As much as I want to chase her, I have to get rid of Penny first.

"Well played," I tell Penny, working my jaw.

She raises her brows. "What do you mean?"

"Come on. You *forgot* your wallet?"

She shrugs. "I was hoping you'd changed your mind. I didn't know she'd be here with you, doing … whatever you two were doing."

"We were closing the bar."

"You were about to fuck her in the same place you'd fucked me."

I snarl. She's right. I was about to screw Sierra where I'd screwed countless other women.

"She's not for you, Maliki." Her hand splays across my shoulder.

I push her away. "Just because we've fucked a few times doesn't mean shit. Just because your mouth has been around my dick doesn't mean you know me."

"When she breaks your heart, you know my number."

CHAPTER FIFTEEN

Sierra

I THROW DOWN MY BAG, tear off my clothes, and step in the shower.

Tears hit my eyes as soon as Penny walked in, but I blinked them away. I couldn't cry in front of her—in front of *them.*

What if he brings her to his bedroom?

I shake my head. He wouldn't do that after what happened on the bar.

I throw my loofah onto the bathtub floor and kick it for good measure. I'm reminded of Maliki's touch as I wash my hair. It was too good to be true. Just when I succeeded in proving he couldn't hide his feelings for me any longer, she interrupted.

No matter what, there's always someone coming between us.

Maliki is seated on my bed when I walk into my room. I screech and tighten my towel around my chest.

"I wanted to assure you I wasn't fucking anyone." He stands. "Get some sleep."

With that, he turns around and leaves.

"Maliki, wait."

"Go to bed, Sierra," is all he growls out.

"SHIT."

I'm late.

With all that transpired last night, I failed to set my alarm for brunch.

I pull a dress over my head, ridding it of wrinkles with my hands, and slip on red wedges. I brush my teeth, braid my hair, and am out the door in minutes. I want to go to this brunch like I want to have mimosas with Louise.

Thank God Maliki is nowhere to be seen. I can't face him yet.

"You're late," is how my father greets me when I sit down at the table.

"I overslept," I say around a yawn.

"If you weren't working at a *bar,* you wouldn't have overslept."

I snatch the carafe of orange juice and pour myself a glass. "I'm not having this discussion." My gaze bounces to my mom's. "I told Mom to inform you of that."

"Oh, she did all right, *but* you're my daughter," he answers with a huff.

He hates not calling the shots, but his life has changed since his affair was exposed. His ass is on the line in every aspect of his life—his career, his family. Hell, even my grandparents are pissed at him. Right now, my father has no one on his side.

My mom brushes her hand against his arm. "Honey, let's wait until after we eat."

"Yeah, Dad. We don't want your sour mood to affect our French toast and eggs," Rex adds with a smirk.

A vein pulses in my dad's neck, and no doubt, he wants to give Rex an ass-chewing, but he stares at me with intent. "We will talk about this."

"Can't wait," I mutter, spreading my napkin on my lap.

I was once a daddy's girl. He wasn't perfect, but he was my dad—the man who fought the monsters in my closet and taught me to ride a bike. Somewhere between me growing up and him growing more successful, he changed—a man I no longer knew but still loved. No matter what, I stood by his side, stood up for him, until he destroyed my mother's heart.

I eat my breakfast while listening to my father rattle on about town developments and my mom about her latest fundraiser. When breakfast is finished and our stomachs are full, I help my mom clean up, moving as slow as I can to delay this unnecessary talk with my dad.

"All right, Sierra, my office," my father says, stepping into the kitchen and straightening his shirt cuffs.

I roll my eyes, follow him to the office, and speak before he has time to shut the door, "Look, whatever you say won't change my mind about working at the bar. I'm working there, and that's final."

The door clicks shut, and he circles his desk, looking more powerful when he sits in the executive chair. My father is a handsome man who's aged well. He's tall with dark hair, only a few sprinkles of gray strands, and he possesses enough confidence you'd guess he was in his twenties. He's wearing a black suit, black tie, and the Rolex that was passed down from his grandfather.

"Not only is working there inappropriate for the mayor's daughter, but it's also dangerous, Sierra."

"You know what else is inappropriate for the town mayor? Cheating on his wife."

He flicks his finger my way. "Touché. This isn't an attempt for me to control you. Maliki's life is darker than the sunshine you're used to, honey."

"Weird. Maliki is my sunshine every time I'm having a shit day, crying over *your* indiscretions and being cheated on. He makes me happy. Do you remember the last guy you *approved* of? He cheated on me in the restroom of a bar." I start pacing in front of him. "And I'm not even dating Maliki. I'm working for him. So, for that reason and our friendship, I'll take *cloudy days* with him because …"

"You have feelings for him?"

I gulp. "Friendship feelings."

He nods. "Be careful."

"I always am."

"That kid, his life wasn't easy. His mother was—" He stops speaking.

"Was what?"

"Mentally ill—in and out of psychiatric facilities—and his father's workplace didn't help the situation. She was paranoid of infidelity, became obsessed with it, and couldn't handle her life—according to your mother, who attempted to mentor her. She tried helping Kelly, but couldn't."

I cross my arms. "Children don't have to take after their parents. I'm nothing like you."

He winces, knowing that wasn't a compliment. "I love you, but I don't want you to be with a man like me, Sierra. I know what a man who can't be held down is—*I'm* one of those men—and it's hard for us. We hurt people." He rests his elbows on the desk. "Your mother filed for divorce."

I stop my pacing to look at him. "What?"

"I wanted to be the one to tell you."

"Why?"

"She fears she's setting a bad example and that you'll take Devin back because she didn't leave me. I suppose we were delaying the inevitable. When she told me about Devin's cheating, I wanted to kill him for hurting you. Your mother reminded me it was no different than my actions. I hurt my wife, my children, and betrayed the town that voted for me. I have to face the consequences for that."

My head is spinning. "What happens now?" *This can't be real. He didn't say that.*

"I'll work on redeeming myself."

"And while you're doing that, let me work on who I want to be."

He lifts a brow. "Which is?"

"Happy."

He nods. "I'll shut my mouth, sit down, and realize I'm not perfect."

"Finally."

Him staring down in shame hurts my heart, and I move around the desk to kiss his cheek. He's a ruthless man, but I love him.

"I'll see you soon, okay?" I tell him.

He nods. "You call me if you need anything. *Anything*. I'm sleeping in my office, but it's time I find somewhere to move permanently. I'm letting your mother keep the house."

I UNLOCK the door of the apartment and walk in, finding it empty. I haven't spoken to Maliki since the girl he desk-banged showed up last night.

Speaking of last night …

What in the ever-loving hell was that?

We kissed.

Maliki Bridges finally kissed me.

For years, I'd wanted to feel his lips against mine.

And it happened with terrible timing.

I was married, and Penny showed up.

Did I overreact last night?

Maybe.

Maliki isn't mine. I have no claim to him.

I have no right to be upset, but I can't stop imagining Penny returning for round two … two hundred … who knows how many times they've banged?

She wasn't startled, seeing me—a clear sign she was staking her claim and making it known they had history.

When I go to the bar in search of him, it's empty. My next stop is the dreaded office—somewhere I haven't stepped foot in since that night. The door is shut. I knock and wait until he calls for me to come in. He pulls away from the paperwork on the desk when he sees me, straightening in his chair, almost appearing as if he's a boss intending to scold an employee.

There's no roadmap for where this conversation will lead. I'm a married woman, frustrated at him over another woman. I'm in the wrong and mortified by my feelings.

"Hey," he says, realizing I'm a mute weirdo gawking at him.

"Hi," I nearly whisper, shutting the door.

"Look, about Penny," he begins.

"Ah, good ole Penny." The mockery falls from my lips in contempt. My eyes shoot from him to the desk, and I cringe. "Okay, I can't talk to you in here." I put my hand up and gulp away the disgust rising.

His gaze shoots around the room in confusion. "What? Why?"

"That desk. I can't even look at it after your whole … sexcapade with *Penny*."

He leans back in his chair and fastens his hands together behind his head. "You mean, after you spied on me?"

"I didn't spy on you."

"I watched the cameras. You didn't take a peek and then scurry along—which, I might add, a sane person would have done. You stayed and enjoyed the show. A show that wasn't yours to watch."

I stutter for the right words. "I was … shocked … horrified … frozen in place." I cross my arms. "Don't twist this around on me. You should've advised me not to work last night if you knew she was returning for another go at desk-fucking."

"I didn't know she was coming last night, *nor* did I invite her to come later. Do you think *forgot my wallet* is code for sex? I was as surprised and pissed as you."

"I wasn't pissed."

"You were pissed. Jealousy looks sexy on you."

"Excuse me? I wasn't jealous of her." I was, but I snort to make myself sound more believable. "I was annoyed, is all." *Irritated that you had my panties wet, offering me something I'd wanted for years, and then bam, Penny the Penis-Blocker showed up.* "I'll be upstairs. We can have this chitchat then."

He drops his arms and shifts in his chair. "Look, I'm sorry." A self-satisfied smile hits his lips. "Not that I have much to atone for."

"Then, you're not apologizing, Fake Apology Giver."

"I'm apologizing for Penny's behavior. I did nothing wrong."

"You're right. You shouldn't have to apologize for desk-banging chicks."

"Don't make it sound like cheap porn."

"It sure looked like cheap porn. If it walks like a duck, talks like a duck, then it's cheap duck porn."

"You're impossible," he mutters. "It was much better quality than *porn.* Yes, I had sex with Penny. No, I won't do it again. It's settled. Let's move forward."

I scrape my hands together. "Conversation over."

I spin around in my wedges and feel Maliki behind me as I dash upstairs. I leave the door open for him and plop down on a stool at the island.

"Now that that's over, you want to tell me what else is on your mind?"

I love how he's not afraid to dig into my feelings, not afraid of me bringing my issues to him. "My parents are divorcing."

Why I'm so overwhelmed is weird. I was happy when my mom said she was leaving my father after news of his affair came out and pissed when she decided to stay.

Now, I feel numb.

Two divorces are happening in my family this year—mine and my parents'.

He stands on the other side of the island. "I'm sorry."

"I …" I stop to clear my throat. "It might be my fault."

"The fuck it is. Everyone in this town knows your father is to blame." He shakes his head. "Don't you dare think that."

"*Yes*, but my mom didn't leave him after she found out about the affair. She's leaving in fear of setting a bad example to her daughters."

"Does her staying with him set a nice example?"

"Every situation is different."

He nods. "I agree."

"It's … *ugh.* It'll be weird, them not being together, you know?"

"Yeah. It was the same when my mom left, but it became our new normal."

My mouth falls open.

Holy shit. Is Maliki getting personal with me?

Do I act like I know what my father told me?

"When did your mom leave you?"

"Yes. When I was six and my sister was nine." His face is blank, offering me not an ounce of emotion.

"Did she tell you she was leaving?"

"Nope. I came home one day, and all her shit was gone. She never came back."

"Do you know where she is now?"

He shakes his head. "I don't care to know. She chose to leave, to not take us with her, and never come back. That's it. I won't fight for anyone's love. She did what a mother should never do, regardless of the situation."

I want more.

I want everything personal he has to offer.

"Why did she leave?"

"I don't know. Years ago, when we were moving my dad's shit, we found her good-bye letter. She blamed it on the bar, on my father making it a priority over his family and not showering her with enough attention. He needed to find out what it was like, taking care of a family, is what she said. I was furious with my father and blamed him for everything. In actuality, it was both of their fault. Her letter proved she didn't deserve me looking for her." He shifts his weight from one foot to the other, shaking his head, and offers his hand. "Come on. We've had enough depressing shit for one day. Let's do something fun."

I perk up in my stool. "Like what?"

"You pick."

"Well …" I draw out.

"Oh shit. Did I stick my foot in my mouth?"

"How about we go shopping for bar selections?"

He shrugs. "Why not? It's a perfect day to get out of town."

I slide off my stool. "Let me change really quick."

He snaps his fingers to stop me. "Cohen is having a barbeque tonight at his house. Come with me."

"Really?"

"Yeah, it'll be fun."

I nod, a smile taking over my face. I walk out of the kitchen and skip to my bedroom when I'm out of his sight.

CHAPTER SIXTEEN

Sierra

"FIRST THINGS FIRST," I say, whipping around and walking backward facing Maliki. "The desk has to go bye-bye."

He tilts his head to the side. "What's wrong with my desk?"

"What's wrong with it is, you banged Penny and who knows how many other women on it."

My answer captures the attention of an elderly couple passing by. The woman gasps, clasping her hand over her mouth as if I were straddling Maliki instead of making small talk, and then moves her hand over her heart. She shakes her head, snatches the man's hand, and pulls him away.

Maliki shakes his head. "You can't trash my desk for that reason."

"Do you possess a sentimental attachment to said desk other than it being your go-to spot for screwing? Family heirloom?" I tsk him. "Which would be disrespectful as fuck to your elders."

"No, Sierra. I'm not having sex on family heirlooms."

Another odd glance comes our way from a passerby. I should've brought this up in the car.

He drops his tone. "Why do you care about the desk so much?"

Because I've been falling in love with you since I was eighteen.

I clear my throat and shrug. "I don't want to hang out with your sex juices if I ever work in your office."

"Sex juices?" A grin plays at his lips. "You're nuts, and please never use the term *sex juices* again."

"Whatever." I loop my arm through his and lead us to the office furniture department in the store we're in. "New desk, here we come." When we reach the spot, I twirl on my heels and gesture to the options. "What look are we going for, Mr. Bridges?"

He scratches his head, and instead of searching out a desk, he fixes his attention on me. "You pick. You're the one demanding it be replaced."

"All righty, I see this is an area you're giving me creative control on." I grab his hand and walk us through the aisles.

"As long as it's not pink or covered in sequins, which seems to be my niece's style, I'm good."

"I wouldn't do that to your desk. The stools, on the other hand …" I grin back at him. "This might be the time to mention, they most definitely have sequins."

He shakes his head, a smile tugging at his lips. "You're such a pain in my ass."

"Get used to it."

"Trust me, I did years ago."

I steal his hat, put it on, and point to a desk. "I like this one. It screams, *Maliki*!"

It's a basic black desk with open drawers. My favorite part is, it looks uncomfortable. That should ward off women from spread-eagling across it.

"Sold." He snatches his hat back.

"COHEN WORKS at the Twisted Fox, right?" I ask from the passenger seat of his car.

We're on our way to the barbeque. Our shopping trip ended with us ordering the uncomfortable desk and office chair, and we have a book of floor and paint samples.

He nods. "He co-owns it with a few of our other friends."

I stiffen in my seat. "We're not going there, are we?"

He shakes his head. "No, it's at his house. I wouldn't have invited you if it were there. It's me and some friends. That's it."

"Cool." I can't believe I'm meeting his friends—friends who aren't in Blue Beech.

Maliki moved out of Blue Beech years ago but came back when he took over the bar. All I knew was, he wanted out of the small town like I did and then was brought back—our reasons different. His was to save the family business. Mine was being around familiarity, my mom, and … *him.*

"DO I LOOK OKAY?" I inspect my shorts, white tank, and red wedges I'm wearing.

Maliki slides his sunglasses off his face and sweeps his gaze over me. "You look perfect."

I grab the handle but pause while taking in the home we're parked in front of. It's a small brick ranch with a bright yellow door and black shutters. The driveway is packed with cars and a motorcycle.

I exhale an uneasy breath. "What am I walking into?"

The excitement of meeting his friends has shifted into nervousness. I'm normally outgoing, the girl who strikes up conversation with others, but Devin's cheating has changed me. I don't want to talk to people or go out in public. I feel taken advantage of, humiliated, and manipulated. My trust in people sucks.

At least we're not in Blue Beech.

"Walking into?" Maliki repeats. "You're walking into a chill barbeque with my friends. This isn't one of your parents' social events. Don't worry about being anyone but yourself."

I rub the back of my neck. "Has Cohen told anyone how we met?"

"Doubt it. Cohen has more shit to worry about than gossiping."

I relax in my seat. "I've decided I already like Cohen."

He pats my thigh, giving it a gentle squeeze. "Don't worry. Just have fun."

MALIKI'S ARM is draped over my shoulders, and I'm pulled into his side when we walk into Cohen's backyard. The gesture shocked me, given he hardly touches me when we hang out. His arm fits around me perfectly, as if it belongs there. I could walk in his hold for the rest of my life and never want to pull away.

"Ki! My man!"

Cohen grins when he sees us, shuts the grill in front of him, and comes our way. "Glad you could make it *and* bring gorgeous company."

I give the backyard a once-over. A group of girls are settled at a table, consumed in conversation, and three men are lagging behind Cohen, moving toward us.

"You must be Sierra," Cohen says when he reaches us. "Maliki said you were coming, and he's told me so much about you. Welcome to my home."

Maliki was right. Cohen is acting as if I were a total stranger.

I laugh, a blush rising up my cheeks. "Whatever he's told you are lies."

Cohen motions toward me and looks at the guys. "Do you

remember the youngster who kept sneaking into Maliki's bar?"

"Yes," one brown-haired man draws out, a lollipop in his mouth.

Another guy's mouth drops open. "Holy hell! This is her?" He shakes his head with wide eyes. "I fucking love this shit."

"Sure is," Cohen replies. "This is Sierra."

He introduces the guys.

Lollipop guy is Silas.

The *holy shit* one is Finn.

The only one not sporting a smile is Archer.

I give them a wave. "Hey."

Cohen wraps his hands around his mouth and yells to the girls, "Georgia! Come here!"

A short blonde rises from her seat and narrows her eyes in our direction. "This'd better be good. We were having a deep discussion about *The Bachelor.*"

"Trust me, it's so much better than that stupid-ass show!" Finn calls out.

"No, it's not," Maliki shouts. "Stay your ass over there!"

Georgia, I'm assuming, proceeds our way, and Cohen signals to me as soon as she joins us. "This is Sierra, aka the underage girl who kept sneaking into Ki's bar."

I hold my hand up to correct him. "Hey now, I was never underage. I was eighteen."

"Eighteen is underage to drink, babe," Maliki says with a hint of a smirk.

"She means not underage to screw," Georgia says, rolling her eyes and grinning at Maliki. "I so called you and her having a thing." Her attention drifts to me, her smile still intact. "I don't know you, but I already like you for the hell you put him through."

Maliki's arm drops from my shoulders. "First off, I never talked about her to you. Your nosy ass eavesdropped on me talking about it with Cohen. I needed advice on what to do other than call the cops on her."

Georgia dismissively waves her hand in his direction. "Shut up. You would've never called the cops on her."

"Eh, he threatened to plenty of times," I inform them, replaying all the times he said that in my mind. "Even threatened to call my parents."

"Shit, dude, not the parent threat," Finn cuts in. "I thought you were cooler than that."

Maliki flips him off.

I shake Georgia's hand when she introduces herself. She's gorgeous, and her look is total nineties. Pink glitter is on her eyelids, and her blonde hair is pulled into two buns at the top of her head. From the smile on her face and the friendliness in her voice, I already like her.

"I hope you brought an appetite," she says. "We have plenty of food."

I eye the food on the picnic tables.

Shoot. It looks like a pitch-in.

"I'm sorry," I rush out. "Maliki sprang this on me at the last minute, or I would've brought something." *Great.* Already making a bad impression.

"Don't worry," Silas says. "We have plenty."

"Maliki already paid me for you two," Georgia says. "They pay, and I normally make—with the exception of the grill stuff."

Maliki's arm returns to my shoulders as we follow her, but I'm pulled away when Georgia snatches my hand.

"I'll introduce you to the girls." Her attention lands on Maliki. "I promise to bring her back."

I nod when Maliki gives me a questioning look and allow Georgia to lead the way.

"She'd better like me when she comes back, you little shit-talker!" Maliki yells behind us.

"I can't make any promises!" Georgia laughs.

When we reach the table, two women smile invitingly, and I take the chair next to Georgia.

"I'm Lola." Lola is a fair-skinned girl with sleek, middle-parted hair.

"And I'm Grace." Grace's name matches her perfectly. Her strawberry-blonde hair is braided into a crown around her head, and she's wearing a loose white dress.

"Sierra." I smile. "I came with Maliki."

Their grins widen.

"Oh, we noticed," Lola comments.

"Do you date Cohen?" I ask Georgia.

"God, no," she replies, scrunching up her face. "He's my brother." She shifts in her seat. "And these are my besties. None of the guys have girlfriends. They're all too chickenshit to have anyone *tying them down*."

Her eyes narrow toward the guys, and I follow her gaze, trying to single out the victim of her glare but can't.

Hmm. Definitely a story there.

"Guys who work in bars," Grace says, soft-spoken, and squeezes Georgia's arm. "It's what you get with them."

Lola clears her throat and motions to me.

"Oh shoot," Grace sputters out. "I didn't mean it like that. *Some* of them. Maliki isn't like that. He doesn't bring different women with him to every barbeque."

"Heck, the man hasn't brought a woman with him, period," Georgia states matter-of-factly. "Until you."

"And that's before we banned them from bringing girls," Grace chimes in.

"Banned?" My gaze darts to each girl in nervousness. "Was he not supposed to bring me?" *I'm so kicking his ass.*

Lola shakes her head. "No, you're totally fine. There was an issue a few years back with one of Finn's girls. She was friends with Cohen's baby mama and talking hella shit about him. It didn't slide well with Georgia, obviously."

I gape at them. "Wait, Cohen has a kid?"

Grace nods. "Noah."

I give the yard a once-over, not spotting anyone under the age of twenty in sight. "Is he here?"

"No," Georgia replies, checking her watch. "His aunt is dropping him off soon."

My mind is spiraling with so many questions. "What about the mom? Is she here?"

Obviously not, but it's the best way I thought to bring her up.

Grace grimaces. "Heather sucks."

I shoot a glance to Georgia. "Why?"

Her pink lips curl in disgust. "A few months before she was due, out of nowhere, she told Cohen she wanted to put Noah up for adoption. Cohen begged her not to, promising to accept all responsibilities and custody. As soon as she gave birth, she ran off to Vegas. Cohen kept his word, is an amazing father, and hasn't spoken to Heather once. Noah has met her a few times when he's been with Jamie but doesn't know who she is to him." She sneers in disgust. "We prefer to keep it that way to protect him."

My stomach clenches. *How could someone do that to their child? Poor Cohen.*

"Wow," I draw out, my eyes glued to Georgia. "Who's Jamie?"

"Heather's sister," Georgia answers. "She has a relationship with Noah."

I peek over at Cohen. "That sounds like one giant ball of headaches."

Georgia shrugs and grabs her beer. "Not really. We're grateful for Heather's absence."

As if in perfect timing, a little boy races into the backyard, tennis shoes stomping against the grass, and takes over everyone's attention.

"Dad!" he shouts, clutching something in his hand and holding it in the air. "You won't believe what Jamie bought me!"

Affection spreads over Cohen's face, and he releases a *humph* when the boy jumps into his arms, squeezing him into a tight hug.

Noah holds the item on display when he's dropped to his feet. "It's an iPod!"

The kid is adorable—a little Cohen with his brown hair and small frame.

Noah's smile can't be contained as he jumps up and down. "It's blue!"

Cohen bends down on one knee to Noah's level. "That's so neat, buddy!"

"Hey, Jamie!" Georgia shouts, causing my attention to slide to a tall brunette woman coming our way.

"Hey," she replies around a yawn.

"You want to stick around?" Georgia offers.

Jamie shakes her head. "I'm working a double tomorrow and in dire need of sleep."

"That's awesome that you're a doctor." Grace shudders. "Blood makes me squeamish."

"Everything makes you squeamish," Finn says, crouching behind her and ruffling his hands through her hair, disheveling her braid.

"Especially you." She reaches up, sticks her palm in his face, and nudges him away.

Cohen and Noah run over to us.

"An iPod?" Cohen asks Jamie. "You didn't have to do that. You spoil him too much."

Jamie laughs—a forced one. "It's for selfish reasons, so I can FaceTime him."

"You always FaceTime me to talk to him. It's never been a problem," Cohen responds with a hint of a frown.

Her face is expressionless. "You're busy sometimes."

He winces before checking himself. "We have plenty of food." His hands sweep toward the table. "Stay."

"Thanks for the offer, but I can't." She bends down to hug Noah. "Make sure you call me, okay?"

Noah hugs her back and then salutes her. "You got it!"

She kisses his head and tells everyone good-bye.

"She is *pissed* at you," Georgia sings when Jamie disappears from the yard.

"She's not *pissed at me*," Cohen imitates in her high-pitched voice.

"Why's she pissed at you?" Grace asks.

"She FaceTimed Cohen to talk to Noah the other day, and some chick answered, asking Jamie twenty-one questions about who she was." Georgia rolls her eyes and shoots a glare at Cohen. "That's why she bought the iPod."

"I need to quit telling you stuff," Cohen mutters.

He shakes his head, grabs Noah, and throws him over his shoulder. Noah breaks out in loud laughter, holding on around his neck when Cohen takes off running.

"Are he and Jamie a thing?" I ask Lola when he's out of earshot.

She shakes her head, scraping a hand through her hair. "They totes should be, but Cohen is too chickenshit."

"You have to admit, it'd be confusing for Noah," Grace chimes in.

"Love is love," Georgia inputs.

Both girls stare at her in sadness.

"Yes, and men are stupid," Grace says while Lola nods in agreement.

I jerk my head back when Maliki comes behind me and whispers in my ear, "You doing okay?"

My stomach flutters. "Yes." There's a slight rise in my voice.

He squeezes my shoulders. "Let me know if you need anything *or* if these heathens give you too much trouble."

The three of them tell him to screw off in three different ways.

"Uncle Maliki!"

Maliki turns as Noah charges toward him and hops on his back.

"I've missed you so much!"

"I've missed you more," Maliki replies with a cheerfulness in his tone I've never heard.

Noah holds on to him as Maliki jogs over to the guys playing cornhole and drops Noah to his feet. They go to one board, and Cohen and Finn take the other. They play while Archer sits in a chair, a beer in his hand, and watches them. Correction: he watches Georgia while pretending to pay attention to the game.

"You two are cute," Georgia says.

"Huh?" I ask, turning to look at her.

She points back and forth from Maliki and me. "You and Ki. You're cute together."

Her comment startles me.

"Oh, no. We're friends."

"For now," Lola chirps. "I've seen Maliki around women at bars, and believe me, babe, he's never checked to make sure they're okay."

"He's also never looked at them like he does you," Georgia adds. "You two will definitely be banging."

I shake my head, wishing I could hide the blush creeping up my cheeks, as tingles sweep up my back and face.

They wouldn't say that if they knew I was still married.

MALIKI PLANTS his hand on my shoulders. "You ready to eat?"

My stomach growls at the mention of food. "Yes, I'm starving."

He holds out his hand, helping me from my chair, and I follow him to the table covered with food. It all looks delicious, and I take one of everything. When I'm finished making my plate and I head back to the table, Archer is in my seat next to Georgia. She's glaring at him, and he shakes his head, chugging his beer. There's only one chair open at the table, so Maliki leads me to a separate two-top table.

"I can't believe you told them about me sneaking into the bar," I say as soon as we sit.

Maliki pops the top of his beer and leans back in his chair. "I wanted Cohen's opinion. It's not like I could ask anyone in Blue Beech, seeing it was you and word would've spread like wildfire. I needed someone to vent to."

"I'm delighted I was on your mind."

"Can I sit with Uncle Maliki?" Noah yells, charging toward us without waiting for an answer.

"Sure," Cohen answers, heading our way with two plates in his hand.

I push to my feet. "I'll find him a chair."

"Unnecessary," Maliki mutters, anchoring his large hands around my waist and dragging me onto his lap. "This one is big enough for two."

Holy shit. Holy shit. Holy shit.

I'm on his lap.

My heart freezes and then pounds like it's prepared to jump out of my chest, so I can hand it over to him. My mind scrambles in so many directions that I'm waiting for it to explode. Maliki is a different man outside of Blue Beech, and I love this Maliki.

Noah falls into my chair when Maliki gestures for him to take it. Cohen drops Noah's plate on the table and sets a bottle of root beer next to it. When his gaze travels to us, he quirks a brow, smiles, and pushes my plate to me.

"Who are you?" Noah asks, kicking his feet against the chair legs when Cohen leaves.

I grin. "I'm Sierra. Who are *you*?"

His attention stays on me. "I'm Noah. Are you Uncle Maliki's girlfriend?"

Maliki rests his hand on my thigh, causing me to take a moment to answer him.

I shake my head, wishing I could curse Maliki. "No, I'm his friend."

Noah scrunches up his face. "You sure look like his girlfriend."

We are in need of a subject change, pronto, and Maliki isn't jumping to stop him from asking these awkward questions.

I pick up my fork. "How old are you, Noah?"

He holds up a hand. "Five *but* almost six."

"Wow, you're old."

"Yes, he is," Maliki says. "I'm waiting for him to sprout some gray hair."

Noah straightens in his chair. "No! That isn't happening until I'm ninety-two hundred."

Maliki chuckles. "Ninety-two hundred, huh?"

"Yes." He grabs his hot dog and points to Maliki with it. "Don't forget you promised to do something fun with me for my birthday."

"I haven't forgotten," Maliki replies.

Noah looks over at me and scuffs his chair closer. "You want to come?"

My back straightens, causing Maliki to jerk behind me. "I'll see if I can."

"You have to since you're his girlfriend," Noah argues.

"I'm not—"

Maliki squeezes my thigh. "Just go with it. You won't change his mind," he whispers into my ear with a slight chuckle.

His hand doesn't move as he changes the subject and asks Noah if he's excited to start school. Noah says yes. Then, he proceeds to talk about his favorite TV show and toys, and he shows off his iPod. When he takes the last bite of his hot dog, he asks Cohen for a cookie. Cohen says yes, and he darts in his direction.

I reclaim my seat and slide my plate to my side.

"You're good with kids," I say, popping a chip in my mouth.

Maliki raises his brow in question. "Did you expect me to be awful with them?"

"No … just some guys aren't."

"Kids are cool. My niece and Liz lived with me before she moved in with her husband."

I click my tongue against the roof of my mouth. "Do you want kids someday?"

"Possibly. It's complicated, having a family with the lifestyle and career I live. My father proved that."

"Then, why did you go into that occupation?"

"It's what I've always known, and I wanted to be a business owner." He shrugs. "But eventually, I'll entertain the idea. I want to make certain I can give them a stable home."

"That means, you'll have to settle down long enough to have a child with someone."

"Yes, it does."

"Do you ever see yourself … you know … doing that? You're not exactly young."

"Nor am I exactly old." He laughs. "According to Noah, I have up to ninety-two hundred years before I start turning gray."

I toss a chip at him. "Shut up."

We're interrupted by Georgia calling our names.

"All right, you two lovers, time for me to beat your asses in cornhole. It's you two against Archer and me."

"Archer is playing cornhole?" Maliki asks with shock.

She lifts her chin, fighting back a smile. "I'm forcing him." She snaps her fingers. "Now, chop-chop, before he changes his mind."

I lean across the table. "I've never played cornhole."

"It's easy," Maliki says. "Just follow my lead."

"Prepare for us to lose."

"YOUR FRIENDS ARE NICE," I say during our ride home.

Spending the day with Maliki wiped out all my family and divorce worries. I didn't think about Devin or my dad or what the hell my future holds. I'm struggling to mask the happiness from tonight rolling through me. I want to savor these moments with Maliki and never forget them—in case the day comes when they stop.

The day *will* come when they stop.

So, for now, I'm going to stay on this ride with him before he kicks me off.

We lost at cornhole … all four games, even when we played against Noah and Cohen. That's right. My ass couldn't even beat a five-year-old at the game. Our night ended with a bonfire and smores. I've never enjoyed myself so much at a barbeque.

Maliki's eyes stay on the road. "They are."

"Georgia invited me to the next one. Hopefully, you'll be in attendance, too."

He chuckles and parks in the rear parking lot, cutting the ignition. "Oh, it's like that now, huh? *Hopefully,* I'll be there?"

"Damn straight."

"Come anytime, and consider Georgia's invite a big deal. She's normally not as receiving to women brought to our barbeques as she was with you."

"Really? Why?"

"She's protective of the people she cares about."

We get out of the car and step into the night, the bright security light glowing above us. I unlock the door, head up the stairs, and flip on lights with Maliki trailing behind me.

"Have you and her ever …"

He shakes his head. "I see her as a little sister. Cohen is a brother to me, and even if I were attracted to her romantically, I'd never touch her. He practically raised Georgia. Hell, he waited a year until introducing us to her—post threatening to rip our balls out one by one if we touched her."

I bite my lips to hide my smile. "And none of the others have?"

He tosses his keys onto the island. "Nope."

"Has she tried with any of them?"

"Don't know. Not my business, and if you learn any different, don't tell me. I refuse to be swept up in that shitstorm."

"Gotcha. I like her and the girls."

"Watch it though. They're quite the troublemakers."

I open the fridge for a bottle of water, my back facing him. "They're convinced we're going to have sex."

"Oh, really?" There's no difference in his tone, and I'm too scared to face him.

"Really," I say around a gulp.

"Do you agree?"

My back straightens, chills running up my spine, and I return the water to the fridge. Hell, I need something stronger. I go to snag a bottle of wine but stop when he keeps talking.

"Look at me, Sierra." His voice has pivoted, now controlled, deep, and demanding.

I do as I was told, shutting the fridge and leaning back against it. His brown eyes are fixated on me, his face hardened, jaw clenched. I've never felt so on display, nor has my pulse been so strong.

"Would you have sex with me?" His smirk is loaded with confidence. He knows my answer. "Answer me straight up."

Act cool.

Act normal.

I gape at him while pulling myself together. "I mean … if you wanted to have sex with me."

"You think I wouldn't want to have sex with you?"

There's no doubt we're attracted to each other.

That we want each other.

I shrug, struggling to answer him without a shaky voice. "You've never seemed interested in my advances, and it'd make our relationship … complicated. It could ruin it, and I never want that to happen." I sigh. "You don't do relationships, and I'm not sure I can have sex and not want more."

The smirk hasn't left his face. "Anything else?"

"Nope. That's it."

He circles the island, invading my space, and stops a few steps away. "Interesting."

"What does *interesting* mean?" I blow out a long breath, my face flushing. "See! I've made it awkward now! Exactly what I didn't want!" I'd love to have his lips on mine again, to feel his body pressed against mine, but it's not worth losing him.

I gasp when he wipes out the space separating us, captures my waist with his strong hands, and tugs me into him. I lose a breath when the erection straining against his jeans rubs against my core.

He cradles my face in his hands. "I can't believe you'd doubt me wanting you."

And his mouth meets mine.

CHAPTER SEVENTEEN

Maliki

SIERRA TASTES FUCKING SWEET.

Sweet but not as innocent as I imagined.

Spending time with her today was incredible.

She met my friends. They loved her. She loved them. Maybe she does fit in my world.

I kiss her roughly, lacking the restraint I should have but don't.

We've delayed this for too long.

She tastes like sweet chocolate and marshmallows when my tongue slips into her mouth, devouring her. My dick stirs when she moans into my mouth.

I've never been so turned on, just making out with a woman.

I need more.

My lips stay on hers while she stays pressed against the fridge. Goose bumps run up her skin when I turn her to rest her back against a wall. My hand nearly shakes when it eases up her tank. Her skin is soft, so damn soft.

"Maliki." My name releases from her lips in a moan, and Jesus fuck, the things that does to me … to my dick.

I cup her breast, thrill rippling through me, and grind against her, rotating my hips.

As a mood killer, a reminder she's married zips through me, urging my dick to calm down, but I shove the thought away.

Fuck that.

She's mine.

Has been since the day her young ass walked into my bar, drinking a goddamn strawberry daiquiri.

"I need you," she breathes out, attempting to wedge her hand between the tight space of our bodies.

I swoop my hand down, snatching her wrist, and stop her.

"Not yet." I fasten her arms above her head and sweep my tongue over her lower lip.

I get to play first.

"Oh my God," she hisses as I drop kisses along her neck, sucking on her soft skin as if it's my favorite snack.

I need more.

"Sierra." My voice is so strained; I hardly recognize it.

"What?" She parts her legs and hooks one around my waist. "I need you, Maliki."

"The first time I fuck you won't be against a wall."

"Why not?" She rubs against me. "Sounds like the perfect plan to me."

"I want to do so many things to your body, and this wall will fuck with my plans. We'll save wall sex for later."

She groans in annoyance.

I chuckle, loving how desperate she is for me. "Do you know what happens now?"

"You pull down your pants and shove your cock inside me?"

"I'm unpinning you, and you're going to strut your sexy ass to my bedroom."

"And you'll join me?"

I unhand her and caress her cheek. "Is that even a

goddamn question?" I fall back a step, giving her space, and clench my fists to stop myself from touching her.

She stares at me with confidence as she passes, her hand lightly brushing against my cock, a smirk hitting her lips.

Shiiiit.

"Goddamn, that ass." I dart my finger over my lips and catch my breath.

She stops mid-step to glance back at me. "Imagine the things you could do with it."

I'm behind her, my eyes roaming every inch of the back of her—her ass, her thighs, her back, her hair. I can't wait to wrap my fist around those blonde strands.

I adjust myself in my jeans, my dick throbbing so hard and pleading to be freed. It's never suffered through so much foreplay hell, and damn, we haven't even reached the good shit yet—only making out and dry-humping like two teenagers after a homecoming dance.

I flip on the light to find her standing at the foot of my bed with a wicked smile on her lips.

I stay in the doorway. "Have you thought about this before?"

She nods.

"You, in my bedroom?"

She nods again, sweeping her eyes down my body. Her smile grows when she stops at my erection straining against my jeans.

My dick screams at me to quit playing games.

I advance closer. "What did we do?"

"Fucked." The word pops from her full lips with no delay.

Shit.

I crowd her. "Is that the best you have for me? We *fucked*?"

She shivers when I stop in front of her. Not another word leaves my mouth as I glide my hands up her shirt and cup her breasts. My cock thickens at the sight of her nipples peeking through the thin fabric.

I tug at the bottom of her top. "This has to go."

She raises her arms with no hesitancy, allowing me to drag it over her head, and I drop it at our feet. Next, I unhook her bra, her breasts spilling out.

"You're beautiful," I comment, stroking a hand over her nipple.

She shuts her eyes, exhaling a deep breath.

"More beautiful than I imagined, baby." I tilt my head down and blow against her nipple, capturing it in my mouth and sucking hard.

I move to her other nipple, peeking up at her when she suppresses a moan, and softly bite the tip. I suck and bite each of her breasts. They're on the small side, and I tend to be a boob man, but I've never seen breasts so perfect.

I can't wait to put my hands and tongue on every inch of her.

"Now, tell me about your thoughts … about us *fucking.* What did I do with you?" I sink to my knees without granting her the chance to respond. "Did I do this?"

She curses my name as I pop the button of her shorts open and unzip them.

"Please, fuck me," she begs.

I trace my finger along the edge of her panties. "Mmm … such filthy words spilling from a pageant queen's mouth."

She grasps my hair when I yank her panties down and kicks them off her feet. "Not a pageant queen, and trust me, this mouth isn't sweet."

I brush my finger along her thigh. "I can't wait to find out how dirty that mouth is."

I also can't wait to get my tongue inside her.

My mouth waters.

I have to taste her.

She trembles, her legs weakening at my first lick, and I grip her ass to prevent her from falling.

"I want you inside me," she pleads. "Do you know how long I've waited for this?"

Does she know how long I've waited to get my tongue between her legs?

I flick her clit with my tongue and hook her leg over my shoulder.

"Every part of you is beautiful." I glide my finger through her folds, back and forth. "You are soaked, baby."

I suck on her clit, drawing a path through her slit with my tongue, and plunge it inside her. She gasps my name, her heels digging into my back.

It's the greatest sound I've ever heard.

I skim my hands up her legs, resting them on her ass. I rise onto my feet, confirming she's steady, and take a step back to admire her.

She's perfection.

I'm impressed at my willpower of not shoving her on the floor and fucking her right here, hard and raw.

She deserves better than wall-fucking and floor-fucking our first time.

She deserves my bed, me taking it slow and worshipping her body.

"Now that you've tasted me, it's only fair I do the same," she says, setting her sharp eyes on me.

I wipe my bottom lip and stand. "How about you lie down and let me have my way with you?"

"Fine, undress then."

She sits on the edge of the bed, her gaze fastened on me, as I shed my shirt and then lower my hands to my belt.

"Jesus, you're slow." She slaps my hand away and reaches for my buckle, and her hands are quick as she undoes it, shoving my jeans and boxer briefs down. "You're, uh … huge," she rasps.

I chuckle. "That's what every man likes to hear. Way to boost my ego before I give you my cock."

She bites into her lip.

"Lie down. I'll get you ready."

She scoots her ass up the bed and drops to her back when I crawl over her.

I slide a finger inside her, not wasting a second. "How many times have you gotten wet, thinking about my cock inside you?"

"You have no idea." She arches her back when I slip another finger in.

I rub her clit. "Trust me, I do." My number is much higher than hers.

"How many times have you jacked off, thinking about me?"

"Too many fucking times to count."

She leans forward, reaching for my cock, and I draw my fingers out of her to fall back against the bed, allowing her to stroke my throbbing cock. She grips it tight, her manicured fingers looking perfect around my cock as she jerks me.

"We've waited too long, Maliki," she says, squeezing the tip.

I pull back, my cock twitching at the loss of her touch, and open my nightstand for a condom, putting it on. I stare down at her—her eyes filled with longing, a small smile on her lips—and my heart rages in my chest. Her legs part wider as I settle myself between them, and she quivers when I drop a kiss to her soft lips.

I swipe my finger across her jaw and grin when her stomach muscles clench. I skim my hand down her neck, between her breasts, and stop at her clit, slowly rubbing it.

We drag in a breath when I position myself at her opening.

The first time I slide inside her is fucking bliss.

She's tight. Perfect. Too perfect for me.

"You feel amazing," I grind out, taking my time as I move in and out of her.

I'll stay inside her for as long as she'll let me.

"No, you feel incredible," she moans out. "I never knew sex could feel *this* good."

Her words give me chills, and I fight back the impulse to pound into her.

If I fuck her as hard as I'm craving to, I'm bound to bust quick.

I maintain a steady pace, my balls smacking against her ass each time I edge in deeper.

"Please," she begs. "Please, fuck me harder."

I grin. "There's that dirty mouth."

"Do you know how long I've wondered about what it'd be like to sleep with you?"

I slow my thrusts more. "How long?"

"Since you kicked me out the first time. I wished you had taken me to your office and let me seduce you."

And slower.

Our words release between pants.

"Seduce me at eighteen?"

Her hips tilt up and grind against my cock. "Just because I was a teenager didn't mean I was a virgin … didn't mean I wasn't attracted to you. I imagined you fucking me better than this."

"Oh, really?" I fuck her harder.

Her arms shoot up. "Yes, just like that."

"Always getting your way."

Satisfaction lights up her gorgeous face.

I quicken my thrusts while struggling to last as long as possible, but her dirty talk isn't helping.

"Yes, just like that." She moans. *"Oh my God. Don't stop."*

With every word, I pound harder.

With every moan, I grow closer.

The bed creaks, hitting the wall, and our moans are so loud. I wouldn't be surprised if the people downstairs hear us.

Let them know who she belongs to.

All I care about is the beautiful woman underneath me—pleasing her, making her happy, making her mine if for only one night.

I flick her clit with the tip of my finger.

"I'm close," she breathes out.

Seconds later, her back arches as she screams out my name.

Four thrusts later, I'm spent, spilling out into the condom, and, "*Fuck, baby*," leaves my lips as they meet hers.

"I WAS GOING to call off my wedding," Sierra says the moment we drop to our backs.

Fuck.

She couldn't even give a man a minute to catch his breath before throwing that bomb on him.

I still. "What?"

"The night before my wedding, when I came to the bar, it was to tell you I was calling it off."

Chills hit me, and I remain silent while turning on my side, my eyes traveling over her naked body. I imagined her being in my bed so many times, jacked off on these very sheets as my imagination grew wild, but never did those include conversations about her marriage.

I should've stopped her from marrying him. We should've ended the game we played for years. I would've never seen her in my bar with an engagement ring wrapped around her finger, and she'd never have watched me fuck another woman. We suffered and risked our happiness out of fear. If we had skipped the games, we would've been here years ago.

I have her now.

And I'm not letting anything or anyone stand in our way.

"Instead of thinking about Devin that night, you consumed me. I went to the bar to tell you I wanted us to turn into an *us* and had for years." She shifts on her side, mirroring my position, and rests her cheek in her hand on her pillow.

She's beautiful. Her cheeks flush as she stares at me with sleepy eyes. Her tangled hair is feathered against the pillow. I love how they're all evidence of what we did. I massage her slender shoulder, and she shivers when I skim my hand down her waist, hauling her closer.

Her warm, naked body against mine is heaven.

She hesitates, questioning if it's wise to venture into this conversation after I was just inside her. I don't want my mistake to ruin this moment with her.

Sex with Sierra is the best I've ever had.

Hell, we went vanilla and fucked in a bed, but no one compares to her.

"When I saw you with her, it killed me." Her voice and body tighten. "I didn't know what to think, what to do, but like I took thinking about you the night before my wedding as a sign, I believed seeing you with her was one too—proof we weren't meant to be. It was a warning you were a man who couldn't keep it in his pants or give me the type of relationship I needed. I was heartbroken, angry, and embarrassed for assuming I could walk into the bar and change everything between us."

"But even after all that, you married him."

She shuts her eyes. "I did."

"Why didn't you tell me?" I trace a finger over the soft skin of her thigh. "Come to me?"

"I couldn't face you after that. All I'd see was you screwing her on that desk."

"And all those years, I couldn't rid the sight of him kissing you and touching you in my bar. You'd be with me and then go to bed with him."

"I know. I'm sorry. I was stupid."

"I ditched town the week of your wedding to clear my head but returned that night. Not going to lie, in the back of my mind, I was hoping you'd come to me. Then, Devin showed up as a pregame to his bachelor party. I knew he was there to rub it in my face, that you'd chosen him, and it killed me. Penny showed up, and … well, you know the rest."

"I was selfish—from the moment I sent you the invite to the wedding, thinking you'd come."

"That invite was a waste of paper. I burned it in the pizza oven."

She laughs.

"Did you think about me when you fucked him the night of your wedding?" I take her chin in my free hand, stopping her from looking away.

"I did," she whispers.

I snake my hand down her waist, pulling her leg up over my thigh, and peer at her. "I thought about you when I was with her, too."

She rises, her hand going to my chest to push me down, and straddles me. I groan, throwing my head back, as she grinds down, her bare pussy against my hard cock.

I cup her breast. "Ride me how you wanted that night. Fuck me how we would've. Give me what we should've had."

She bites into her lip, grabs a condom from my nightstand at my direction, and then fucks me hard.

"Don't stop," I mutter.

"Don't make me."

"I love looking at you like this," I say, smacking her ass. "All mine."

CHAPTER EIGHTEEN

Sierra

I'VE HARDLY SLEPT.

Every time my eyes attempt to shut, I force them back open, scared of falling asleep and waking up to discover this was all a dream.

Our legs are tangled, and Maliki's bulge presses against my ass as he stirs in his sleep.

His arms tighten around my waist.

"Good morning," he grumbles into my neck, running his hand up and down my leg.

"Morning," I squeak out.

He rests his hand on my waist and falls to his back, taking me with him, and situates me so I'm straddling him. He reaches out to clip a strand of my bedhead hair behind my ear, his gaze concentrating on me.

I settle my hand on his bare chest and release a deep, weighted sigh.

"What's wrong?" he asks.

It's always better to rip the Band-Aid fast.

Here goes.

"Do you regret what happened last night?"

He squeezes my waist. "Why in the living fuck would you

think that?" He reaches up, sliding his hands over the curve of my jaw, and cups my chin when I attempt to break eye contact.

"From the beginning, you've made it clear you A.) aren't interested in a relationship like that with me and B.) aren't interested in a relationship, *period.*"

"I didn't want to corrupt you."

"Corrupt me?"

He nods. "We come from different sides of the tracks. At first, not going to lie, in my eyes, you were a young teen getting her rocks off on being rebellious against mommy and daddy."

"Wow," I draw out, my brows scrunching. "I'm thrilled you thought so highly of me."

"Hey, that was my first impression."

I squirm, the panties I slipped on after our last round rubbing against his bare cock. I'm not as comfortable naked as he is. "What do you think about me now?"

He tips his head back when I shift back and forth and groans. "Even when I met you and thought you were rebellious, I thought you were sexy and funny. I still think those things along with how amazing you are, and I'm so glad you walked into my bar that night."

I grin. "Corrupt me."

He leans back to snag a condom from the nightstand, and my breathing heightens as he puts it on. He wastes no time sliding my panties to the side, slipping his cock inside me, and I have the best morning sex of my life.

I GRIMACE when I read the text.

Devin: We need to talk. You're still my wife.

I was so occupied with my parents' issues, my new jobs, and Maliki that I neglected the husband situation.

That's right. I forgot I was married.

Or maybe I've put it in the back of my mind, so I don't have to tackle the whole divorce thing.

"What's up?" Maliki asks.

"Devin texted me."

He frowns. "And?"

I cover my face with my hands. "This is humiliating."

"Why?"

"Uh … I'm married."

He scratches his cheek. "You're divorcing him, *right*?"

"Yes."

"Good." He takes a bite of a carrot and points to my phone. "Text him back and tell him that."

I ignore the text and shut off my phone.

TONIGHT IS my first shift of working with Maliki since we had sex.

I'm like a lovesick teen.

Our eyes briefly catch when I peek over at him and grin.

"You slept with him, didn't you?"

I shift my attention back to Ellie, who's perched on a stool, nursing a glass of wine. We haven't hung out since dinner the day I left Devin.

I make a poor attempt of hiding my grin with my hand.

She laughs, reaching across the bar and slapping my arm. "You hooker! You screwed him and didn't tell me, your best friend. What the hell?"

I blow out a long breath, still unable to rid myself of my smile. "I can't call you *in front of him*. That convo needs to be saved for when we're alone."

"Uh, you can trek your little ass to the bathroom and call me … or at least shoot your girl a text. It's rude and against friendship rules for me to find out at the same time as all these wasted people here."

I jerk my head back. "Wait, what?"

She rolls her eyes. "It's obvious. You're eye-fucking him, and he does the same between every drink he makes."

I perk up, my heart leaping. "Really?"

She whistles. "Girl, you've got it bad. He has it bad. I demand every single detail, please and thank you."

"I'm off tomorrow. Margaritas?"

"Can't. I'm babysitting."

I raise a brow. "Someone trusts you with their kid?"

"It's my niece, so if I lose her or something, I won't go to jail." She shrugs. "My sister is moving home, and I was given the option to babysit or help move. Considering physical labor isn't my jam, I chose babysit." Her eyes brighten. "Oh, *instead* of drinks, you can have the pleasure of helping me. You've volunteered with kiddos. You know how to change diapers and all that stuff."

I shake my head, fighting a grin. "I'm not changing diapers."

"*Kidding.* The little heathen is, like, six. Consider it practice for when you and Maliki make little ones."

I hold my palm up. "Seriously, don't go there."

"Oh, I'm going there." She grins and then downs her wine.

"ELLIE SAID it's obvious we had sex," I tell Maliki. "That everyone at the bar knows."

We're closing as usual, but tonight, it's different. We exchange flirtatious glances and brush against each other as we cross paths.

He chuckles, his lips stretching into a broad smile. "Then,

maybe you shouldn't eye-fuck me all night, huh?" He steps closer and pokes the tip of my nose. "That makes it obvious."

"Oh, *puh-lease*. You eye-fucked me all night. And not only tonight but *every night*."

"I won't dispute that." He spans his arm around my waist. "You know what's nice?"

I shiver when his hand wanders to my ass. "What?"

"Now, I can do more than eye-fuck you."

I grin. "Oh, yes, that's definitely nice." I encircle my arms around his neck to tug him my way.

He bows his head, brushing a gentle kiss over my lips. "I have an idea."

"Hmm?"

"You. Me. The apartment. We'll save the closing for later." He swoops his tongue into my mouth to suck on mine.

"Why wait?" I peek down and notice the erection through his jeans.

His hands leave me when I hop onto the bar—the same place he pinned and kissed me the night Penny ruined our moment.

He raises a brow but doesn't speak.

I pat the bar and signal for him to come closer with my finger. "I want you to screw me here."

"Sierra." My name leaves his lips in warning, and he exhales audibly.

"Maliki." I imitate his tone. "Finish what you started before *she* showed up. Let me mark my territory. Now, when you look at this spot, you'll be reminded of me—where you laid me onto my back and fucked me until I couldn't breathe."

"Shit," he hisses through clenched teeth and advances a step, stopping in front of me and standing tall. He snags my waist and tugs me to the edge of the bar, my core rubbing against his hardness. He releases my waist, his hand drifting up my side and shoulder, and he moves my hair to the side, his lips brushing against my ear. "How do you want it, baby?"

I rub my thighs together, feeling my wet panties, and desire screams through me.

"Fuck me hard, right here, right now. Own me, Maliki." The words exit my mouth in harsh gasps.

He wraps my hair in his fist, tugging it back. "Jailbait, I've owned you since you were eighteen."

I lick my top lip and lean forward until my mouth is almost resting against his. "Prove it."

His lips claim mine, heavy and heated, and he widens my legs, giving him enough space to stand between them. He tightens his hold on my hair, yanking my head back, and his lips roam my neck.

My pulse beats hard in every spot he kisses and licks. I struggle to breathe when he grabs my ankles and pulls me toward him, my ass hanging off the bar.

"I hate when you wear these short shorts," he says. "It drives my imagination wild, thinking about licking and sucking your tight pussy." He rakes a finger across my core over my jeans. "Is that why you wear them? To torture me?"

I lower my head to stare at him, his eyes mischievous as they harden on me. "Maybe."

His mouth replaces his hand, resting his lips on my jeans and blowing on them. I open my mouth to beg him for more, but his hands are faster than my words.

In seconds, he has my shorts unbuckled and shoves them along with my panties down my legs. I help him drag them off my feet, and he falls to his knees, resting my thighs on his shoulders. I squirm when his hand squeezes my ass, holding me still, and his tongue dives deep inside me.

My nails dig into the bar and move to his hair, pulling at the strands while he plunges his tongue deep inside me, playing with my clit, and then his fingers meet his tongue.

The roughness of the bar is hard against my back. I'll be sore tomorrow, but I don't care.

I dig my heels into his back and beg for more.

Then, I gasp because I can't take it anymore.

My skin tingles against the wood when I arch my back, and my body trembles as I release onto his tongue.

He lifts, wiping his hand across his mouth, and I shake my head.

"I can't handle it anymore." Deep breaths leave my stomach. "You can't … there's no way I can … Jesus, that was incredible."

His hands rest on my knees, and he carefully settles my legs back down. "You can."

He snatches a condom from his wallet before dropping his pants, his dick hard and long as it comes into my view, and it twitches as he places it at my opening.

"You want me to own you with this cock here?" he asks, raising a brow.

I gyrate my hips, pleading with him, and grab his ass to come closer. I wrap my fingers around his cock, raise my hips, and position him at my opening.

He's moving too damn slow.

He waits, allowing me to take control, and throws his head back when I push in the tip. His eyes fixate on my hand as I play with myself with his cock, moving in just an inch, and his breathing is harsh and ragged, but he doesn't thrust himself in. He lets me play my game as he grows harder and harder underneath my fingers.

I release his cock, my hands running up his chest, and cup his shoulders.

Then, he grabs my ass, holding me up, and pushes inside me.

It's the best damn feeling everywhere.

Maybe because we're doing it here—a forbidden place.

Maybe because I know he's had other women here, and I want to erase them.

Maybe because I've sat at this bar, night after night,

fantasizing about this that I never want him to stop as he plunges in and out of me.

Sweat builds along his forehead, his gaze pinned on our connection.

"God, you feel so good," I moan.

His attention flicks up to meet my eyes. "You're perfect, Sierra. So tight and so perfect."

It doesn't take long until his thrusts turn harder and faster, my hips moving at the same speed as we slam into each other. My eyes shut, my head dropping back, and I yell out his name while collapsing against the bar.

He continues his thrusting, groaning, until he releases inside me.

Our breathing echoes through the bar.

It takes a moment to gain control of myself. "That was amazing."

He gives me a quick peck. "You're amazing."

CHAPTER NINETEEN

Maliki

"I'M BACK," Liz sings, walking into my office. "How big of a mess are you in with troublemaking Barbie?"

"Don't call her that." I narrow my eyes at her from my desk.

Two weeks have passed since Sierra and I had sex.

It's been a fucking amazing two weeks.

Liz shuts the door. "Your answer tells me she hasn't broken your heart yet."

I recline in my chair, crossing my legs, and play with the pen in my hand. "How's Dad?"

"He's Dad. He and the wifey reconciled, and she's surprisingly not terrible."

"What happened to divorcing her?"

"It was his fault for their issues. He was scared she'd leave him like Mom did and pulled away. They talked and seem okay now."

"Good." I fidget with the pen between my fingers. "I have something to tell you."

"What's up?"

I massage the back of my neck. "I'm renovating the bar."

"Oh, cool." She smiles. "I'd love to help."

"Actually—"

Sierra walks in mid-sentence, her hands filled with a notebook and paint samples. Liz's smile wipes off her face, turning into a glare.

Without bothering to glance up, Sierra starts talking, "So, I've gone back and forth with the taupe color you picked—and by picked, I mean, pointed and said, 'That one,' without bothering to look at other options. I don't see it working with the floor we ordered. I know you like it, but *blugh.* I promise to find something better. You'll love it."

All the color drains from Liz's face while Sierra continues her rambling.

"I also have furniture options, and stop me if I'm going too far, but *maybe* we can tear down a wall?"

Liz's gaze pings from her to me. "Tear down a wall?" she shrieks.

The notebook drops from Sierra's hand, paint samples fluttering on the floor, and her eyes shoot straight to me in panic.

"When you said renovating, I took that as a fresh paint job," Liz spits out.

"We are doing new paint," Sierra remarks.

Liz shoots her a hard look. "I meant, not changing everything."

"*Technically,* we're not changing everything," Sierra answers. "We're preserving the bones of the bar, just altering a few things, making them better."

"The bar doesn't need to *get better.*" Liz turns back to me, her face serious. "Why wasn't this discussed with me?"

"Liz, not here, not now," I caution.

"I'll go … look at other ideas," Sierra mutters.

I tilt my head her way with a small smile, and she backs away, hurrying out of the room.

"What will you hire her for next? To sleep with you?" Liz seethes as soon as Sierra disappears.

"Don't go there." My tone is harsh. "Leave Sierra alone."

"You've already slept with her, haven't you? Jesus, Maliki!"

"That's none of your fucking business."

"You're making a mistake."

"Then, it will be my mistake. I'm a big boy."

"You're going to let her ruin our family's legacy."

"Our family's legacy?" I explode. "What legacy is there to be proud of, Liz? The one where our mother was clinically depressed and regularly institutionalized? Or is it when she abandoned her family? Is it our father neglecting to care for his children as he should have, passing that responsibility on to you, or when he nearly went bankrupt and lost this *legacy?* What goddamn legacy are you referring to?"

Her face softens at my hard blow. "You know what I mean. The bar has been in our family for generations without any *renovations*, and you never mentioned changing anything until *she* came along."

"Let me remind you, I rescued this bar from going under." I slam my hand on the desk. "I didn't want it. You knew that, but you begged me to come home and save it—to keep it in the family and make it my own. That's what I'm doing. If you have such an issue with it, I'll gladly sell it to you."

"You're an asshole." She stomps out, the door slamming behind her.

"AM I FIRED?" Sierra asks.

I took a breather in my office before coming out.

How dare Liz throw out *family legacy* bullshit.

"No," I answer.

"Maliki, I don't want you and your sister arguing over me."

"We're not. We're arguing because she's stubborn and she was rude to you." I kiss the top of her head, smelling her strawberry shampoo. “Don’t worry about Liz. She’ll get over it.”

She looks up at me. “Or kill me in my sleep. Does she have a key to my bedroom?”

“Your bedroom is in my bedroom now, and no, she doesn’t.”

She frowns, sighing. “You know what I mean.”

I lean down and press my lips against hers. “Don’t”—another kiss—“worry”—another kiss—“about”—another kiss—“her.”

CHAPTER TWENTY

Sierra

"IT'S BEEN FOREVER since I've been here," I say, walking into Ellie's apartment.

"You've neglected your bestie while on Operation Dodge Your Husband," she teases.

"A successful mission so far. Has he been here?" I assured Ellie I don't expect her to stop Devin from coming over. It's not fair to Corbin.

"A few times." Her tone softens. "He misses you."

"Ellie," I warn.

She holds up her hand, palm facing me. "I'm not suggesting you take him back. I'm simply reporting what I've seen when he's here with Corbin. I don't want you to get back with him, *but* there is no doubt he regrets cheating."

My throat burns. No matter what, I care about Devin, but not only can I *not* forgive him, but I also can't walk away from Maliki.

We're interrupted by a small brown-haired girl wearing a yellow sundress and a daisy clip in her hair. "Aunt Ellie's friend!" A smile beams on her face when I spot her sitting on the floor behind the coffee table, surrounded by crayons and coloring books. She holds up a book, showing off a picture of a princess scribbled with different colors, and squeals in excitement. "Look what I colored!"

I lean down to her level and take a long look at it. "Oh my goodness! That's so pretty!"

She sits up straight and giggles.

"See, you're better with kids," Ellie comments. "I'll whip up some mac and cheese while you watch her not color in the lines."

I shake my head. "You're awful."

"I know." She shrugs and heads to the kitchen.

"And make me a bowl!" I call out behind her. I plop down next to the tot, grab a coloring book from the stack, and snag a few crayons. I open the book and flip to a picture with Barbie and Ken.

"I'm Molly." Her voice is bubbly as she grips a crayon and shows it to me. "Purple is my favorite color!"

I choose a crayon and grin. "I'm Sierra." My voice lowers as I lean in closer. "And guess what."

She giggles. "What?"

"Purple is my favorite, too."

Her face brightens. "Really?"

I nod. "Really."

"Will you be my friend?"

I bump my shoulder against hers. "Uh, duh."

"Yay! We can play dolls after this."

"I'VE ALWAYS LOVED WATCHING you with kids."

I glance away from the TV to find Devin standing behind me. "What are you doing here?"

Molly looks between the two of us, curiosity swimming in her eyes. I can't exactly be rude to him in front of her.

He points to the patio with his chin. "Can we talk?"

Hell no. "Sure."

I stand, and he follows me outside.

His shoulders are tense when he shuts the door behind us, and his scowl hits me. "I've called you nonstop, Sierra. I'm your husband. I know you're angry with me, but at least show me respect and answer my calls. Hear me out."

I cross my arms. "You cheated on me. What do you expect? I don't want to talk to you. I don't want to see you."

"What do I expect? I expect you to at least hold a goddamn conversation with me. You're my wife! We got married, exchanged vows, promised to love each for the rest of our lives—for better or worse." His words come out in forced restraint.

I scoff. "*For better or worse* doesn't excuse you sticking your penis in Louise."

"It was *once*. One fucking time, and I was drunk. *Please.* I've given you time. Hell, I've even sat back while people walk around, saying you're screwing Maliki. *Him*. Out of all people, you had to run to him."

"I'm not talking about Maliki with you."

"Are you sleeping with him?" he grits out.

"That's none of your concern."

He drops down on a chair, taking my hand, and a sob leaves him, surprising me. Sadness clutches my heart. I've never seen Devin this emotional.

He scrubs a hand over his face and uses his free hand to point to Molly through the window.

"You see that little girl in there?" he asks. "We were supposed to have that. How many times did we talk about kids in our future?"

I jerk my hand back, unable to look at him as tears swell in my eyes.

His shoulders slump. "I fucked up, and I'm sorry. Whatever you did with him, it's in the past. We'll start fresh and consider this a speed bump in our marriage, act like it never happened."

I shut my eyes for a moment, an attempt to hold myself together. I can't flip my shit with Molly watching us. "You can't have a family with a man you don't trust."

He scowls and releases a spiteful laugh. "You think *he'll* give you a family? Where would you raise your children? In an apartment above a place filled with drunks? You're worried about trusting me. What do you think you'll get with the town's biggest bachelor, huh? He lives in that bar, and we've both seen how well he attracts the ladies. Do you honestly think he'll stay faithful or that he'll even *want* a family?"

"Don't go there."

His words hit too close to home. That's what happened with Maliki's mom—she couldn't handle being the bar owner's wife—and the girls at the barbeque said the same about bartenders.

"I'm owning up to my fuckup and begging you. Let's go to counseling. I'll do whatever you want to make this work. *Please.* I don't want to lose you."

Tears fall from my eyes. "I can't … maybe this means we weren't meant for each other."

He shakes his head in disdain. "You haven't filed yet. That has to mean something."

"I haven't had a chance to."

"I won't sign."

I retreat a step. "Don't do that."

"Do what?"

"Drag this out."

His eyes darken in frustration. "I'll fight for my marriage."

"You should've fought for it then!"

He abruptly stands. "You'll never have a family with him. Think about that before throwing everything you've ever wanted away. You know where to find me, and I swear to God, I'll forget anything you did with him if you come back to me." His lips graze my forehead, and the patio door squeaks when he opens it to leave.

I fall back in his abandoned chair and wrestle with Devin's words running through my mind. He made valid points. Maliki said his job would interfere with having children, and he couldn't give them a stable home. I sniffle, wiping the tears from my eyes, and catch my breath.

"Are you okay?"

I inhale a breath and look over at the door where the tiny voice came from. Molly has it open a few inches, enough room for her head to poke through, and holds the handle in hesitation. She waits until I give her a head nod and opens the door all the way, stepping on the porch with me.

"I'm fine, sweetie," I answer, fighting back sniffles.

She wraps her arms around me. "My daddy says to always hug people when they're sad and crying. It'll make them happy again."

I hug her back.

Maliki is older than me and has never settled down with a woman, never mentioned living anywhere but his apartment, never seemed to want to move on from the bachelor life.

Where will our relationship be in a month?

Six weeks?

A year?

Will we even have one?

LIZ IS behind the bar when I walk in.

Great.

I've already dealt with Devin today.

Now, her.

We've rarely been around each other without Maliki around, and she's made it clear she's not a fan of mine—his presence or not.

I should've taken the back entrance, but I wasn't sure if Maliki was working.

She sourly stares at me while setting the clipboard in her hand onto the bar. I twist on my toes to head upstairs, but her voice stops me.

"You know how long I've wanted to bitch-slap you?"

Whoa. I expected an insult, smart-ass comment, definitely not bitch-slap talk.

"No, but you do it, and I'll slap you back," I quip.

"I see why my brother is infatuated with you." Her tone is surprisingly sincere as a hint of a smile presses against her lips.

Whoa. I didn't expected that … whatever it was … either.

I hitch my purse onto my shoulder. "Will there be any bitch-slapping going down?"

She shakes her head. "Maliki would never talk to me again if I laid a hand on you."

I stay quiet, unsure of where she's going with this uncomfortable-as-hell conversation.

She lifts her chin. "Are you divorcing him?"

I nod. "Yes."

"My brother is in love with you."

I retreat a step, wincing, and force a laugh. "I don't know about that." Another laugh. *Please sound amused, not scared that she might be wrong.*

"I do. I know him, and he's in love with you. He might not admit it, but when you got married, it nearly broke him. Make him happy. He deserves it."

"You're crazy," I stammer.

I have no doubt Maliki cares about and is attracted to me. He's told me how much he wants to be together, *but* I'm still unsure of where our relationship stands. Does he even know how to have a relationship?

"No, you're blind or too afraid to admit it like he is. You're scared he'll break your heart like your ex, but that won't be Maliki. If you were another woman, eh, I wouldn't say that, but it's you. My brother has been obsessed with you for years."

I gulp, unable to form the right words.

"In other news, I'm extending my leave from the bar. The bartending job is all yours for as long as you'd like."

I smile weakly. "Thank you … for letting me keep my job."

She picks up her clipboard. "You're welcome. He's upstairs."

I walk up to the apartment and find Maliki in the bedroom, undressing, his well-defined back facing me. I gulp when he pulls his pants up.

I step forward, wrapping my arms around his waist, and hug him from behind. "Hey you."

After what Liz told me, I should be on top of the world, but I still can't stop thinking about Devin's words.

I rest my head in the crook of his shoulder, and he turns to kiss me.

"Hey, how was your day with Ellie?"

"We babysat." I pause to hold up a finger. "I babysat while Ellie watched me and texted."

He chuckles, grabbing his shirt and pulling it over his head, causing me to frown. Now that I've seen him without his clothes on, it's my favorite sight. Like a child, I hate when he takes my favorite show away.

"Who trusted you with their kid?"

"Hey, I'm exceptional with kids, thank you very much. It was her niece, Jessa's daughter. You remember her; you two had a thing."

He throws his head back and groans. "You never neglect to bring up the *few* women I've had *a thing* with."

"I'm certain there are more than *a few* that I know nothing about."

Maliki has always been quiet about his history with women. All I know is, he's never had a serious relationship.

He grimaces. "I haven't spoken to Jessa in years. It's been months since I touched Penny. Hell, since I've slept with anyone but you. Trust me on this, Sierra. *Please.* I'm not like Devin or your father." He wraps his arms around me, his mouth meeting mine, and smiles against my lips. "You're all I want. All I need."

CHAPTER TWENTY-ONE

Maliki

I'M DRINKING a cup of coffee when Sierra walks into the kitchen, whistling with a pep in her step.

I set my mug down and raise a brow.

She's always been eager and ecstatic, but after Devin's cheating, it's faded out some, and I hate that.

"So … I did a thing," she reveals, her tone bubbly.

"Yeah, and what kind of thing?"

"I met with an attorney and filed for divorce."

I jerk my head back. Not what I was expecting, but *motherfucking yes.*

Excitement spirals through me. All of my doubts of Sierra going back to Devin and us being a fling have vanished. Her filing has opened the gates of us developing a deeper relationship than sex.

Fuck, who am I kidding?

Our relationship has always been more than sex.

We formed a deep connection before I even touched her.

My grin is so large that I'm surprised it hasn't fallen off my face. "Let's celebrate. I'll take you out."

"Really?" Happiness and surprise register on her face.

It hits me that we haven't done much outside of hanging

out at the bar and the apartment. Sure, we went shopping and to Cohen's but nothing like a date. She deserves more from me.

I nod. "Really."

She skips around the island to plant a kiss on my cheek. "I can't wait."

Devin cheating might've broken her heart, but it's the best damn thing to happen to mine. I was right all along. He wasn't the man for her.

I am.

I FASTEN my gaze on Sierra sitting across the table. "Mikey won't stop pestering me about renting my apartment. He's driving thirty minutes back and forth to work and whining about his lack of sleep and gas money."

Tonight has been incredible, and we're only at the beginning. I brought her to Clayton's, a five-star restaurant outside of Blue Beech. Clayton's is the preferred spot for anniversaries, proposals, birthdays, and celebrations.

And tonight, we're fucking celebrating.

Sierra is cutting the Devin cord, and I can't wait to throw that sucker away.

"You'd better tell Mikey I'll crack a bottle over his head if he attempts to steal my roommate position," she replies.

Shit. She's not going where I wanted this conversation to go.

Mikey won't steal her roommate position.

He'll move in. We'll move out.

"We're more than roommates," I correct.

She taps the tip of her chin. "Right … we're … bedmates?"

"More than that, too."

She looks damn gorgeous tonight. She doesn't dress up

much around me, given the bar is so laid-back, and I love the casual look on her, but she looks stunning. I nearly fell on my face when she walked out of the bathroom in a short red dress that showed plenty of leg and strappy black heels, and her hair is down in loose curls. Her lips are painted a bright red. The lipstick seems to be the only makeup she wears.

I can't wait for the day that red lipstick stains my cock.

I shift in my chair, just thinking about it.

I'm ready to explain my reasoning for bringing Mikey's whining up, but as soon as I open my mouth, she's already talking.

"Have you ever had a relationship?"

"No," I respond without hesitation. "Well … not before you."

My honesty startles her, her bright lips lifting into a wild grin. "Are you saying …"

"Am I saying we're in a relationship? Yes." I cock my head to the side. "If that's okay with you?"

She gapes at me. "We're doing this for real?"

I don't know who's more excited—her or me. This is a serious step for me—wanting a relationship. I couldn't see myself doing this with anyone but her.

"You're divorcing Devin, correct?" I ask.

"Absolutely," she rushes out.

"Then, it's settled."

"Holy shit," she whispers. "I'm in a relationship with Maliki Bridges. My teenage fantasies have come true."

I chuckle. "Oh, really?" I fold my hands together, rest them on the table, and lean closer. "Did you write about me in your diary?"

"Yes." Her voice turns soft and almost childish. "*Dear Diary, Maliki smiled at me today*." She cracks a flirtatious smile. *"Dear Diary, Maliki said he hates annoying teenagers, and I'm an annoying teenager."*

"You have to admit, you were an annoying teenager."

"You have to admit, you were an annoying bar owner," she counters with amusement. "And that you drank before you turned twenty-one."

"I won't deny that."

"See! Why was it such a big deal for me to drink?" She snatches up her martini, gives me a *cheers,* and takes a long sip with a smirk.

"The difference is, my dad was the owner then and didn't care if I drank. I owned the bar when you tried and *did* care."

She rolls her eyes and drops her empty glass onto the table. "FYI, and side note, I am a high-maintenance girlfriend. Just wanted to give you a heads-up. This is your first test: I'm drinking *a lot* of martinis tonight. I might be annoying."

"And I don't give a shit. High maintenance, annoying—which I have dealt with for years, mind you—or not, you're still mine."

"I CAN'T EAT for another week," Sierra declares when we walk out of Clayton's, dodging bodies in the busy crowd.

We've run into three people from Blue Beech, and luckily, Sierra had drank enough martinis that she didn't stress about what they thought about her being married.

Me? I couldn't care less.

Let them report back to Devin.

"Even if it's an ice cube," she goes on, "I'll die." Her head falls back in a groan. "And thank goodness you barely drank, so you can be DD tonight, *boyfriend.*"

I grin like a motherfucker at her last word.

I gape down at her as she stays in my hold. "You're going to regret drinking so many martinis tomorrow, *girlfriend.*"

She wobbles in her heels a bit, and I tighten my arms around her shoulders, keeping her from falling.

"Nope. I'll be ecstatic I drank all those martinis." She licks her lips. "Martinis are my jam, and I can't wait to bring more recipes to the pub. I'll turn all the beer and whiskey drinkers into champagne and martini connoisseurs."

I chuckle. "Good luck with that, babe."

I hand the valet our slip and focus on her, admiring the woman who's become everything to me, while she babbles on about different martinis—something along the lines of Key Lime and Blood Oranges.

This damn woman has buried herself so deep in my fucking veins that there's no way I can cut her out.

I wave off the valet when he goes to help her into the car, doing it myself, and rush over to the driver's side.

"I wonder if the bar is busy tonight," she comments, leaning back in her seat.

"We won't know until tomorrow when I check the figures," I say, pulling out of the parking lot.

"Ah … the boss won't be going down to check on business?" She gasps. "I can't believe Maliki, the workaholic, will let that slide for a night."

"The boss won't even be in the building." Even though it's dark and she most likely can't see me, I smirk her way. "Tonight, it's you and me, babe. No bar chaos, no employees, nothing other than room service and us relaxing in a hotel suite."

She perks up in her seat. "Seriously?"

I nod, loving how excited she is. I should've spoiled her like this sooner. I'll have to make up for my lack of taking her out.

"Uh, shit," she mutters, and by her tone, I wasn't supposed to hear that.

"What's up?"

She shakes her head. "Nothing."

"Sierra," I warn.

"I don't want to feel like a Debbie Downer, and I know I won't be wearing any clothes tonight—"

"Correct on that assessment," I can't help but chime in.

"I'm worried about tomorrow. This dress and heels aren't exactly comfortable to wear then."

"I packed a bag while you were showering."

"You went through my things?"

"Don't worry. I wasn't *too* nosy … didn't find your diary filled with *I Heart Maliki* and *Mrs. Bridges* written between hearts."

She laughs. "I can't wait to write in that journal about how I sucked and then straddled your dick tonight."

"Jesus." I grip the steering wheel tighter in fear of driving off the road. "You can't say that shit to me when I'm already struggling to pay attention."

Good thing the hotel is only minutes away.

SIERRA'S MOUTH is on mine as soon as we walk into the hotel room.

I suck in a breath as her drunken hands fumble with my belt.

The bags I'm holding drop out of mine, hitting the floor.

Yes.

The hotel room was an amazing idea.

I flip on the light.

She backs me toward the bed, and my heart nearly gives out when she shoves my pants down. Her lips have never met my cock, and my heart quickens from me just thinking about it.

She drops to her knees and tugs down my pants, and my swollen cock springs free.

Shit. I might come before she even puts me in her mouth.

She peeks up at me, a teasing smile on her lips before she

licks them. I groan when she wraps her lips around the crown of my dick and takes me all the way in, the tip of my cock hitting the back of her throat as she starts sucking me.

The best goddamn blow job I've ever had.

I dig my fingers into the bed while watching my cock move in and out of her mouth. I suck in a breath, grab her hair, and pump my hips to the same pace she's sucking.

I'm close.

As bad as I want to see her swallow my cum, I need to be inside her more.

"Stop sucking me and take off your clothes," I rasp out. "Then, fuck me."

As I grab a condom, I see her lipstick on my dick and grin.

I waste no time slipping on the condom as she gets naked.

She straddles my cock and rides me.

My life has never been perfect.

Never will be perfect.

But Sierra has made it damn near close.

Too bad I don't know it's going to all fall apart.

CHAPTER TWENTY-TWO

Maliki

I'M SEARCHING real estate online while Sierra is shopping with her mom. To say the market blows in Blue Beech is an understatement. Finding a place might take a while, so I haven't mentioned anything to Sierra yet.

No matter what, I'll find a new home for us. We need privacy and space from the bar. From experience, this isn't a stable place to raise a family either.

That's right.

I'm already thinking about having a family with her.

I want her to be my wife and the mother of my children.

I never thought that was something I'd say.

I shut my laptop and drop it next to me at the sound of a knock on the door. I don't get very many visitors here, given it's in the back lot and most people see me at the bar.

I open the door to find the last person I expected.

She gapes at me, her face brimming with stress.

What the fuck?

I have no clue why she's here or what to say.

"Hey, Maliki," she says, looking high-strung.

I cross my arms. "Jessa, this is a surprise."

She scowls at my harsh tone. "Can I come in?"

"Sure." I retreat a step while doubting if it's a good idea, making sure there's ample space between us, and shut the door. "What's up?"

"I need to tell you something."

"So, tell me."

"I, uh …"

Jesus. She needs to stop this stuttering shit and explain herself. I can't risk Sierra coming in and seeing her here.

I snap my fingers in her face. "What do you need to tell me?"

I'm acting rude, which is unnecessary, but why is she standing, speechless. in my doorway? Her uneasiness makes me worry she's about to start some shit. The faster she explains why she's here, the faster I can go back to house-hunting.

Until something hits me.

An abrupt wave of nausea smacks into me. "Is Sierra okay?" It's reaching, but if something is wrong with her, Ellie could've asked Jessa to relay the message.

"Sierra?" She glances around the apartment. "Why are you worried about my sister's friend?"

"Why else would you be here?"

"*Again,* why do you care about her?"

"Cut to the chase and spit it out, Jessa. I have shit to do that doesn't involve your manipulative games."

"Manipulative games?" She snorts. "I'm manipulative? You're the one worried about a *married* woman. I see your type hasn't changed."

"I had no idea you were in a relationship when we fucked," I seethe. "You and Pete were off and on as much as you changed your panties." I clench my jaw. "*Now*, for the umpteenth time, why are you here?"

"There's something I've been hiding from you."

"Tell me what this *something* is."

"You have a child," she blurts out.

I explode in laughter. "Good one. Did Devin put you up to this?"

"It's true." She shakes her head and pinches her lips together. "I got pregnant when we were sleeping together."

I rub the back of my neck. "Bullshit. I always wrapped up." Sierra is the only woman I've gone raw in.

She continues shaking her head while firing back her argument that I'm her baby daddy. "Tom Petty concert. The backseat of your car."

My mind scrambles back to that night.

Broken condom. *Shit.*

She promised she was on the pill.

"I got pregnant." She rocks back on her heels. "By the time I found out, I was back with Pete."

I hold my hand up, swallowing loud, and sink into a chair at the kitchen table, growing light-headed. "I'm so fucking lost right now."

She takes the seat across from me. "Pete would've left me if I was pregnant with another man's baby, so I told him she was his. Our relationship was solid, and I knew a relationship with you was off the table because you're … well, *you*."

"Jump to the part where I have a child," I grind out. "And why I'm just now finding out."

She slightly lifts her chin. "She's six years old. Pete's mother has never been a fan of mine and always questioned the paternity of Molly. She took it upon herself to swab my daughter's cheek and send it to one of those stupid mail-in labs. Pete found out the truth and filed for divorce. Now, I'm back in Blue Beech, and you deserve to know the truth."

"Oh, *after* Pete left you, I deserve the truth. How fucking convenient is that?"

"I'm telling the truth, Maliki!"

"You've always been a liar, Jessa."

"I swear, I'm not lying."

"Just because she's not Pete's doesn't mean she's mine. Who knows how many men you slept with behind our backs?"

"She's yours. One hundred percent. You might think I'm a vindictive bitch, but I love my daughter."

I grind my teeth and keep an eye on the door, as if I'm waiting for Sierra to walk into this mess. "If you loved her so much, you would've told me years ago, so she wouldn't be fatherless."

"She had a father. Pete. You and Pete were the only men I slept with, *and* I was only screwing you during the time. Believe me, I knew you'd treat me like this and still told you."

"I want a paternity test," I bite out.

"That's no problem."

Her answer falls from her lips in seconds, shocking me.

Maybe she is telling the truth.

She stands and runs her hands over her black dress. She rests them on the table with a stern look on her face. "And FYI, if you're screwing my sister's friend, be careful. She was arguing with her husband the other day while watching Molly. She cried, and they kissed. If I were you, I'd check on your sidepiece." She stops to put her finger to the corner of her mouth. "Or are you her sidepiece, given she's married?"

I fight with myself from throwing whatever I can grab across the room. Too much is being flung at me.

I might have a child.

Sierra was with Devin.

They kissed.

My hands shake as I maintain my composure. "All I'm talking to you about is a paternity test. Otherwise, keep your mouth shut about my life."

"I'll figure it out and get back with you."

I nod.

I'm speechless.

She leaves without another word, and as soon as the door

shuts behind her, I snatch a coffee cup on the table and chuck it across the room.

I'm not believing anything until I see results.

But if it comes out positive, that means she's hidden this part of my life from me for six years.

I calculate the timeline of my relationship with Jessa while cleaning up the glass and then slump down on the couch, staring at the wall.

Jessa has always been a fan of games. We went to high school together, fucked a few times, and then I moved away. We reconnected a few years later and fucked some more. Since I wasn't living in Blue Beech, I didn't know she was engaged to Pete.

"Off and on," is what she said, and I was young and dumb and ran with the *off*, thinking with my dick.

We fucked, plain and simple, and I cut her off when she turned crazy.

I rise to my feet, pour myself a drink, and return to the couch. My mind drifts to Sierra and what Jessa said about her being with Devin at Ellie's. She never mentioned their encounter.

Why would she hide that from me?

I'm being smacked with too many bombshells.

I might be a father.

Jesus fucking Christ.

SIERRA STOPS dead in front of me and presses her lips against mine. "Sorry I'm late. Please don't fire me, boss man."

Please don't leave me if Jessa's telling the truth.

I kiss her again. "Only if you make up for your tardiness later."

She flips her straight hair over her shoulder. "Duh."

I grab a towel and smack her ass with it. "Now, get to work."

She salutes me, bends down, and smacks my ass in return. "I missed you today."

As much as I don't want to ruin the mood, the words have been resting on the tip of my tongue since Jessa left. "Jessa said you and Devin had a moment at Ellie's. You never told me that."

She freezes in step. "Jessa? What were you doing, talking to Jessa?"

Shit. "She came into the bar before you got here, you late one, you, and told me." I hate lying to her.

"Well, Jessa can kiss my ass because she's lying." Her face reddens. "She probably wants to start screwing you again now that her husband left her unfaithful ass."

I wish I weren't avoiding her gaze, but I can't look at her. I'm afraid she'll see the lies in my eyes. "Why'd he leave her?"

She shrugs with a frown. "Something about her lying to him about being the father of their daughter. It's sad because the little girl is so adorable, and now, Jessa stuck her into this weird position of not knowing who her dad is." She kisses my cheek. "Be happy you dodged that bullet."

"Trust me, I am." *At least I thought I'd dodged it.*

"Yep, because then you met me. By the way, Devin was begging me to stay with him at Ellie's. I made it clear I wasn't and then filed for divorce the next day. That lying tramp can kiss my ass, and she'd better stay away from you."

"I love when you get all territorial."

CHAPTER TWENTY-THREE

Maliki

Two Weeks Later

MY HANDS SHAKE as I stare at the envelope—the paternity results.

The day after Jessa broke the news, we went to get a paternity test. She brought her—maybe *our*—daughter in first and left, and then I went in. It isn't healthy to include the little girl until paternity is established. Jessa could be lying, and the little girl is already confused after learning the man she believed to be her dad for years isn't. I need to be positive before breaking the news and further confusing her.

Jessa called the bar, looking for me this morning, which resulted in a glare from Liz. I ordered Jessa to never do it again and reluctantly gave her my phone number. She's already texted me five times.

I decided not to tell Sierra until the results came. Our relationship is perfect, and I'm scared this news will lead to problems, given she can't stand Jessa. She wouldn't be happy to find out Jessa is the mother of my child.

I pace back and forth and then tear it open.

I lose my breath as I read … *99.9% positive paternity.*

I drop the paper on the floor.

Holy fuck.

I'm her father.

CHAPTER TWENTY-FOUR

Sierra

"ALL RIGHT, I'll let you know. Love you."

I bite the inside of my cheek when I hang up the phone, setting it on the couch next to me and scowling at it as if it were evil. I'm lost on what to do.

"Not a good call?" Maliki asks, strolling into the living room and handing me a coffee mug.

We had our morning shower, and he went on coffee duty while I returned the missed call from my father.

I slouch against the cushion. "I have yet to decide."

He moves my phone and takes its place. "What's up?"

"My dad found an apartment. I can move in by the end of the week."

The room turns mute until Maliki clears his throat. "You can stay here for as long as you want. You know that, right?"

I nod. "It's just … we're not exactly *just roommates* anymore. What if things change between us? I'll end up in the same situation as I was with Devin." My situation was better with Devin. We co-owned the condo. I could've stayed, but here? It's Maliki's. I have no claim.

"The only turn our relationship will take is in the right direction of growing stronger."

"No one plans for relationships to fall apart. Devin *didn't* plan to cheat when we married."

I didn't *plan* on divorcing him after three months of marriage.

My father didn't *plan* on cheating on my mother.

I trust Maliki, but never say never.

His jaw clenches. "You and Devin didn't work out because you belong with me, not him."

I scrub my hand over my face. "My father needs an answer by the end of the day, or the landlord will rent to someone else. It's the only place available, and if I don't take it, who knows how long it'll take for another one to open up?"

"What if we rent it together?"

My mouth falls open. *Together? As in him moving out of the apartment?* I grin at the thought of us being in our own new space, but then reality crashes through.

I shake my head. "The only reason the apartment was offered is because the landlord is an associate of my father's. My father wouldn't allow him to rent to *us*, nor would he be okay with you staying there."

He nods in disappointment. "It's your decision, babe. If it counts for anything, I want you here as much as I can get you. If you're scared of breaking up and need a backup plan, go ahead. I won't be upset. As for me? I'm not doing anything to fuck this up. Now that I have you, I won't risk losing the woman I love."

"What?" Good thing I'm sitting, or his words would've knocked me on my ass. I stare down at my lap, studying my hands, unsure if I'm fighting back a smile or a sob.

"Look at me, Sierra."

That's Maliki's thing—always wanting me to look at him, to keep that eye contact. He wants to read me—read my eyes, my heart, every emotion bleeding through me.

When I do, there's a tenderness on his face I've never seen.

His eyes are soft with affection when our eyes meet. Maliki has never been a softie.

He smiles. "Even with you being a pain in my ass, I fell in love with you."

"Really?"

He nods. "I think it's been obvious for a while."

I laugh. "And I think it's been obvious I love you."

His voice turns arrogant as he cracks a giant grin. "Oh, babe, I know."

I roll my eyes. "Shove it."

He wraps his arms around my shoulders, drags me into him, and kisses the top of my head. "This is the best way for us to say it—romance with a hint of sarcasm and teasing."

"That's our style." I grin. "You know what else is our style?"

"Hmm …"

I pull away, and he relaxes against the couch when I straddle him. I skim my hands up and down his chest and lean forward until our lips are nearly touching. "You've had feelings for me for a long time."

He gulps. "Probably. I was just too pissed at myself for wanting an eighteen-year-old."

I gasp when his hand falls to my ass, catching it and pulling me into him. "I was *grown.*"

He clenches his jaw while I grind against him. "Yes, eighteen—old enough to gamble and do porn is what you said. You don't understand what those words did to me."

My lips part as he cups my chin and brings my mouth to his.

"I wanted to make a point," I whisper against them.

"And you certainly did with my imagination."

I gulp when he teases my top lip with his tongue. "Good thing because I love you, too, and I'm sick of feeling like a stalker."

"It was fun, being stalked by you." His hands anchor on my waist to pull me to my feet.

I'm hardly stable when he throws me over his shoulder and heads toward the bedroom.

"Let me show you what you'd be missing every day if you left. Don't think I won't do *plenty* of convincing with my tongue on the matter."

THREE HOURS LATER, when I'm good and orgasmed out, I call my father back.

"I'm not taking the apartment," I blurt out when he answers.

Maliki loves me.

He said those three incredible words and then brought me to his—no, *our* bed and made love to me with his fingers, his tongue, and his cock.

"Sierra," he cautions. "Don't be foolish."

Am I being stupid?

I won't turn my back on this with Maliki.

Let's hope it doesn't come back to bite me in the ass.

"I want to be with him."

"How about you be with him *while* having your own place?"

"Look on the bright side. I'll save money on rent."

Hopefully, this persuades the man who's a spitting image of *money talks.* He's a lover of the dollar, so maybe he'll understand from that perspective.

"I'll pay your rent until you get on your feet. Problem solved," he promptly fires back.

"Dad …"

"Don't *Dad* me. What excuse do you have now?"

"I'm happy, living with him."

He blows out an exhausted breath. "This is a mistake.

Let's hope I can find you something when you change your mind."

"I won't."

"Don't be so sure of that."

"*Gosh,* quit being so negative on love."

"I have a meeting and have to go. Love you. You have by the end of the day to change your mind. Think about it."

"Love you, too."

CHAPTER TWENTY-FIVE

Maliki

THREE DAYS HAVE PASSED since I learned I'm a father, and I still haven't wrapped my mind around it.

What's worse is that I've been an absentee father, thanks to Jessa.

I hate her and now have to figure out a co-parenting plan.

After Sierra leaves, I give Jessa permission to come over.

I've kept my phone off when I'm with Sierra because Jessa has made it her mission to blow it up.

It's such a dick move.

Sierra told me she loved me.

We made love.

And now, I'm letting Jessa step into our home.

But what else can I do?

I sure as shit can't meet her in public or in the bar. This needs to stay private until we make a plan.

This isn't an easy fix.

My daughter thought a different man was her father for years, and now, I'm supposed to walk in and say, *Surprise! I'm your dad.*

An annoying smirk is on Jessa's face when she drops the results onto the table. "I told you, asshole."

I pluck the paper back up, fuming, and point to my chest with it. "I'm the asshole? Not you for hiding the fact I have a goddamn daughter? Not only that, but you also made her believe she had a different father for years! How fucked up is that, Jessa?"

"You didn't want me!" she shrieks.

"That doesn't mean I wouldn't want her!"

"Oh, please," she sneers. "You, a father, especially at that time? You would've said you weren't ready."

"Fuck off. Don't say that shit." Anger spreads through my body. "Where do we go from here?" Enough with the bullshit. We need to figure out the *now* shit.

"You tell me. Apparently, you're calling the shots and not answering my calls. Do you want to be in her life?"

Is that even a question? "Fuck yes, I want to be in my daughter's life."

"What about your little girlfriend, huh? Have you told her yet?" She rolls her eyes and shifts her weight from one foot to the other. "God, I hate seeing her around Ellie's. I do everything in my power to avoid it."

"Trust me, I'm sure she does the same with you."

She perks up, a sly grin on her face. "Does that mean she knows?"

"None of your business." I rest my elbow on the table and rub my forehead with both hands, warding off the Jessa-ache.

"Oh, she doesn't. This will be interesting. Want to tell her together?"

"Shut the fuck up," I grind out.

"When do you want to meet Molly?" She parks her hands on her slender hips.

"We need to ease her into this." *Shit. I need to ease into it myself.* "She knows Pete isn't her father?"

She nods. "She doesn't know about you yet. She's asked a few times who her *real* dad is, but I want us to do it together. Until I find a home, I'm staying at my grandparents' while they're in Florida. You can come over tonight and meet her. Six o'clock okay?"

"Sure. I'll be there. Do I need to bring anything?"

She licks her lips. "A bottle of wine would be nice."

"Our daughter doesn't need wine for me to visit her," I sternly reply.

"Whatever." Her gaze flicks upward. "It would be nice for me to get through this stressful night."

I walk her to the door. "Good-bye, Jessa."

She waves with too much enthusiasm. "See you tonight."

I HATE MYSELF.

"Hey, babe," I say to Sierra over the phone.

"Hey," she chirps. "I'm about to head home. Do you need anything while I'm out?"

Home. She's coming home, and I'm about to fucking lie to her.

A sour taste sets in my mouth. "I'm good. I wanted to let you know that I'm not working tonight." I need to leave before she gets here. I can't face her.

"Uh-oh, the boss is calling in?" she teases.

I force myself to chuckle. "Cohen needs help at the Twisted Fox." I cringe at how easily the lie comes out. "They're short-staffed, and the others are on vacation."

I went through lies all day today. I need to tell Sierra about my daughter, but things are so damn good between us. Not to mention, she turned down an apartment for me. She was right. It'd put her in the same position as Devin. I need to figure out the perfect path to spring this on her and pray she doesn't freak out.

Shit.

Not only is the change to our lives a daughter, but it also involves Jessa—a chick she can't stand.

Fuck. I don't even know why I'm hiding it.

I'm a pussy. That's it.

"You can't have Mikey do it?" she asks, snapping me away from my worries.

"It's too hard, explaining the ropes on a night shift. I helped Cohen open his bar and know my way around it."

I hear the disappointment in her tone. "Oh, okay. I'll see you later then. If you need an extra hand, I don't mind tagging along."

"I'll ask him and let you know, okay? Love you."

"Love you, too."

I hate myself more when I hang up.

Even worse, I have a message from Jessa giving me the address with a smile-face emoji.

I'M SWEATING BULLETS.

My mind is scrambling.

I'm suffering from more anxiety than I have in my entire life.

I'm about to meet my daughter.

My heart races as I park down the road from Jessa's grandparents. I don't need anyone seeing my car there.

I gulp, my hands sweating when I knock on the door.

It swings open, and I jerk back as soon as I see her.

She's beautiful.

My daughter has dark hair, identical to mine. It's pulled into tight French braids with red bows on the end of each one. She's wearing a purple unicorn shirt, polka-dot pants, and unicorn slippers.

Her mouth pops into an eager smile. "Hi! Who are you? Mommy tells me not to answer the door for strangers, but sometimes, it's a Girl Scout selling cookies. I *love* Girl Scout cookies, and I told Mommy I want to be one, so I can eat all the cookies in the world."

Holy shit.

She's adorable.

"But you're a boy, and boys aren't allowed to be Girl Scouts. You have no cookies. Bye-bye."

I stop her from shutting the door.

"Whoa, I'm a friend of your mom's, and sadly, I don't have cookies. I'll bring some next time though."

A friend?

Way to confuse her more.

She wavers and keeps the door cracked. "Mom!" she yells. "There's a man without cookies at the door! He said he's your friend!"

Jessa comes to the door with a wineglass in her hand. "Molly, honey, this is Maliki, the friend I told you was coming to dinner."

Dinner? I didn't agree to fucking dinner.

Jessa is wearing a tight red dress, baring plenty of cleavage, is barefoot, and her hair is pulled into a tight ponytail. There's no denying she's an attractive woman. It's what drew me to her and caused me to fuck her so many times. I ignored her craziness in exchange for her hotness.

"Come in," Jessa says, waving me in, and Molly stands behind her. "I didn't see you pull up."

"I parked down the street."

"Of course. You don't want anyone to see you."

My heart leaps when Molly bounds down the hallway. I follow her into the living room where she has coloring books sprawled over the coffee table and dolls lined up the couch. I glance at Jessa in hesitation, asking for permission, and she smiles with a head nod in Molly's direction.

My steps are slow, and I settle down next to Molly on the floor, keeping distance between us. "Whatcha doin'?"

"Coloring," she says, stating the obvious while snatching a crayon.

Her head tilts to the side as she colors a unicorn the same color as the one on her shirt.

"What are you coloring?"

She holds up the book and points to it with the crayon. "This is a unicorn and the castle she lives in."

I control my shaky breath. "Wow, you color really well."

"Thank you! I've been practicing real hard because I'm going to start school soon! My daddy said I need to color in the lines before I go!" She drops the crayon and frowns. "Well …" Her eyes shoot to Jessa. "My old daddy said that. He doesn't want to be my daddy anymore."

I inhale a breath, and Jessa rushes over to squat down next to Molly.

"Honey, I told you that's not true."

Tears fill her eyes. "I don't know why I don't have a daddy … but Mommy said I'll get another one."

I freeze, and swear to God, tears prick at my eyes.

Jessa fucked this up before giving me a chance.

My gaze flicks upward to give Jessa a glare.

She turns away, her attention returning to Molly, as she wipes loose strands falling from her braids away from her face.

I stand.

"Honey, why don't you finish coloring your picture, and Mommy will be right back, okay?"

"Okay," Molly says in a soft-spoken voice.

I follow Jessa into the kitchen. I keep my voice low, but there's no hiding the anger in it. "You're confusing the shit out of her! A different daddy? Where's she expecting to get one? From goddamn Santa Claus?"

She holds her hand up toward me. "Chill out. What was I supposed to do? She wouldn't stop begging to call Pete, and he doesn't want to talk to either of us. I needed to find a way to explain his absence. Otherwise, she thought I was keeping her away from him."

"There were better ways."

"You know of a better plan, Mr. Sudden Parent?"

"Don't do that." I scrub a hand over my face. "You're right. I don't know."

"You should thank me. I made it easier for you. Now, she knows Pete isn't her dad, and you won't have to explain that to her." She smiles as if her plan is gold and won't further fuck up our daughter's head.

"Where do we go from here then? Since you have it figured out?"

"I made dinner. Let's eat, conversate, help her get comfortable with you, and go from there."

JESSA MADE over-boiled spaghetti and burned garlic bread.

I hardly touched my food while listening to Molly, my daughter—*fuck*, it's weird saying that. Sauce is on her face as she rambles about enjoying dance and how she wants to be a cheerleader and then an astronaut when she grows up.

I nod, captivated by her every word, not wanting to miss one.

"What do you think?" Jessa asks, pouring herself another glass of wine after we clean up after dinner.

I've turned down a glass of wine or whiskey five times. Molly has gone back to her coloring in the living room.

"I think she's ready," she adds, shocking me.

"You do?"

She nods.

I trail behind Jessa into the living room. She asks Molly to sit on the couch and takes the seat next to her.

"Sweetie, do you remember when I said you have a different daddy?" I've never heard Jessa speak so soft.

Damn, she went straight for it.

Molly blinks at her in disbelief and rubs her eyes. "Yes …" She drops her hands and rests them in her lap. "But … I don't know why Daddy can't be my daddy anymore. I liked him being my daddy. I love him!" Her cheeks turn red as tears fall down them.

Tears hit Jessa's eyes, and she hurriedly wipes them away. I have no doubt she loves our child.

They cry while I struggle to control my own emotions.

Struggle to not console them.

I knew this would be hard, but I didn't think it'd be this painful.

My heart knocks against my chest while breaking at the same time for the little girl I hardly know. I'm livid with Jessa but also with myself.

What if she's telling the truth of knowing I wouldn't have wanted anything to do with Molly?

Regret slams into me like a headache.

Jessa pulls Molly into a hug and mouths to me, *Tell her.*

I respond with a *what the fuck* look.

I'm the last person who knows how to do this.

I move closer and sink to my knees in front of them.

Is it too early?

Hell yes, it is.

It's too late to stop now.

I suck in a breath to stop my tears, focusing on Molly, and scratch my neck. I don't speak until she pulls out of Jessa's arms.

"Molly." I pause to clear my throat. "I know what your mom said is confusing. I was confused when she told me, too. You loved your daddy, and I know he loved you. But you also have another daddy who loves you, and that's me."

Molly's eyes widen in more disbelief. "Huh?"

"Honey, Maliki is your real daddy," Jessa explains more confidently. "Pete was what we call a stepdad. He was your daddy when Mommy was married to him." She kisses the top of her head. "You have two daddies, and Maliki will be yours from now on, okay?"

From what it seems, Pete was a good father to her.

Until he tossed her out of his life as if she meant nothing.

It'll look like I took that away from her.

Shit!

Molly gapes at me with brown eyes, her mouth open. All I can manage to give in return is a lame attempt at a reassuring smile.

I feel so guilty.

I hate myself.

Hate Jessa.

Her tears don't stop. "So … you're my daddy now?"

I nod. "I am."

"What if I want my old daddy back?"

My eyes are damp.

I want to fucking kill Jessa for putting us through this.

"Sweetie, this is your *real* daddy," Jessa stresses.

Molly frowns, and that makes a man feel like shit. "My *real daddy*?"

"He's always been your daddy," Jessa goes on.

Her eyes pin to me. "Why weren't you my daddy before? Where was you when I was smaller?"

Jessa squeezes her. "He didn't know he was your daddy, and that's Mommy's fault." She takes Molly's small hand in hers. "I'm so sorry, honey."

Wow.

Shock rushes through me at Jessa's honesty—for her taking the blame.

We wait for what feels like forever for Molly's response.

She sniffles, her face unreadable. "Can I have my doll, please?" Every ounce of the excitement she's had all evening vanishes.

I frown.

Jessa nods, handing her a doll, and Molly grips it to her chest while sprinting down the hall.

"That didn't go over so well," Jessa whispers.

I stand and shake my head in disbelief. It wasn't supposed to go down like this. "Way to confuse a six-year-old."

She sighs. "It went better than I'd expected. Sure, she'll have questions, but she's more in shock and scared than anything."

I stumble back a step. "Scared of me?"

"No, of the situation. I bring in a stranger and say, *Hey, here's your father, not the one you've called Daddy for years.* She needs to spend time with you, not see you as a stranger. She needs familiarity."

"I agree." I sit down, drop my head between my legs, and calm my anger before lifting it. "It would've been much easier had you told me in the beginning."

Her eyes downcast. "It's over. We can't change what happened."

"My daughter thinks another man is her father," I hiss. "Why did you hide it?"

"What was I supposed to tell Pete? I was pregnant with another man's child but wanted to be with him? He would've left me."

"Speaking of Pete, what about him? I'm sure he's on the birth certificate as the father. That's another issue."

She shakes her head. "He's heartbroken, and he refuses to see her. He says it hurts too much and has already filed for divorce. He's done with both of us."

"Ah, he left you, and now, I'm your next option. What you did was inexcusable."

Sadness cloaks her face. "She deserves a family like she had before."

"Let me make this clear: this does not mean we'll be a *family.* I can hardly look at you for hiding this from me, but I have to for my daughter. A daughter I hardly know because of your selfishness."

"I'm sorry, Maliki! If I could take it back, I would."

I only shake my head.

"I loved you, you know. Then, you left me."

"We were young, dumb, and I had my own shit to deal with. *You* had your own shit to deal with."

She rolls her eyes. "Too young and dumb? Look at who you're dating. Someone young and dumb."

I sneer at her. My heart clenches, reminding me how I lied to Sierra tonight. "Don't. Don't even fucking bring up or disrespect Sierra."

"I have a say of who's around my child."

"Sierra is part of my life. Molly is now part of my life. Eventually, they'll interconnect."

"Let's confuse her more." She throws her arms up in the air. "Here's your new dad *and* his girlfriend."

We need a subject change.

"Why don't we stop talking about my girlfriend and check on our daughter?"

Jessa rises. "Follow me. I know how to fix this."

I follow her into a bedroom with a full-size bed where more dolls take residence next to Molly. Her eyes are puffy, and she doesn't look up when we walk in.

"Molly, honey, how about some ice cream?" Jessa asks.

Molly's head flies up as if Jessa had told her the Easter Bunny were here. She wipes away the snot under her nose and grins. "Really?"

"Really. It was your dad's idea. He wants to make you a bowl."

Molly's attention flies to me, and I grin. "Come on. We'll make your favorite kind."

She drops the doll and jumps to her feet. "Can we watch cartoons while eating our ice cream?"

"Sure," I answer.

Ice cream makes her happy.

I need to remember that.

Shit, I'll spend every dollar I have on ice cream if it makes her feel better.

We make giant bowls, and she grins when I sit next to her on the couch.

I'M WOKEN up by my phone buzzing in my pocket. When I glance down to retrieve it, I find Jessa snuggled in my lap, nearly on top of me. She's awake with the remote in her hand.

"What the fuck?" I snap. "Why didn't you wake me?"

She peeks up at me with puckered lips and innocent eyes. "I didn't want to be rude. You looked exhausted and in need of sleep."

I shift to stand, but she moves quicker and straddles my lap.

Jesus Christ.

"Why don't you stay here tonight?" She rotates her hips, her lips nuzzling into my neck, and I nearly vomit.

If her goal is to get my dick hard, she's confused.

"Jessa," I bite out, "I don't want to push you off my lap, but if you don't get up in the next five seconds, I will."

She moans and rolls her hips.

I grab her ass and dump her onto the floor.

Her eyes bulge, staring up at me, flustered, from the floor when I stand.

"I warned you."

She brings herself up while huffing, "Where does she think you are tonight anyway?"

"None of your business." I tug my phone from my pocket, my pulse quickening. "When can I see Molly next?" I can't wait until she becomes comfortable enough with me that I won't have to deal with Jessa around.

"Whenever you want. Maybe you can have lunch with us tomorrow?" She holds up her finger. "Oh! We're going to the city in a few days to shop for school clothes. She's nervous about going to school. Maybe it'll be a good experience for you to bond, and you can put her at ease."

I nod. "Email me the details. I don't want you texting me anymore. Lunch tomorrow sounds good."

"Email, huh? You'd better tell Sierra dearest before she catches you in your lies."

I point to her, fuming. "Stop with the fucking Sierra talk. I won't say it again."

"Why? If you're so *serious*, why won't you tell her? Are you ashamed of our daughter?"

"I'll see you tomorrow." I halt, noticing Molly isn't on the couch, which means Jessa put her in bed while I was sleeping.

When I walk out the door, I check my phone.

Cohen's text is what woke me up.

I scroll down the screen.

My stomach drops.

Six texts from Sierra.

I check the time.

It's after midnight.

Fuck!

CHAPTER TWENTY-SIX

Sierra

I TRUST HIM.

That's what I repeat to myself while waiting for Maliki to come home. I wish he'd asked me to take his shift tonight instead of Mikey. It would've calmed my nervous thoughts.

I attempt to work on designs for the bar but can't concentrate.

He's hiding something from me.

I could've tagged along with him to Twisted Fox, and the panic in his voice told me he didn't want me anywhere near that bar tonight.

Why?

I've texted him a few times and received one reply, saying he was busy and would be home around nine o'clock when a replacement came.

Nine o'clock was three hours ago.

I don't call or text him again.

Screw that.

I shut my computer, debating on sleeping in the guest bedroom tonight. I decide otherwise as I yawn, plug in my charger, and climb into bed, worry dancing through me.

I fidget, staring at the alarm clock, watching the night grow later and later.

I stiffen when I hear the front door unlock and then open. I remain still and silent, listening as he walks into the room, undresses, and slides into bed.

His arms wrap around my waist, and he pulls me into his chest.

I twist away.

Fuck that.

"What the hell, Sierra?" he bursts out.

I whip around as he lifts and shove his chest. "You tell me! You're coming home from the same bar my husband cheated on me at, smelling like some cheap whore's perfume." Spit flies with my words. "At least Devin had the decency to hide it."

He moves away to turn the lamp on.

We're on our knees, staring at each other in shock.

"You honestly think I'd hurt you like that?" He holds his finger up, his brows furrowing. "And your soon-to-be *ex-husband.* Let's get that straight right fucking now. I have nothing to *have the decency* to hide."

"And I'm your soon-to-be ex-whatever-I am," I fire back with venom in my words.

His chest hitches. "Don't say that shit."

"I want to see Cohen's tapes," I challenge, resulting in him flinching.

"You don't trust me. *Wow.*"

"Not when you come home this late. *Wow.*"

He runs his hands through his hair. "I swear to you, on everything, I'd never cheat on you. If I ever even thought about touching another woman, I'd end things between us first."

Tears trickle down my face, sticking my hair to my face, and he brushes the strands aside.

"I love you. I fucking love you to no end and will never

jeopardize losing you. Do you hear me?" He catches my chin in his hand, forcing me to look at him, and massages my face with his fingers.

I swallow rapidly. "Okay." As much as I want to carry on this conversation, I'm drained and terrified of where our relationship will go from here.

I've wanted Maliki for as long as I can remember, and he's already slipping away.

I sniffle. "Please don't play me for a fool."

"Never happening." His jaw flexes, and he drops his hand from my face. He gives me a quick peck on the lips and pulls himself out of bed.

"Where are you going?" I rush out, crawling to the edge of the bed, wishing the desperation weren't there.

His jaw remains clenched. "Shower. I apparently smell like some women's cheap perfume, and I'm not about to bring that shit into our bed."

He kisses the top of my head, and nausea balls up into my stomach as I lie back down, my back facing the bathroom.

Maliki's arms wrap around me again when he returns. He smells like clean soap, and his hair is wet. His lips brush against my ear. "Please trust me, baby." He drops kisses along my neck. "I've never given you a reason not to."

I don't push him away this time. "You've also never done anything this sketchy."

His hand slips between my legs, and I wish I didn't spread them wider.

"Why would I want another woman when I have this?" He sinks two fingers inside me. "When I come home to this? You're all I want."

He grabs my jaw, pulling my head back to kiss me.

I let him.

Even though I don't believe him.

I gasp when he slides himself inside me.

Even though I don't believe him.

I allow him to make love to me.

Even though I don't believe him.

I'm on the road of heartbreak again, but I can't seem to jump off the ride like I did with Devin.

THE NEXT MORNING, Maliki makes love to me.

He's gone all day, supposedly at the Twisted Fox, but he makes it back in time to work at the pub.

Weird.

THIS MORNING, he gives me an orgasm before dropping his bomb.

He makes us breakfast before ruining my day.

"Hey, babe," he says, giving me a quick peck on the lips and sitting across from me at the table. "I'm going to the city to sample new product with Cohen. Liz offered to cover my shift, so you'll be working with her tonight. I won't be gone late."

I take a bite of toast and consider what response to give while chewing.

Rip him a new asshole?

Act like everything is okay?

Leave him?

"That's cool," is what I choose to go with as an idea pops into my head. I keep my tone calm. "I've put off going to the mall. I need some makeup and bras. I'll ask Mikey to take my shift. It shouldn't be a problem. He always wants money, and we can make a day of it. Maybe have dinner when you're done."

This is a test.

He drops his bacon, startled, and scoots his plate away

from him. "Make me a list. I'll pick up whatever you need. We'll make a date to go into the city sometime next week. Sound good?"

Hell no.

"Make you a list of *bras and makeup* I need?" I deadpan.

He nods, refusing to meet my gaze, and plucks a slice of bacon from his plate.

I roll my eyes and am the next one to push my plate up the table. "I need to shower."

He stiffens in his chair and stops chewing. "We showered an hour ago."

"Yeah, well, I didn't think you'd lie to me an hour ago."

He curses as I walk away but doesn't stop me.

CHAPTER TWENTY-SEVEN

Maliki

"YOU'RE SHITTING ME," Cohen says over the phone after I tell him about Molly.

I had to give him a heads-up. I need a favor.

I shake my head even though he can't see me. "Nope."

"Wow," is all he says, stretching the word out for seconds.

Cohen is the only person I've told. No one in my family knows. I have to handle my own shock and come to terms with everything before releasing the news into the world. Cohen won't ask as many questions as Sierra and my sister.

At least, I hope not.

I've never exactly held a secret this large.

I followed Sierra when she stomped away from breakfast to shower. She wouldn't listen to a word I said as I went into detail about this stupid-ass nonexistent product I was lying about testing. She turned away, giving me her back, as I begged her to trust me. I debated joining her, thawing out her cold behavior with an orgasm, but wasn't going to risk a razor to my balls.

I will fix this.

I will tell her.

I don't know why I'm being so chickenshit.

As bad as I want to stay here with her, shower with her, work with her, I also want to see my daughter.

The more relaxed Molly becomes with me, the faster I can kick hanging out with Jessa to the curb.

"What did Sierra say?" His question breaks me away from my thoughts.

I scratch my head. "I, uh … haven't told her yet."

"Now, you've really got to be shitting me. What the fuck, Ki? Did you break up?"

"No, we're good. I'm waiting for the right time."

"Not only have you known about this for weeks, but you also told me before her? I understand you're inexperienced in the relationship department, but that's not how one functions—a healthy one, at least. Hiding you have a kid sure as fuck isn't healthy! Think about this: her ex cheated on her. The longer you hide this, the worse damage it'll cause."

I've never heard Cohen so pissed off at me.

"I need to ask for a favor," I remark, desperate to switch the subject.

"Don't ask me to participate in your lies."

"I'm not doing anything wrong," I hiss. "I'm going shopping with them, and I need you to cover for me."

"Fuck you."

"Please. I'm going through some shit, but I want to get to know my daughter."

"Fine, but when this comes back to bite you in the ass, I don't want to hear you whine about losing her."

I spent yesterday with Molly playing board games and was introduced to her stuffed animals. I haven't known her long, but she's already growing into my heart.

I'm building a relationship with my daughter while my relationship with Sierra is crumbling.

EVEN THOUGH I told Sierra that Liz is covering my shift tonight, I haven't asked my sister yet.

"Hey, can you cover for me tonight?" I ask Liz, walking into the bar.

Liz drops the clipboard she's doing inventory with onto the bar. "Why?"

"Cohen and I are looking at new whiskey in the city. We won't be gone long, just for the day." And just like that, another lie slips from my lips so easily.

She shakes her head. "I call bullshit."

"I call not bullshit." I crack a smile in an attempt to lighten the mood. It doesn't work.

"I know when you're lying to me."

Do I tell her?

"You had another woman call the bar the other day, acting shady, and there's tension with you and Sierra." She shakes her head, staring at me in near disgust. "Here I thought, she'd be the one playing you, yet it seems to be the other way around."

I flinch at the truth in her words. "I'm not playing her."

"What's going on then?"

Here goes.

I start pacing. "Do you remember Jessa?"

"Bitch-face Jessa? Yes."

I stop to face her. "I got her pregnant."

She falls back a step, her back knocking into the shelves, and thankfully, nothing falls. "What do you mean, you got her pregnant?"

I shake my head, nerves rippling in my stomach. "Not recently. In the past, when we used to hook up. She came over a few weeks ago and broke the news. I have a daughter."

"And you believe her?" she says with a laugh and a snort.

"I didn't until I got a paternity test."

"Holy shit." She releases a hard breath. "Have you told Sierra?"

"Not yet," I croak out.

She throws a towel at me, and I barely dodge it. I deserve to get hit though.

"You're an idiot," she snaps. "You can't hide something like that from her. What would you do if it were the other way around?"

"I doubt Sierra will find out she has a secret baby she never knew about."

"Shut up, dick. You know what I mean. This is a big deal. It changes your life and everything around it."

I bow my head. "Trust me, I know."

She walks around the table, slumps onto a stool, and gestures for me to do the same. "What are you going to do? Does she know you're her dad?"

I hoist myself on the stool next to her and nod. "I met her the other day. It's hard on the both of us. She'd thought another man was her father for years."

Her hand flies to her chest. "Whoa, that's messed up." She pats my back with a stern look on her face. "You'd better tell Sierra. News travels fast in Blue Beech."

Another person knows.

And I still haven't told Sierra.

ALL THE MADNESS of my day vanishes when Molly races toward me with a glowing smile on her face.

She jumps up and down. "I can't wait for us to go shopping today! Mommy said I can get new clothes." She stops and claps her hands. "She said we can look at American Girl dolls, too! I've wanted one for forever and ever."

I had Jessa meet me at a gas station twenty minutes out of Blue Beech. She smiles and gives me a hug when she sees me. I grit, patting her shoulder, and pull away as fast as I can.

"Do you think she can ride with me?" I ask.

"I thought we could ride together," Jessa says.

"Yes!" Molly squeals. "Let's all ride together in the cool car!"

I groan, covering my face. "All right. We'll ride together."

Fuck my life.

We pack into the Camaro, and as soon as I turn the radio on to get through this hell of a ride with her, Jessa leans forward and changes the station. I've never been so annoyed with someone. Spending time with Molly is supposed to be fun, but Jessa is driving me nuts, and I haven't even pulled out of the parking lot.

The good to come out of Jessa's music changing is Molly starts animatedly singing in the backseat.

I check my phone when a text comes through.

Cohen: I still vote you tell Sierra.

I groan.

"Is that your girlfriend?" Jessa asks. "It's not safe, texting and driving, *especially with our daughter* in the car."

I drop my phone in my lap and clench the steering wheel.

God, why are you testing me?

When Jessa realizes I'm not going to talk about Sierra, she stretches her legs out and sighs. "Molly needs some clothes, and she asked for an American Girl doll. Do you mind paying for them?"

I shake my head. "That's no problem."

She nods. "We'll need to figure out child support payments, too."

I nod. "I'll call my attorney and have her get in touch with you."

She bites into her lower lip. "I'm broke, Maliki, so the more you can help us, the better. I was a stay-at-home mom, and now, without Pete, I have no income."

I don't mind supporting Molly.

"Start looking for a job then," I remark.

"As soon as she starts school, I will. I want her to make a smooth transition."

I BUY Molly four new outfits, new tennis shoes, and an American Girl doll.

We grab lunch in the food court, and Molly holds my hand and skips as we walk out to the parking garage to leave.

"You know what would be fun?" Jessa asks.

Never having to speak to you again.

"If we stayed in the city tonight," she continues when I don't answer. She turns to look at Molly in the backseat, a smile on her face. "Wouldn't that be fun, honey?"

"Yes!" Molly squeals.

Fucking great.

"No," I grit out without looking at Molly. I can't see the disappointment on her face.

This is where I draw the fucking line.

"Oh, come on." Jessa smacks my arm with a laugh. "It'll be fun." She whips around to look at Molly again. "Ask Daddy pretty please for us to stay in the city."

What the flying fuck?

CHAPTER TWENTY-EIGHT

Sierra

"I THINK Maliki is sick of me," I say. "We've been a *thing* for three months. Maybe that's his cutoff time. He can't handle a relationship this long."

"Are you on drugs?" Ellie asks. "It's clear how much he loves you when I see you two together. You've been into each other for years."

"He's acting shady."

I shrugged off all Maliki's attempts at conversation while I re-showered.

I don't like liars.

He stuck around until I got out, kissed me, and left.

Since then, I've restrained from texting or calling him.

He texted twice, asking what I was doing.

I've ignored them.

What's he doing? is the better question.

"I love you," Ellie carries on, "but you don't trust anyone because of Devin cheating, which is understandable."

I take a lengthy drink of water and settle the bottle down on the table. "Maybe you're right."

"I'm always right." She grins and pops a cracker in her mouth.

Even if he isn't cheating like Devin, he's hiding something.

Our conversation is cut short by Corbin *and* Devin walking into the apartment.

Devin stops, his eyes dilating when he notices me. "Shit, Sierra. I didn't know you were here."

He appears in better shape than I saw him last. He hasn't attempted to contact me again since our patio talk. Maybe he's moving on like me.

My chest caves. *I hope not with Louise.*

Ellie scowls at Devin before shifting the look to Corbin.

Corbin flings up his arms. "We didn't know you were here! Ellie never told me she was coming over. I thought the coast was clear."

"It's fine." I swish my hand in the air. "I was about to leave anyway."

"You don't have to do that. The cheater can go," Ellie replies.

"I need to work," I comment, rising up from my chair and grabbing my keys.

"I'll walk you out," Devin offers.

"Not necessary." I glance at Ellie. "I'll call you later."

I say good-bye to them and don't stop Devin as he walks behind me.

"I don't want to sign, Sierra," he says as soon as we make it outside.

I swing around to glare at him. "Please, it's over." I can't deal with him on top of this Maliki madness.

"You're in love with him, aren't you?" His voice loses power at the end, and his eyes are gentle as I meet them with mine. "You don't want to be with me because of him."

My stomach knots. "This isn't about him. This is about your unfaithfulness. We'd still be together had you not done what you did. Maliki has nothing to do with this. Us not being together is all on you."

His broad chest hitches. "You're right."

He turns around without another word and walks to his BMW, shaking his head. He leans into the seat, opens the glove compartment, and grabs a folder. I stay silent as he drags the forms from the folder, a pen falling out, and goes to the last page.

I stagger back a step when he places the paper against my car and signs it.

"Here you go," he says, holding it out to me. "Be prepared for him to fuck you over worse than I did." He falters a step after I take them. "We could've made it work. Think about that before you sign and throw us away."

He goes back inside the apartment without another word.

I rest my back against my car, catching my breath, as my heart twists in my chest.

"Be prepared for him to fuck you over worse than I did."

Devin already knows what's coming.

I study the divorce papers when I slide into my car.

Am I doing the right thing?

I toss them into my passenger seat and call Maliki.

No answer.

THE CROWD HAS DIED down when Maliki gets to the bar.

Relief strikes through me that he's here.

Anger follows next.

I shouldn't have been afraid he wouldn't come home tonight.

That's not a healthy relationship.

He drops a kiss on my cheek, says, "Hey, babe," and runs upstairs for a quick shower.

When he's finished, he comes down and does paperwork in the corner, keeping his eyes on me.

I'm drained when my shift ends, and I ask him to close

with Mikey, so I can shower. I slide into bed without waiting for him to come up.

When he does, he wraps his arms around me, as always.

"I wasn't sure you'd come home tonight," I whisper into the darkness.

His arm twitches, his body stiffening against mine. "What?"

"It seems you're doing everything in your power to avoid me."

His lips trickle down my neck. "I love you, Sierra. You believe me, right?"

I nod.

"Whatever you're gathering in that pretty little head of yours, it's not what you think."

"Why are you being sketchy?"

"I'm working it out. I promise."

"Let me help you."

"You being here helps me."

I'm too exhausted to argue.

CHAPTER TWENTY-NINE

Maliki

THIS HAS TO STOP.

Sierra is breaking down with each day I carry on this lie.

She hardly speaks to me in the morning.

I feel like a piece-of-shit boyfriend.

No, I *am* a piece-of-shit boyfriend.

What happened after the mall trip proved this will only get worse.

I'm still pissed about Jessa's sleepover attempt, causing me to look like a jackass in front of Molly. No exaggeration, I declined sixteen times.

I was fuming the rest of the way home.

It got worse *when* I got to the bar and saw the crestfallen look on Sierra's face.

The words are sitting on the tip of my tongue, but I can't set them free.

I almost did last night, but it wasn't the right time.

The right place.

The right way.

I can't do it while she's slinging drinks.

I can't do it after she's wiped out from a long night.

I grab my phone.

This shit is long overdue.
No more lying or sneaking around.
She'll be pissed, but I hope she understands.
Me: Date night tonight?
Sierra: Ooh, sounds good! I've missed you.
Me: A night in the city?
Sierra: That sounds perfect.

CHAPTER THIRTY

Maliki

"WHAT'S THAT SMILE FOR?" Ellie asks.

The eager grin hasn't left my face since Maliki texted me. "Maliki and I are going out for the night."

Her smile grows just as wide. "Does that excitement mean he's no longer being Shady McShaderson?"

My smile falters an inch. "Somewhat, but I see this as promising." I shake my head. "I've been dumb, waiting this long to demand answers."

"I don't see him cheating on you. He looks at you like you own his world."

"I'm not as worried about cheating as I am him wanting to break up with me. I'm scared he wants to end our relationship, and since he doesn't know how, he'll pull away until I cut the cord."

"Doubt the man is taking you on a date to break up with you. Stop being paranoid."

"I'm sick of you telling me to stop being paranoid."

"Then, stop being paranoid."

"Aunt Ellie!"

Molly comes running into the kitchen, an eager smile

glued to her face. She wraps her arms around Ellie's legs, and Ellie squeezes her shoulders.

"Hey, I didn't know you were coming over," she says.

"I need you to babysit." I hear her grating voice before seeing her. "Mom isn't home, and I need to run errands."

"Okay," Ellie says to Jessa. "A heads-up would've been nice."

"I texted, but you didn't answer," Jessa fires back. "Molly asked to hang out with you."

"I'm watching cartoons!" Molly says before rushing into the living room.

"It won't be long," Jessa continues. She turns to leave but halts when her eyes meet mine. "Oh, hey, Sierra."

I narrow my eyes at the smugness in her tone. "Uh, hey. How's your moving going?"

My mama taught me never to act rude … unless someone pisses you off. So far, Jessa hasn't hit that level.

She fidgets with her necklace. "Oh, it's going. I thought it'd be terrible, moving home, but I've enjoyed catching up with *old friends*."

"That's good." *Please stop talking to me.*

She smirks. "How's Maliki today?"

What the fuck? "He's fine." I still. "Why?"

She slaps her hand through the air. "I haven't heard from him since last night. I know we had a long day yesterday, but we normally talk every day, so this is unusual. I might stop by the apartment and make sure he's okay."

My ears ring, my stomach knotting. I've never been a violent person, but I want to punch her in the face.

"What are you talking about?" I snap.

She releases a mocking laugh. "He still hasn't told you we hang out?"

"Hang out where?"

"At my house … sometimes his apartment." She shrugs. "Whichever is more convenient."

"Excuse me?" I shriek. "He went to *your house*?"

She nods. "Not yesterday though. We went to the city, had lunch, spent time together."

Ellie slides between us, and my stomach sinks.

"What are you doing, Jessa?" she asks, her tone filled with warning. "Don't come into my home and play games with my best friend."

I rest my hand against my chest while doing a shitty job of controlling my breathing, controlling my aching heart, and restraining myself from not clawing her eyes out.

"I'm not the one playing games." Jessa cackles, sharpening her attention on me. "Why are you so offended the father of my child was at my house?"

"What?" Ellie and I scream simultaneously.

Ellie aims her finger toward the door. "Leave. I'll watch Molly."

Jessa laughs, pleased with herself, and ignores Ellie. "You don't know yet, do you?" She squints, a hard smile passing over her lips. "I've told him to tell you for weeks now, but that's how Maliki is, you know? So secretive, lets no one in. That's why it didn't work out with us last time, but we're doing better now that we're older."

I shut my eyes. *No. No. This isn't happening.*

He would've told me if he had a kid.

My eyes tighten. "Nice try."

Jessa scoffs. "I'm serious. He's Molly's father." All eyes are on her when she drops her bag on the counter, rummages through it, and pulls out an envelope. She slaps it down next to me. "Don't believe me? See for yourself."

It takes everything I have to control my hands from shaking when I pick up the envelope and pull out the paper.

I read it once.

Twice.

Another time for good measure.

I see his name.

He's a 99.9% match.

Molly's cartoon in the background is the only sound in the apartment.

I check the date on the test. It was done over three weeks ago, and he never told me.

Three weeks!

Hell, he's known for longer since that's when he had the test.

The secrecy makes sense now.

"How did you get this?" I stammer, hating how weak I sound.

"I went to his apartment, of course," Jessa answers. "He's spruced up the place, hasn't he?" Her hands go to her chest. "We normally hang out at my place though. There's more room."

I grip the paper. "Stay the fuck away from my boyfriend."

"Boyfriend for how much longer?"

I take a step toward her, nearly in her face. "I'd be a bigger bitch if your daughter wasn't here."

Ellie squeezes between us again, and we both stumble back.

"It's okay," Jessa says over Ellie's shoulder. "It's not like she'll see you around much."

"Jessa, stop!" Ellie yells.

Jessa doesn't. "Where do you think he was the other night when he came home late?"

My face falls.

Jessa grins, knowing she hit a spot.

It was her perfume.

It was her scent he went to the shower to wash off.

It all makes sense.

I shove the paper in my bag and storm past her.

"Hey!" Jessa shouts behind me. "You can't take that!"

Ellie is calling my name as I leave her apartment and sprint to my car.

I STORM into the bar with the paternity test in my hand.

"Oh shit," Liz yelps, standing next to Maliki at the bar.

Maliki's eyes are wide, all the blood draining from his face, and he scrubs a hand over it.

"We need to talk," I grind out.

He nods, and I lead the way to our apartment.

No, *his* apartment.

An apartment he allowed Jessa to come into who knows how many times.

I shove the paper into his chest as soon as he shuts the door and faces me. "Care to explain this?"

He doesn't bother looking at the paper as it floats to the floor.

He knows what it is.

"I planned to tell you tonight," he says.

I scoff. "You *planned* to tell me the day I confronted you? How convenient. Why wasn't I told weeks ago?"

"I had to know if she was mine."

"You've known she was yours for a while. Not only did you keep this from me, but you've also been hanging out with Jessa behind my back." Tears sting the backs of my eyes. "You came home, smelling like her perfume. You were never helping Cohen, were you? You weren't in the city with him. You were with her."

"I was with my daughter," he corrects, grinding his teeth.

"And her!"

"I had no choice!" His voice rises. "Molly didn't know me! I couldn't walk in and expect her to be comfortable. Jessa had to be there."

"You could've told me." I choke back a sob. "I would've helped you work through it. I would've been with you like a *girlfriend* should."

He draws in a breath, his body tensing. "It was complicated."

My pulse slams into my throat as all rationality flies out the door. "I can't." I shuffle back a step. "I can't do this."

He winces. "Can't do what? Be with a man who has a child?"

Hell no. I won't allow him to turn this around on me.

It's my turn to raise my voice. "No, be with a man I don't trust."

He scowls. "You don't trust me?" His shoulders straighten. "Before this, I never lied to you. Not once. Hell, Sierra, you're fucking married, and I've accepted that!"

"Not for long. The divorce will be finalized this week." My answer is firm. Flat. No expression shown.

He blinks. "What?"

"Devin signed the divorce papers. You'd know that if you came around."

His face softens. "Why didn't you tell me?"

That flat voice rises a few notches. Okay, a lot of notches. "Why didn't you tell me you had a child?"

"I was scared it'd become an issue, like it fucking is right now. You're young, Sierra."

"Screw you. Don't you dare use that as an excuse for your fuckup!" My chin trembles, my voice shaky. "I'd have accepted you in any way I could have you—daughter, no daughter, twenty damn daughters. I would've held my arm out and helped with your baggage because you've accepted mine, but that acceptance ends at lying." My voice cracks. "I should've known when you came back smelling like her, when you went MIA for hours, when you weren't working in your own goddamn bar!" Tears swim in my eyes, and I jerk my head to the side, wishing I could rid myself of them. "You and Jessa can make yourselves a happy little family and stay the hell away from me."

Maliki's eyes glaze over. "I don't want Jessa."

"Yet you've been secretly hanging out with her."

"Don't do this. Don't fucking walk away from us, Sierra."

I whip around, and he's on my trail as I storm toward the bedroom. I scoop up what folded clothes I see, not even caring what they are, and shove them into my bag, overfilling it. Items fall, but I don't care.

Like with Devin, I'll buy new shit.

Maliki stays at my heels as I leave the room, pleas falling from his mouth. "Don't do this. Don't fucking walk away from us."

I don't stop until I'm at the door.

That's when I face him.

And when I nearly break down.

No, I *do* break down.

Our sad eyes meet, neither one of us wanting to be the first to waver.

Disappointment swims in his.

I don't know if that disappointment is toward me for leaving or himself for lying, for doing this to us.

"I thought you were different," I finally whisper.

His eyes shut. "I am." He swallows hard. "I thought you loved me enough not to walk away because I have a daughter."

I point to him, tears blurring my eyes, and my anger resurfaces. "Fuck you! Don't you goddamn dare try that excuse to make yourself feel better." I shake my head and snort. "I always fall for the cheaters."

"I'm not a goddamn cheater," he grinds out. "She tried, but I stopped her before it went anywhere."

I withdraw a step, nearly tripping over myself, my back hitting the door. "She *tried*?"

"Sierra—"

I cut him off, "Let me put this in perspective. How would you feel if I told you I went to the condo and Devin *tried* to fuck me? You'd want to know, wouldn't you?"

"Fuck yes!"

"Exactly!"

His hand curls around my arm when I turn to leave. "Please," he begs. "Don't do this, baby."

I shake my head, sobbing.

"Don't throw us away like this." His voice breaks. "Please, for the love of God, drop your bag and don't leave me."

I attempt to control my sniffles. "We need time apart, and you can spend that time getting to know your daughter."

His hold softens on me, his hand massaging my arm. "I can be with you and spend time with her."

I shake my head and jerk away from him. "I'm sorry."

"You're walking away the second there's a bump in our relationship. I'm going through some shit, and I stayed by your side when you were going through the same."

"You wouldn't have been by my side if it involved still being around Devin."

"Our circumstances are different."

"True, you have a woman from your past who had your baby, claiming you're sleeping together. Just like Devin, you don't care about trust in relationships. I learned my lesson with men I can't trust. You need time to spend with your daughter. Do that."

I can't believe I gave up my apartment for a man.

I'm never doing that shit again.

Lesson fucking learned.

And with that, I walk out with tears falling down my cheeks.

CHAPTER THIRTY-ONE

Maliki

I'VE NEVER BEEN a man who fails.

Who quits.

I'm learning today I'm also a man not afraid to beg the woman he loves not to leave him.

My pulse drums against my throat as I follow Sierra down the stairs and through the bar, biting my tongue to keep my mouth shut in front of customers. As soon as we're outside, customers be damned, I'm still pleading with her.

Begging her not to leave.

She doesn't stop until she makes it to her Lexus. "Maliki, just—"

Weight settles on my heart as I take in the hurt on her face.

I did this to her.

Now, I need to fix it.

"Look at you!" I yell. "Neither one of us wants this! I've never made you doubt my feelings for you, my loyalty to you. Not once!"

"Until today. Why did you smell like her? Why were you there until after midnight?"

"Don't fucking believe her lies," I hiss, lowering my voice as people start walking into the bar.

Her sadness swerves into anger. "You might've turned her down then, but what about the next time and the next? When you're with her, *seeing your daughter*, all I'll think about is whether you're sleeping with her. Had you not hidden this or stayed at her house until midnight, things would be different. I don't trust you and refuse to let myself go through that pain again. You lied about this, something I would've understood. Who knows what else you've lied about?"

I duck my head down to her level, my arms spreading to each side of her body, my hands resting on her car. "Please."

She shoves me away, opens her door, and gets in.

She leaves me.

As fast as Sierra railroaded herself into my life, she's walked out.

LIZ IS WAITING for me in my apartment.

I don't know how long I stayed in the parking lot, praying she'd come back, but all I saw were customers ready to have a good time.

I've called.

I've texted.

I've left voice mails.

She's gone.

I should've never hidden it.

That much is obvious.

I didn't know what to do. I'd never had to answer to anyone, to explain to anyone, never shared a life like I did with her.

"I told you this would blow back in your face," Liz says, frustration in her tone.

"She left. You should be happy." I plod around her and yank a bottle of vodka from the cabinet.

"*Please*, I don't feel sorry for you. I feel sorry for her."

In seconds, a shot glass is in my hand, and I fill it to the rim with vodka. "I thought you hated her."

One shot down.

She pushes her hands into her pockets. "Me, too, but now, I hate you. I thought she'd hurt you, not the other way around. You, my dumbass brother, are to blame for losing her."

Another shot knocked back.

I'd offer Liz some, but who knows how long I'll be drowning in my pity?

I slam my glass down. "I did it because I didn't want her to worry about me with Jessa. She was already having trust issues. I fucking did it because I finally had a woman I'd wanted for years and was afraid of losing her."

She snatches the glass from me, pours herself a shot, and downs it. "All of those reasons are what made her leave. Had you told her about Jessa and your daughter, she'd be here. You were a dumbass."

Another shot.

"How did she find out?" she asks.

"Fucking Jessa," I answer through clenched teeth.

"I never liked her. I might've hated her more than I did Sierra back then."

"Join the club."

"You'd better go rip Jessa a new fucking asshole."

"Trust me, I plan to."

"When do I get to meet the little one?"

"Now that the news is out, whenever, I guess."

Another goddamn shot.

CALLING her drunk is a bad idea.

Fuck good ideas.

I've already proven I exceed at bad fucking ideas.

"What the fuck is wrong with you?" I scream at Jessa over the phone.

"I've been waiting for your call," she replies.

I slam the shot glass on the island.

"She needed to know, and you didn't have the balls to tell her. It's not like I went to Ellie's, planning to break the news, but she was there, and I figured, *Why not?*" Her voice is chipper. Goddamn chipper after ruining my life.

Why not?

Her words only fuel the fire burning inside me.

"You're telling me, you walked around with a copy of our paternity test?" *That's some weird, manipulative shit.*

"I never took it out of my purse."

I stay quiet.

"When will we see you next? Molly has been asking about you all day. I thought it was smart to wait on your phone call, given what happened."

"My attorney will be in touch." No longer will I be a participant in her mind games.

"What?"

"I'm establishing rights to my daughter. I want to see her without you breathing down my neck. You keep making shit complicated, and I'm a simple man. Molly knows who I am now, and I can see her without you."

"I want us to be a family. Molly deserves that."

The vodka is close to coming up while I listen to the phoniness in her voice. "Get it through that dense skull of yours that there will never be an *us*."

"She left you, didn't she? I told you Little Miss Perfect wouldn't accept this. Hell, I'm sure she never intended to stay with you. You were the bad-boy fling before she went back to her straitlaced husband. He cheated, and she wanted to play, too. Don't think I haven't overheard them talk."

I pull my phone away to find Liz calling.

"Gotta go." I hang up with Jessa and answer Liz's call.

"Hey," she says timidly.

"What's up?"

"Sierra's brother is here to collect her things. Is it okay to let him up?"

"Yeah."

I hang up.

She really is walking away.

Seconds later, there's a knock at my door.

I'm not sure which brother I'll find on the other side.

"Dude, you fucked up," a kid I don't recognize says, walking into the apartment, uninvited, his shoulder hitting mine.

Since I know Kyle, I'm guessing this is Rex.

"I'm well aware," I grumble. "I need you to talk to her for me."

He shakes his head. "Dude, I don't know you or what happened or what to tell you. What I do know is my sister's trust in people is shit, and beware, she holds grudges like a motherfucker now. I don't know if there's any talking to her that can be done to change her mind. You saw how quickly she left Devin's ass. She doesn't play games."

"Ask her to call me."

"You hurt my sister. I'm not relaying shit."

The little shit has a mouth on him for being twenty pounds less than me.

I clench my fists. Punching her brother won't get me back in her good graces.

"Look, dude," he says, noticing the switch in my mood, "give her a few days. We all know she loves you. It just depends on how much."

I give him her bags, making sure I don't pack *everything*, and search for another shot glass when he leaves.

WORKING WAS A BAD IDEA.

I'm near as drunk as the people ordering drinks from me.

But hey, I can work under pressure … under alcohol … under heartbreak.

I have to work, or I'll go nuts upstairs, thinking about her.

I've always thrived on solidarity and silence, but suddenly, I hate it.

The man who never needed anyone needs *her*.

I miss her—her presence, her scent, her laughter.

I miss my rebellious princess—the woman who pushed my buttons from our first meeting, who challenges me and pushes a smile out of me more in one day than I used to in months.

I miss her when I close the bar.

I miss her when I slide into bed.

I miss her and can't fucking sleep.

CHAPTER THIRTY-TWO

Sierra

THREE DAYS HAVE PASSED since I walked away from Maliki.

Three long, miserable-as-hell days.

He keeps calling.

I keep ignoring.

"Hey, babe," Ellie says, walking into Rex's apartment with ice cream, hot wings, and wine. She glances around. "Your little bro's pad isn't as bad as I imagined." She drops all her items, including hand sanitizer, on the floor next to the couch.

I called my father and asked if the apartment he'd offered was available. It wasn't. I needed a place to stay and asked Rex if his offer was still open. My baby brother doesn't ask questions. I'm closer to him than any of my other siblings.

He shares the three-bedroom apartment with another roommate, who welcomed me with open arms. It's a total bachelor pad with large TVs, video games, and movie posters as the wall decor, *but* they do keep it clean and are respectful.

I hop up from the couch to put the ice cream in the freezer and grab two plates from the set Devin's uncle gifted us on our wedding. Next, I open a drawer for the wine opener and snag two wineglasses.

Instead of avoiding Ellie's apartment in fear of running into Devin, it's now Jessa I'm dodging.

Ellie blows out a long breath when I hand her a plate. "Damn, am I in one crappy position."

I open the bottle of wine and pour myself a full glass. "I don't expect you to take my side over Jessa's."

"She's in the wrong though."

I gulp down my entire glass and pour hers. "You really didn't know he was Molly's dad?" The question has been lingering in my head since Jessa's big reveal.

From Ellie's reaction when Jessa broke the news, it seemed Ellie was clueless, but I never know. She could've been protecting her family.

"Hell no. I would've told you the moment I found out. My sister led our entire family to believe Pete was Molly's dad. Hell, she made it seem like what she and Maliki had was just a fling. I told you my sister had slept with him. That wasn't a secret. I never knew it was more than that, and I definitely didn't know my niece was his. I can't believe I missed it though. I mean, he looks nothing like Pete."

I nod even though I don't know Pete.

I do feel bad for the guy though.

Not only did he think Molly was his, but he also had to deal with Jessa on the regular.

I shiver, just thinking about it.

"Have your parents said anything about me?" I ask.

"Jessa and I got into a screaming match at my parents', and she called me unfaithful because I'm friends with *the enemy*. She told them about Maliki and you, and it was a shock to everyone. The way she did it was shitty, and I hope this doesn't change our relationship."

"I hope so, too." I drop two wings onto my plate. "I can't believe your sister and I are fighting over the same man."

She crosses her legs. "Technically, you're not. Maliki doesn't even see Jessa because he loves you."

The problem is, he has to see her.

"HEY, HONEY."

I smile up at my father from my chair and stand to hug him.

He wraps me tight, patting my back, and straightens his suit before taking the chair across from me.

"I'm searching for an apartment for you," he says, diving straight in with no good-morning chat. "I offered the last guy nearly double in rent, but he said no. When you sign a lease, it's hard to back out."

He pauses when the waitress comes to take our order.

"I can look outside town," he continues when she leaves. "Leaving Blue Beech for a while might help you."

I nod, taking a sip of my orange juice. "You're right."

He frowns. "I hate seeing you like this."

"Like what?"

His face creases in concern. "Sad. Heartbroken. It seems it keeps happening to you."

"There's nothing—"

He cuts me off, "I know when something is wrong with my daughter. Is this about Devin or Maliki?"

My cheeks blush. "There's no way I'm discussing my love life with you."

He holds up his hand. "Tell me what they did, and I'll offer my opinion. I'm the epitome of a bad man. I'll let you know if they stack up or if there's reason behind their actions."

"It's Maliki. He has a secret kid … *just like you.*"

I recoil in my chair, my appetite disappearing, and notice the change in my father as well. He holds his hand to his lips, shuts his eyes, and then slowly opens them back up.

My situation is so similar to my mom's.

Maliki has a child and kept it a secret.

Sure, there are a lot more differences than similarities, but my broken heart can't stop comparing the two.

He raises a brow, finally speaking, "Maliki has a kid?"

I nod. "A daughter."

"Did he know about her?"

"No."

"That changes things. Our situations aren't similar."

CHAPTER THIRTY-THREE

Sierra

TWO WEEKS HAVE PASSED since my fallout with Maliki.

"Your brother and I totally understand if you don't want to come," Chloe says. "It won't hurt our feelings."

Her engagement party is tonight.

At Down Home.

I wave off her offer. "No, it's fine. I'll avoid Maliki. Everything will be good."

Yeah, right.

I fake a smile.

"What's going on with the bar's remodel?" she asks.

"All the hard work is done. We already selected flooring and paint. The contractors were scheduled, and I sent copies to Liz. The contractors will show up, do their job, and I'll check on them while Maliki is gone from the bar. Liz has agreed for me to come in on his days off."

"Maliki is okay with that?"

I shrug. "Don't know. Don't care."

Lies.

Chloe whistles. "Oh Lordy, your life is becoming more interesting than mine."

"WHY THE FROWN, NEW ROOMIE?"

Josh, Rex's *and* my roommate, crashes next to me on the couch, a wild grin on his face.

Rex glances up from his video game—a video game he's *developing*. "Boy problems." He pauses his game, tosses the controller to the side, and turns to face us. "Maliki problems."

I wince, just hearing his name.

It possesses so many good and bad memories.

"You going to the party tonight?" Rex asks.

I nod.

"You sure that's a good idea?"

It's stupid, but as I have for so many years, I'm going there even though it's a bad idea. I've become a professional at ignoring warnings to steer clear of Down Home Pub.

"I can't miss my brother's engagement party because of boy problems, and it's not like I hate Maliki." I wrinkle my nose. "We just aren't right for each other."

Wrong.

We are right for each other.

You can be right for someone and it still not work out.

Romeo and Juliet.

Cleopatra and Mark Antony.

Minus the whole dying thing.

"Maliki," Josh says, breaking me away from my thoughts. "He's the bartender at Down Home, right?"

"Yep," Rex answers for me.

He didn't ask questions when I texted him that I was moving into his spare bedroom, nor did he when I asked him to pick up my stuff from Maliki's. All he did was tell me he was here if I needed to talk.

That's the thing with my brother. He puts up this funny, not-give-a-shit act, but deep down, he's one of the most caring men I know.

Josh props his feet onto the coffee table, his eyes cutting to me. "Want to know of a good way to get your mind off him?"

Yes, please. "Nope," is what I answer though.

Josh drinks cheap beer, pisses with the bathroom door open, and has an obsession with *The Sopranos.* Not taking relationship advice from him.

He thrusts his thumbs into his chest. "This guy."

I swat my hand through the air. "Go away before I call your mother."

"*Shit,* if I bagged a girl like you, my mother would be a very happy woman."

"And mine would have a heart attack."

"Shut up. That's my sister," Rex says in agitation.

Josh ignores Rex. "What did Maliki do? Want me to beat him up?"

A smile tugs at my lips at the same time Rex snorts and says, "Maliki would squash you, dude."

Again, Josh ignores Rex. "You've had an older man. A guy your age. Why not try a younger one this time around?"

"I wish I could tell you to go home," I tell him.

He scoots closer to curve an arm around my shoulders. "I am home, babe."

I roll my eyes and shove him away.

Josh looks at Rex. "It sucks you can't go out tonight, man. We need to score you a fake."

Rex shrugs. "It's all good. I have plans with Carolina."

"Ah, sweet Carolina," Josh sings. "That's my girl right there."

"She's not shit to you," Rex growls with a glare.

Josh glances at me. "I warned Rex if he doesn't make his move on her in six months, I'm asking her out."

Rex tenses. "You'll be smothered in your goddamn sleep."

"Why aren't you two a thing?" I ask, happy the attention is off me. "I've never understood that."

"She's my best friend, and I don't do girlfriends well. I

won't ruin what we have because I'm a dumbass when it comes to relationships."

"Yet you won't let me ask her out," Josh says. "You also don't want *anyone else* to have her."

"Yes, because none of you pricks deserve her."

"Neither does someone afraid to ask her out."

"Fuck off." Rex turns around and goes back to his video game.

My father wasn't happy when he found out Rex had swapped out his political science major to computer science, but I'm proud of him. He has a dorm at Iowa State, but since he only has classes three days a week, he commutes from his apartment. He hasn't even graduated and already scored an internship at some huge tech company.

Josh twists to look at me. "If you need a make-him-jealous man, I'm your boy."

Rex isn't old enough to get into bars yet, but Josh is. They met each other at Iowa State, kicked it off, and became roommates. Josh is cool and flirtatious as hell but means no harm.

"Dude, be careful," Rex says. "Maliki will kick your ass."

CHAPTER THIRTY-FOUR

Maliki

SATURDAYS ARE the pub's busiest nights.

I hoped the bustling crowd would hinder my thoughts of Sierra—and then I remembered her brother's engagement party is *here* tonight.

I've been scanning the bar all night, unsure if Sierra is coming. I've spotted a few of Kyle's friends and her cousin but no sign of her. She might sit this one out. I frown, hating my bullshit might prevent her from celebrating with her brother.

It's been a tough week overall and a busy week for my phone, given how many times I've called and texted Sierra … and dodged Jessa's phone calls. It pisses me off how damn quick Sierra threw us away when she'd fought for us for so long.

That's not me placing all the blame on her.

This is all my fault.

I was stupid, and Sierra is afraid of getting hurt again.

Sierra hasn't returned to the bar since she walked away from me. Although she's talked to Liz. How the fuck that happened is beyond me, but Liz knows the schedule of the renovation, and she agreed to take all of Sierra's shifts. Liz has taken Sierra's side in our breakup.

I'm numb as I move around the bar, going about my regular routine.

A vodka and Sprite.

Bud Light.

Corona.

A guy from high school mentioning an old memory.

I yell out an order for a basket of hot wings to the kitchen.

Same shit, different shift.

Only Sierra isn't here.

I got so used to us working together. The bar feels hollow without her.

My back goes straight, and I overpour the drink I'm making when I see her. I don't move, nearly in shock, when she comes to the bar.

I walk away, ignoring a customer, and meet her, wishing the bar didn't divide us.

She's more anxious than she was the first time I busted her here.

"Hi," she says, her voice nearly a whisper.

She looks damn gorgeous.

She also looks tired.

My chest caves in, as I know that tiredness is most likely from my dumbass actions.

I stare at her, tongue-tied for a moment, scrambling for the right words to not fuck this up.

"Are you ready to come home?" I decide to go with a playful tone. "Or are you here to get your job back?" I'm trying to stay composed, but my heart is heavy as it constricts in my chest.

"I'll pass," she says with unreadable eyes. "I'm here for the party, and I don't want it to be weird between us. I'll order all my drinks from Liz and steer clear of this side." She gestures toward my area of the bar.

"Why did you come over here then?"

"To give you a heads-up."

"I call bullshit."

"Whatever, Maliki. Call bullshit all you want, but it's the truth."

I open my mouth to explain why I'm calling bullshit, but I'm cut off when she keeps talking.

"Also, I don't know if Liz told you, but everything is scheduled for the remodel. I'm doing all my communication through her." Her lips are pressed into a firm line.

Liz already shared this info with me.

I fix my stare on her. "Liz doesn't own the bar. *I do.* Not communicating with your client is unprofessional."

She narrows her eyes at me. "Whatever. I'll maintain a *professional* relationship until the remodel is over. I've appointed Liz as my assistant, so all communication will go through her. How's that?"

"I'd much rather deal with the woman I *hired.*"

"Don't make this difficult."

Trust me, I'm trying hard not to.

I pinch the bridge of my nose. "I miss you, Sierra. We need to talk about this. I know you're young, but—"

She inches up her hand, stopping me. "Nope, don't blame this on my *age*. I'm smart enough to know not to get hurt again."

"If you get hurt again, it won't be by me."

"You already have. I won't take that risk again."

I gulp in an exasperated breath. "Anytime you're in a relationship with someone, you risk heartbreak. Have another relationship, but you can't guarantee it won't happen again. With me, you have a fucking guarantee I'll do everything in my power to never hurt you again. I've never made you doubt my feelings for you. Never. Remember that."

"Maliki—" Her eyes narrow as she stares over my shoulder.

"Hey, babe," Jessa says behind me, and I shit you not, I'm shocked my back doesn't break with how tense my spine goes.

"Molly is knocked out. Do you want me to bring your dinner down?"

My pulse slams into my neck, and my eyes don't leave Sierra.

"Wow," Sierra snarls. "Never doubt you, huh?" Her fingers dig into the wood of the bar.

"It's not what it looks like." The words slowly leave my mouth.

She scoffs, "Piss off, Maliki."

I hop over the bar when she turns to leave, knocking down napkins and baskets of food, and follow her. I call her name louder with every step through the bar. When we make it to a clearing, I snatch her wrist and whip her around to face me.

She smacks my hand and wriggles out of my hold. "Don't. I'm here for my brother and Chloe. I won't let our drama ruin their party. This isn't happening tonight."

"Well, well, look what we have here." A hipster-looking dude comes up and slings an arm around her shoulders, blind to what he's walked into. "My hot-ass roommate."

What the hell?

My temples throb.

Sierra tenses before relaxing when he drags her into his scrawny-ass chest.

"Who the fuck is this?" My voice thunders through the bar, catching the attention of customers around us.

Luckily, there's a band playing that covers some of my anger.

The dude has the balls to hold out his hand. "Josh." He cocks his head toward Sierra. "New roommate. New friend. Hopefully, future boyfriend."

My hands clench.

"Josh," Sierra drags out in warning. "Now isn't the time."

The smirk on the dude's face drops when he sees the temper in mine.

He pulls away, takes a glance at me, and squeezes her arm. "I'll be at Kyle's table."

"Your new roommate?" I hiss when he walks away.

She nods. "I'm staying with Rex and him." Her lips twitch into a smile, and I wince at her sudden mood change. "Will you make me a drink? Liz looks busy over there."

My brows crinkle. "Sure."

Her smile stays intact as we walk back to the bar. "Tequila."

I pour her a shot.

She knocks it back. "Two more."

I pour her two more.

Her smile turns cold. "Thanks. I can't wait to take these with Josh." She grabs one in each hand and smirks. "Enjoy Jessa's gross dinner."

My eyes stay pinned to her as she walks straight to Josh's table and hands him the shot, and they take them together.

I march over to Liz. "I'm taking five."

She nods, her eyes moving to Sierra.

Asshole's arm is back around her.

Liz squeezes my shoulder. "She's doing it to piss you off. She wants to hurt you like you did her."

"I'm well aware." *It's fucking working.*

MOLLY IS CRASHED out on the couch, and Jessa is in the kitchen, not making shit when I walk into the apartment.

"I warned you not to pull that shit," I bite out.

My attorney hasn't come through with the custody paperwork yet, so I'm still tortured by Jessa when I visit with Molly. She came over for pizza before my shift, Jessa's annoying ass right behind her. We hung out, and she asked to stay and finish the movie we'd been watching. I figured they would've left by now.

"What shit?" she asks, playing coy.

"That stunt you pulled when you saw me talking to Sierra."

She releases a hard laugh. "God, Maliki, it's time for you to say good-bye to your little sorority-girl fling. She won't be with someone like you long-term. Stop wasting your time. She's been friends with my sister since they were kids. I've seen the guys she dates, the ones she's brought over for group dates in my parents' basement. They aren't you. You're a rebound."

"You need to leave," I grit out.

She reaches out, brushing her hand over my arm, and I jerk away in disgust. Her face falls. She's not used to being turned down.

"Come on, Maliki. We had something—good times, hot sex."

"That was in the past. You were a *fling*. That's it. I want a relationship with Molly, but you? I want nothing to do with. I've been nice, but you've played nothing but games. All I want from you is to be mature and co-parent with me."

"Molly needs a stable home, and my grandparents are returning this weekend. There's not enough room for the two of us there without being too cramped." It's as if she didn't hear what I'd just told her.

"If you feel you can't provide somewhere for Molly to stay, she can live with me. *Only her*. Not you. If you need a place to live other than your parents', I can help you find an apartment, but you're not moving in with me."

"You have a guest bedroom."

"It isn't available for you."

I HUG MOLLY GOOD-BYE, knock back a shot of whiskey, and return to the bar. I've left Liz long enough to deal with the craziness tonight and feel like an asshole.

I immediately shoot my attention to Sierra.

She's at the same table with her douche-bag roommate.

He holds up his shot glass and gestures to Sierra with it. "She's coming home with me tonight, gentlemen!" he drunkenly slurs. "Be jealous!"

I charge toward the kitchen, open the door, and yell inside, "Mikey! You're on bar duty!"

I leave without waiting for a reply. Mikey needed extra cash, so I told him he could work in the kitchen. Thank fuck I did that and can bail from this place.

"I'm out of here," I tell Liz.

I can't make a scene here. Can't punch a dude in the face here.

I'm a business owner, a father. I have to change my mindset about shit.

The asshole kisses her cheek next.

On second thought, fuck this shit.

CHAPTER THIRTY-FIVE

Sierra

"OH SHIT," is all I hear Chloe say before Maliki captures my elbow, hoists me up from my stool, and hauls me outside, the crowd watching with curious eyes.

"What do you think you're doing?" he snarls, unclasping me when we make it to the edge of the parking lot.

What does he think he's doing?

"Enjoying my night," I fire back.

"Bullshit." Temper flashes in his eyes. "You're *enjoying* making me miserable."

Yes, that, too.

I internally shrug.

He deserves it.

I've been miserable since our breakup. It only seems fitting it's the same for him.

"Whatever. You know nothing," I somewhat slur, realizing how much I've had to drink now that I'm standing, no longer supported by the barstool. "Better yet, maybe I should play games with you like you did me."

He thrusts a hand through his hair. "Jesus Christ, you're plastered."

"That's your fault."

"*My fault?* I didn't shove those drinks down your throat."

"I never planned to drink this much, but I needed to erase the image of your baby mama, the one you were … whatever with behind my back, coming down from *your* apartment." I struggle to keep my voice strong, and it cracks near the end. Heartbreak clutched at my heart when I saw Jessa.

He shakes his head. "What happened with Jessa isn't what you think."

I flick my hand through the air. "I don't care. I'm leaving."

"You're not going home with that kid, FYI."

"*Excuse you,* that's where I live, FYI."

He stands tall with his arms crossed. "You're drunk. He's drunk. Not happening."

"I'll sleep where I damn well please." I tap my finger against my lip. "Hmm … maybe I should sleep with my *new* roommate. This one might not break my heart."

"Do you want to be responsible for that kid getting his ass kicked?" His pissed off glare lifts into a smile. "Not to mention, he's too young for your liking."

I want to slap that stupid smirk off his face. My head throbs, and the liquor is making its strike to my brain. "Where am I supposed to sleep then, huh?" I regret my question as soon as it drops from my lips.

"You can crash in the guest room."

I release a cold laugh. "Oh, yes, that sounds like a blast. Maybe I can eat Jessa's dinner to sober myself up. Is she still up there?"

"Jessa came over *with Molly*, so I could visit with *Molly*. I don't give a shit about Jessa. Barely spoke to her until after she pulled that shit. She said it to provoke you, and you fell for the bait."

I scoff, "Whatever."

"I'm already taking care of one kid, Sierra. Don't act like that."

"Screw you," I hiss, turning and walking around the

building. "I can't believe I was dumb enough to fall for every word that came out of your lying mouth. I swear, it's always the cute ones. Cute guys break your heart. I need to switch up my type, pronto."

He grabs my arm, stopping me from walking back into the pub, and leads us toward the apartment. I don't jerk away, but I do throw a string of curses alongside each step we make.

He releases me when we make it to the stairs, standing behind me, and blocking me from going back to the parking lot.

Fuck it.

I turn and stomp up the stairs. He remains quiet while following behind me as I swing open the door that leads to the apartment stairs, surprised it's unlocked.

"You had me walking around, looking like a fool." My stomps grow louder and harder when I make it to the apartment, my muttering continuing, "You're like every man in my life—like my father, Devin—"

I'm abruptly cut off, and I yelp when Maliki grips my shoulders and twists me around to face him.

His face is inches away from mine, his dark eyes settled on mine. "Don't you dare compare me to them."

I shove him back, destroying our eye contact. He can't witness my impending tears.

"Why? You're no different." I retreat another step and stare up at the ceiling, blinking and silently yelling at my emotions to stop being such a pansy.

"You and I both know I'm nothing like that. I *never* touched anyone but you when we were together."

I dip my chin after I've calmed down the tears and bumped up the anger, catching on to the past tense of his words. "Oh, but what about now that we're not together?"

"Still haven't touched anyone. Don't want to touch anyone." He raises his arms. "Now that we have that cleared up, drink some water and sleep that bullshit off. We'll talk in the morning."

"Fine," I snap, maintaining my stomping game into the living room. I kick off my shoes, snatch the pillows on the couch, and hurl them across the room. Next, I start grabbing cushions and chucking them.

"What are you doing?"

"Sleeping, like you told me to." I throw the last cushion down. "No way am I sleeping in a bed you could've screwed her in." My drunken mind doesn't believe him. My wonderful, pessimistic friend—aka tequila—is screaming he's a liar. "I don't want to sleep here, but it seems it's the only choice I have, considering you threatened physical violence on my new roomie."

He stays quiet, standing in the corner, and I drop down on the couch.

I suck in a breath. My intoxicated anger has shifted to intoxicated sadness. "Why did you make me do it?"

"Do what?" he asks in a strangled voice.

"Make me fall in love with you." I sniffle, a failed attempt to suppress my tears.

"I should ask you the same." He releases a hard sigh. " There's no damn reason for us not to be together."

I lift my head, and my back is stiff as I sit against the bare couch. "Losing Devin was nowhere near as painful as losing you. I offered you too much of my heart." Tears swell in my eyes, and I wipe them away with the back of my arm. "I would've accepted you having a daughter, accepted her into my heart, because she's a part of you, and I love every part of you. You never gave me that chance, and now, we'll never have that chance again."

"Sierra," he gently says.

I stretch on the couch to my side, turning my back to him. "Forget it. I'm over it, and I need sleep."

All I hear is a sharp sigh from him, and the room turns miserably silent.

Minutes pass.

No words.

Did he leave?

I reposition myself, still facing the rear of the couch but allowing myself to peek behind my back.

My throat tightens when I see Maliki sitting on the floor by my feet, his elbow resting on his knee as he massages his forehead.

The air turns heavy as we remain quiet—a silence that's too loud.

Finally, I yawn, my eyes feeling weighted as I shut them.

I don't know how much time passes before he lifts me in his arms and puts me in his bed.

I'm too exhausted to fight it.

MY THROAT IS dry and scratchy when I wake up.

My pounding head is calling me an idiot.

I rub my forehead and glance around his bedroom.

Relentless jerk.

He's nowhere to be seen, but I hear clattering in the kitchen. I slide out of bed, brush my teeth with the toothbrush Maliki didn't give Rex, and rub my sleepy eyes decorated with old mascara off with a washcloth.

I make a stop at his closet, snag one of his tees, and find a pair of my panties in the drawer I was using. Yes, I'm walking out half-naked, but whatever. It's nothing he hasn't seen.

Maliki's head rises, his attention moving from the sizzling pan to me when I wander into the kitchen.

How much shit-talking did I do last night?

I don't realize those words actually left my mouth until Maliki answers me.

"Oh, you definitely expressed yourself, Jailbait." He forks out bacon strips from the pan and drops them onto a plate with a napkin covering it. He grabs another pan and cracks two eggs inside it.

"Oh, we're back to Jailbait now, huh?"

He turns to snag a water bottle from the fridge, motions for me to sit, and slides the bottle to me when I do. "Drink this."

"All right, Dr. Hangover. Do you know how many times I've been plastered? *Way more drunk* than I was last night?" Sorority life hurts your liver.

"I won't dispute that, but next time, make sure you're only plastered around me."

"I thought drunk people annoyed you?"

He scoops the egg on a plate, drops a few bacon strips on it, and hands it to me. "They do. You're not just a person to me, so I don't mind."

I slump down in my stool and start eating.

I miss you.

And just like the shit-talking comment, that wasn't supposed to come out either.

He doesn't eat. He just stares at me, leveling his elbows on the island, even though he made himself a plate. "Fix it then. Pack your shit and move back in."

"You need time."

"I need you."

"You've had a serious life change," is my next argument.

"Still doesn't change the fact that I need you. If anything, *this* is when I need you the most—when I'm going through some shit."

"I wish you had needed me when everything started," I mutter. "Or at least told me."

"If I could take it back, I would."

"But you can't."

His face falls. "Tell me this, do you trust me?"

I swallow.

"Do you trust me, Sierra?"

I shake my head. "I don't trust anyone anymore." Not my family, not my exes, not even the lady at Sephora when I went there last week.

My new life philosophy is, *Don't trust anyone*. Maybe I should get it tattooed.

His lips twist downward. "Never doubt your trust in me."

I pick up my fork but drop it seconds later. "I never doubted you before, but you can't honestly stand there and defend what you did, say that it didn't hurt our trust."

He nods. "You're right, but I'd never jeopardize my relationship with you for her or any other woman. I promise."

"Maybe you want to have your cake and eat it, too?"

"Wrong. I wouldn't be pushing through these problems, begging you not to leave me, if I didn't love you, if I wanted another woman."

"I know," I whisper. I take a large bite, wishing for this conversation to be over. My head needs to be clear when we sit down and have a mature talk about our relationship.

"How's staying at Rex's?"

"Not as disgusting as I thought it'd be. He's actually pretty clean."

"And the other guy? The roommate?"

I keep my focus on my eggs. "What about him?"

"Don't play coy with me."

I glance up at him. "What if I was fucking him?"

He flinches. "Excuse me?"

"What if I was fucking him?"

His face hardens. "Don't fuck with me, Sierra." His fork clangs against the plate when he drops it and circles the island, grabbing my stool and swiveling it so I'm facing him. "If you want a boy who plays beer pong with his friends and doesn't know how to please anyone but himself, go right ahead, but we know that's not what you want. Is it?" He rests his hands on my thighs.

My stomach turns inside out as I struggle to control my composure. "I said nothing about *dating him*. I've stopped confusing sex with love."

He releases a harsh laugh. "Then, why are you here, huh? Why were you in *my* bed last night and not his bunk bed with Spider-Man sheets?"

"I hate you, and in case you forgot, I was taken into your bed unwillingly."

He travels a hand up to my chin, raising it, and tightens his hand resting on my thigh, smirking. "You would've rather been in his bed last night?"

I gulp. "Yep."

I'm not sure how the sneaky jerk does it, but somehow, someway, he—or his hands—convinces me to stand at the same time his mouth meets mine.

His tongue slides into my mouth, tasting like coffee and vanilla and a man I've missed so damn much. Our knees knock into each other's as he backs me against the same wall we visited the first night we had sex. That memory only turns me on more.

Seconds ago, I was lying about wanting for sleeping with another man.

Now, he's drifting his hand up my shirt, his fingers exploring my stomach.

"You want to be in *my* bed. Not his. You're lying. Admit it," he grinds out against my mouth, his hand dipping to the band of my panties, panties that are soaked and waiting for his hands, his mouth, his cock—anything of him.

I ignore him, and his hands move when I pull his sweatshorts down.

"Admit you're lying," he repeats, slightly pulling away.

I don't.

He yanks up his pants, taking a step back. "Then, no dick for you."

"Are you kidding me?" I snap, my heart picking up speed.

"Nope." He's fighting to control his breathing, control his hands from touching me, and there's no controlling his erection.

I shove him back. "I don't want to touch anyone but you, you bastard. You want to know why?" I don't wait for him to answer. "'Cause I fucking love you!"

He grins. "There's my girl."

I squeal when he grips my waist, lifts me into his arms—my legs wrapping around him—and walks us to the bedroom. I'm thrown onto the bed, bouncing up while he undresses. He crawls up the bed, pulling my shirt off, and slips my panties to the side, two of his fingers diving inside me. My back arches as he works me, and right as I'm about to lose it, he pulls them away along with my panties and positions himself between my legs.

I moan when he shoves himself inside me.

"The only girl I want in my bed." He pulls out and slams inside me.

"The only woman I ever want to be inside." Another thrust.

"The only woman I'll ever love." Another thrust.

"The only woman I want to spend the rest of my life with."

His slams get so rough, so hard, as if he's pushing his words deeper and deeper inside me so I have no choice but to believe them.

CHAPTER THIRTY-SIX

Maliki

BEING inside Sierra again is like going back to heaven after being punished in hell.

There's no damn way I'll ever want any woman over her.

She's perfect—stubborn as hell but goddamn perfect.

We're sweaty against the sheets, attempting to catch our breaths, but each time I push myself inside her, we lose them again.

She hooks her legs around the indent of my hips, drawing me closer, and digs her heels into my back when I obey.

"Your nails," I say.

She pushes her chest against mine, her mouth hitting mine, and rakes her nails down my back.

I grind my teeth.

I love when she marks me.

If she leaves me after this, I'll have the marks of her being here again, if even for a few days. I feel her pussy clench against my dick as her nails claw at my skin, and she yells out my name.

"*Fuck*, you feel good," I groan with my release.

When her eyes open, I brush her hair from her face and stare down at her.

"Jesus, you're beautiful. Thank you for letting me touch something so perfect," I whisper.

"YOU ready to hand out more truths?" I ask Sierra while she sucks in a few breaths and falls down on her back next to me.

She takes a moment before glancing over at me. "Hmm? What truths?" She narrows her eyes. "You can't make me orgasm like that and then expect a deep conversation. That's cheating."

I chuckle. "I can give you another one, sentence by sentence, if you'd like?"

She throws her head back "Oh my God. I would die, and then we couldn't have that conversation. I'll take an hour-by-hour orgasm."

"I'll give you whatever you want."

She grabs the blanket and draws it up our naked bodies. "I'll actually take sleep and *then* another orgasm." She yawns. "Can we save all serious talk until then?"

I pull her into me, taking a chance, and she has no problem with snuggling into my side.

All the tension I had of losing her releases.

She's mine, and I'll hand her every damn secret, every thought in my head, every move I make if it means keeping her.

I MADE HER HOT WINGS.

Correction: I went down to the kitchen and asked the cook to make her hot wings.

They're her favorite, and she deserves as many of her favorites I can give her for making me so goddamn happy.

I set the basket in front of her, and a thought hits me.

"So, are we made up?" I ask with an eager smile. "I gave you the truth, orgasms, *and* hot wings. There's no way you can turn a man down after that."

She swallows her bite and cleans her hand with a napkin before answering, "If we do this, it needs to be complete honesty going forward." She grabs another wing, dips it in ranch, and takes a bite.

"Complete honesty," I agree with a nod. "I owe you an apology. I should've never kept secrets from you, especially one of that magnitude. Hiding that from you and hanging out with Jessa behind your back was fucking stupid." I blow out a breath. "I was scared to tell you, for fear of losing you. I needed the right plan. It needed to be at the right time, and whenever I tried to convince myself it was, I would chicken the fuck out."

"You really were planning to drop the bomb on the dinner date?"

I nod. "I figured if I wined and dined you, you'd surely accept it. Plus, I'd give you orgasms." I wink.

"Had you revealed you were hanging out with Jessa behind my back, I would've thrown that wine at you." She wipes the sauce off her mouth. "You know I wasn't upset about you having a daughter, right? It was the whole secrecy and Jessa part that hurt me."

She's not lying. Sierra has too much heart to do that. I only said that to cast the blame on someone else even though I was in the wrong.

"I want you there with me," I say. "In Molly's and my life."

She grins. "She's such a cute girl. When I babysat with Ellie, she was so sweet."

I smile at her words. "She is. Jessa is worried about her starting school in a new town. We enrolled her in dance, so hopefully, she'll meet some friends before the year starts."

"Call someone who has a daughter her age." She stops to

think. "What about Dallas Barnes? His daughter is a total sweetheart and looks to be around Molly's age. She's always at events with her grandparents, given they're so involved. Maybe we can schedule a playdate. I'll ask my brother to see if we can set something up."

"I don't know why I waited to tell you for so long. You're already perfect at helping me with this."

A SELF-SATISFIED SMILE is on Sierra's face as she kicks her feet against the floor. "I told you this flooring would be amazing. *Plus,* the maintenance is child's play compared to hardwood."

I was reluctant on switching over to tile. Tile can make a room appear cold. The pub isn't cold. It's a relaxing experience. Sierra, the determined woman she is, found tile that looks exactly like wood. I wasn't even able to tell when she first showed me. No more constant worrying about spills causing damage.

I do a once-over of the bar. It looks so damn good. I've lost count of the number of times I tried calling her to tell her that when we weren't talking. She did a kick-ass job—from the flooring to the paint scheme and the furniture. She had the brick walls behind the bar painted, changing from red to a subtle gray. That same color brick is wrapped around the outside of the bar, and she left the tops untouched to keep the authenticity. The new kitchen appliances were installed a few days ago as well as the kegs. The new taps are coming tomorrow, and I can't fucking wait.

"And the paint matches *perfectly,*" she sings out. "We *are* missing the furniture *you* said you'd assemble."

"I didn't think it'd be that complicated. I opened the boxes and found five thousand pieces. How the hell do they think that's cool?"

She settles her gaze on me, attempting to put off a serious look but it fails when a smile cracks along her lips. "I told you so."

I wrap my arm around her shoulders. "Care to help a man assemble furniture?"

She dramatically groans. "I guess."

I smack her ass. "I love you."

CHAPTER THIRTY-SEVEN

Sierra

"I SWEAR, Jessa won't be showing up here," Ellie says, snagging a doughnut and dropping it onto her plate.

We haven't seen each other in days. I've been swept up in Maliki, moving my things back to his apartment, which wasn't much, and wrapping up the bar's remodel. I have a busy week ahead of me and came over to spend time with her this morning, doughnuts and pineapple smoothies in hand.

"She's still not talking to me over the whole *I'm hanging out with the enemy* nonsense." She lifts her chin and rolls her eyes. "I've never been tight with her. Hell, I'm closer to you than her, and she's in the wrong. So, the enemy is who I shall hang out with."

"It doesn't matter. I'll see her later today." I take a gulp of my smoothie to hide the dread on my face. "We're hanging out with Molly later."

She drops the doughnut in her hand. "Holy hell. You're meeting Molly as *the girlfriend*?"

"Sure am."

I'm nervous about seeing Molly, and I would rather shave off my eyebrows than be around Jessa. Fingers crossed I won't see her since we're picking Molly up and taking her out for the day. Jessa tried weaseling her way into tagging along with Maliki, but he wasn't having it.

"This is a big step! I'm happy for you!"

I pick at my doughnut. "I don't know why I'm nervous. I've babysat her with you. It's not like she's a stranger."

"You're nervous because you'll be her stepmom one day."

My eyes widen. "I don't know about that."

"I do."

MY KNEES ARE BOUNCING as I sit in the passenger seat.

"I hate I wasn't here for you last time," I tell Maliki.

He briefly glances at me before returning his eyes to the road. "It might've been for the best. Jessa broke the news to Molly terribly. She sprang it on her without warning. Molly was upset and confused."

Of course Jessa did.

My heart aches for them. "It probably would've done more harm than good. I would've been another person added to the confusion."

He nods. "She's comfortable with me now, and I've talked about you with her."

"I'm sure Jessa loved that."

"I've started tuning out Jessa when it's not Molly-related." He hesitates before continuing, "I forgot to explain the day I went to the city without you. I took Molly shopping for clothes and a doll."

That's random.

But I did say no more secrets.

"Way to piss me off more about Jessa right before I see her."

He chuckles. "Yeah, bad move on my part to start throwing out confessions right now. I just don't want everything out in the open, so anytime I think of one, I'll clear that shit up fast."

"Appreciate that."

He pulls up to Jessa's parents' house. After their grandparents returned, Jessa moved in with them. I had been here countless times during my childhood with Ellie.

He shifts the car in park. "Ready?"

"Absolutely." No longer is nervousness crashing through. I'm excited to hang out with the little girl who will be such a huge part in our lives.

The front door opens after Maliki knocks, and Molly stands in front of us with an eager grin spread along her face. Her eyes travel from Maliki to me, her smile growing wider.

"I remember you!" she squeals. "You're Auntie Ellie's friend! Sierra! You were nice and colored with me!"

I blink at her, taking in the similarities between her and Maliki.

I see it.

She has his nose.

His lips.

I grin down at her. "And I remember you! You color so well and watch the best cartoons!"

I like kids. My mom had our family regularly volunteer with them, growing up. It's one of the best things she ever did for us. All my siblings have hearts of gold when it comes to children.

She hops from one foot to the other. "Are you my daddy's girlfriend?"

"What's she doing here?" Jessa snaps, coming to the door, standing next to Molly, and breaking our warm vibe. Her arms are crossed as she fixes a glare toward me.

I ignore her, not even firing a fake smile her way. Today is about having fun with Molly.

"I don't know if Molly should go, given you brought your

flavor of the week. I made it clear I want to be careful who my daughter is around," Jessa barks before anyone replies.

"You had no issue when Sierra babysat her with Ellie," Maliki hisses.

"That's different. She was Ellie's friend, not her new father's *girlfriend.*"

Maliki tenses at the *new father* blow. "I won't argue with you in front of her. We can talk later." He leans down to Molly's height. "Ready to go?"

Molly squeezes between her mom and grabs Maliki's hand. "Yes!"

She skips hand in hand with Maliki to the car.

I don't peek back at Jessa, but there's no doubt she'd stick a knife in my back if she could.

MALIKI HELPS Molly into her seat before we get in and turns to look at her. "Did you decide what you want to do today?" He told Molly she could choose.

Molly straightens in her seat. "Can we go to the movies, and can I get a gigantic bucket of popcorn, and then can we paint my nails like Sierra's, and then she can maybe braid my hair later? I *love* my hair braided."

Maliki eyes me in question.

I twist back in my seat to smile at her. "Sounds like we have a plan."

She's giggling when we turn around, and I snatch my phone from my purse to check movie times. The theater is thirty minutes away, so we have plenty of time to decide. I rattle off the movies and let her pick.

We raid the concession stand when we get to the theater, scoring a bucket of buttery popcorn, M&M's, Mike & Ike, and slushies.

Molly will definitely be in a sugar coma.

With me right alongside her.

Molly takes the seat between me and Maliki, and I can't help but crack a smile at Maliki. He's about to sit through a two-hour-long animated children's film for his daughter. He doesn't complain once, even when he watches the movie trailer with a horrified look on his face.

As soon as I fall down in my seat, I pour the M&M's into the popcorn and offer it to Molly.

"I've never had that before," she says, glancing up at me with an arched brow.

I push the bucket closer. "It's the best. I promise."

She grabs a handful, and her eyes brighten as she swallows it down. She immediately goes for another handful.

Maliki shakes his head at us with a smile.

Molly turns to look at Maliki. "You want to try some?"

His smile grows. "I'll let you two have it all."

"Your dad doesn't appreciate the art of sprinkling sugar on top of everything," I whisper to her, and she breaks out in laughter.

MOLLY TAPS HER CHIN. "Hmm … there are *way* too many colors. I can't pick only one." She does another scan of my nail polish collection. "Can I pick however many I want?"

"Yes, ma'am, *but* we have to stop at ten." I wiggle my fingers in the air. "Unless you have an extra thumb somewhere." I grab her hand to inspect it.

She bursts into giggles. "No!"

She spins to look at Maliki. He's in the chair, watching us. *Beauty and the Beast* is playing in the background, there's an array of fingernail polish bottles scattered around us, and Molly's hair is braided into four braids.

"Can you paint my nails while Sierra does my toenails?" she asks him.

My mouth falls open.

Maliki shifts in his seat. "Sure, but I can't promise they'll look pretty."

"It's okay. If they don't, Sierra can redo them."

I laugh, my hand going to my stomach, as Molly hands him ten bottles and another for "glitter on top."

"I THINK it went well with the exception of Jessa losing her shit when she saw me," I say after we drop Molly off at home.

To minimize the baby-mama drama, I gave Molly a hug at the car and stayed behind while Maliki walked her to the door. I wouldn't let Jessa taint the fun we'd had today.

I grin over at him. "I learned something else about you today."

"Yeah? What's that?"

"You are a terrible nail-painter."

"Yes, I've been told that by a six-year-old."

CHAPTER THIRTY-EIGHT

Maliki

I GROAN when the name flashes across my phone.

If only I didn't have to answer.

I briefly wonder when is too young for a phone.

Noah has an iPod.

Maybe I can do the same with Molly and tell Jessa to only call on emergencies or to set up visitation.

"Hello?" I answer.

"I don't want that whore around my daughter," is the first thing she says.

Jesus. I scrub my hand over my face.

Jessa's bullshit isn't what I want to deal with today.

"First things first. Don't you refer to Sierra like that again, do you hear me? Don't you mutter a bad word about her to me, or we'll have serious issues," I snap.

She scoffs, "She's married, for God's sake. What does that teach our daughter?"

My stomach drops. I hate being reminded that Sierra married someone other than me. "The divorce papers have been signed by both her and Devin," I bite out, shaking my head. "Not that I need to explain shit to you about my relationship, so unless you called about Molly, it's time for us to hang up."

"Uh, yes, you do need to explain and ask my approval if you want to see your daughter."

I clench my fingers around my phone. "Take me to court, Jessa. I fucking dare you."

I don't tell her, but my attorney is already drafting a document. I want Molly's last name changed to mine, three days a week of visitation, and a set child-support payment. But if Jessa wants to play games with me, I don't mind asking for more.

I hang up and shop for an iPod online.

"HEY, MAN."

I turn to find Dallas Barnes hopping onto a stool at the bar. "Hey. What can I get you?"

It sucks Dallas doesn't frequent the pub as often as he used to, but it's for a good reason. He went through a rough patch after his wife died from breast cancer. Not only was he going through hell, but he also had to take care of his daughter.

So, on the days his daughter, Maven, was with her grandmother, Dallas would come here to drown his sorrows. Sometimes, we talked. Sometimes, we gave each other a head nod, and I gave him his space. He's a good man who found love again. We were all surprised as hell when Willow came into town, pregnant with his baby after a one-night stand. She was a town outsider but helped replace Dallas's pain with happiness.

He smiles. "Whiskey, neat."

I make his drink and set it in front of him. "How's the family? Kiddos?"

"Good." A shit-eating grin spreads along his lips as he thrums his fingers against the glass. "Speaking of kids …"

Ah shit, here it comes.

"Word has hit town, I take it?"

He nods. "Word has definitely hit town, thanks to your baby mama. She did things *way* different than Willow." He shakes his head. "Sierra told Lauren your little one is around Maven's age and starting school here. Maybe Maven can put her at ease, having a friend there." He takes a drink and laughs into his glass before pulling it back. "Want to schedule a playdate?"

I chuckle. "Look at us, scheduling fucking playdates."

"Playdates are the easy part. You wait until you're singing along with Disney songs and having tea with stuffed bunnies and—I shit you not—holding straight conversations with them. Winnie-the-Pooh loves extra honey with his tea, and her American Girl doll prefers coffee with extra cream." He takes a drink. "And be careful about the people you have her around. My pain in the ass sister is the one who introduced her to coffee."

"Lauren does love to stir up trouble."

"That she does. I told her to wait until her little one grew older. I'll be getting her right back."

I pour him another drink and hand it to him, lowering my voice. "How'd you do it? Raise a daughter by yourself?"

Technically, I have Jessa but don't consider her a part of my team until she cooperates with co-parenting and keeps her opinions to herself. I understand her concern, but it's not like Sierra's a bad person, nor did Jessa have an issue with her being around Molly until she found out I was dating her.

Dallas raises his glass and his brow at the same time. "You're not raising her on your own. You have Sierra."

CHAPTER THIRTY-NINE

Maliki

"IS JESSA COMING TO THE FESTIVAL?"

I shrug at Sierra's question. "Maybe."

Didn't ask. Don't care.

I tend to tune Jessa out when she's not talking about Molly, but I might've caught the end of her saying she was coming.

"She has a new boyfriend and has been too busy making his life more miserable than mine. I'll take it," I add.

Jessa has become tolerable now that she's grasped Sierra isn't going anywhere. The signed custody agreement and the new boyfriend have helped, too.

"Good riddance," Sierra mutters. She aims to steer clear of Jessa as often as she can.

We turn around when Molly comes into the kitchen.

"You ready for the festival?" I ask.

"Yes!" Her excitement dies down, her smile replaced with a frown. "I won't have any friends there to play with me though." Her attention shoots to Sierra. "Will you play with me?"

"Duh," Sierra replies. "There will be a lot of kids there. I bet you nine million dollars you'll meet new friends and then ditch me to hang out with them."

"No way. I *love* hanging out with you. You and Aunt Ellie are my best friends in the whole wide world," Molly argues.

"You and Ellie are my best friends in the whole wide world," Sierra replies.

"Hey, what about me?" My palm goes to my chest as I fake offense. "Don't I get a friendship bracelet in this mix?"

Molly shakes her head. "You don't paint your nails, Dad. You have to do girl stuff to be best friends. You're my dad who gives me pizza and takes me swimming!"

Dad. It still sounds surreal, being called that.

I'm a dad.

It took Molly a while to call me that—understandable—and the first time she did, swear to fucking God, it was music to my ears. My chest lightened, and I held myself back from jumping in the air with a raised fist.

We get into the car and make the short drive to the benefit festival. Dallas texted me the other day and invited us. His family is throwing it to benefit a local who was recently diagnosed with cancer.

It'll be my first time at a benefit.

I've donated bar gift cards to them but never *attended* one.

It's a family thing—full of fried food, face-painting, and children's games.

Not a pastime for a bachelor.

We park in a lot separated by orange cones, and I help Molly out of the car. She walks at my side, swinging her arms up and down while naming off everything she wants to eat and do and see.

For a small town, there's a full house—well, full parking lot and clubhouse. The local pizza shop owner is playing DJ, blasting some kid shit I've never heard. It might be the music Dallas was talking about—Disney stuff.

Chloe swings her arms in the air to get our attention and waves us over to their crowded table.

Chloe and Kyle.

Willow and Dallas.

Lauren and Gage. Gage is Kyle's best friend and partner at the station.

The six of them are seated at the table.

I've known the guys for as long as I can remember. It's nice, seeing them all happy.

Maven, Dallas's his little girl, is sitting next to him. She grins wildly when she sees us.

"Hi!" she chirps, her eyes on Molly as she waves with a caramel apple in her hand. She pats the seat Dallas is occupying next to her with her free hand. "Come sit by me. My daddy got an extra caramel apple, and you can have it."

Dallas moves down a seat and slides his old one out for Molly to sit. Molly peeks over to me, and I nod. Her eyes are wide as she scurries over to Maven and jumps in the open seat.

"I'm Maven," she says, scooting the plate with the caramel apple to her. "I like your hair." She flips her attention to Willow, Dallas's girlfriend, on the other side of her. "Can you do my hair like that tomorrow?"

Willow smiles. "Sure."

Sierra and I take a seat. Maven dances in her chair while eating her apple, and after a few minutes, I notice Molly doing the same, caramel on the side of her face. I'm so excited to see Molly so comfortable that I'm close to dancing in my damn chair, too.

If someone had told me this was what my life would be, I would've laughed and kicked their wrong ass out of my bar.

Conversation is happening around us, but my focus is on Molly and the glowing smile on her face.

"There's a jump house," Maven announces after finishing her apple. "After you're done eating, we can go play in it! They're so fun!"

Molly keeps on grinning while chomping on her apple.

The little tykes have sticky hands when Maven asks permission for them to go play.

Dallas and I nod at the same time.

Maven grabs Molly's hand, and they run toward the bounce house, joining the group of children.

I suck in a concerned breath, my eyes glued to my little girl.

This is the first time I've had her and she's *away* from me. Even if it is only across a yard, I'm still nervous.

What if she gets bullied?

What if someone kidnaps her?

What if someone accidentally kicks her in the face in that jump house?

"Relax," Dallas says, as if he were reading my mind. "I promise they're not as breakable as you think."

Willow nods. "Just wait until you have a little one. You'll truly be crazy and uptight. I'm pretty sure I'll be the epitome of one of those helicopter moms."

I glance over at Sierra, and her attention is on Molly, too.

I beam with pride.

I can't wait to have babies with her.

"I'll be there, right beside you," Lauren adds. "I thought being a nurse would make me more easygoing, but nope, I'm paranoid."

Gage throws his head back. "You have no idea."

My focus switches to Rex when he plops down in Maven's abandoned chair.

"Hey, what are you doing here?" Sierra asks.

"Carolina," is all he says while looking exhausted.

Sierra glances around. "Where is she?"

"Volunteering around here somewhere," he answers, rolling his neck back and forth. "She forced me to come do all the heavy lifting."

"Speaking of Carolina," Kyle says, unable to control his

grin as we all watch Carolina come our way, a stern face pointed toward Rex.

"Oh shit," Rex says, rubbing a hand against his brow. "I might be in trouble."

"Hey, Carolina," Lauren sings.

Carolina smiles and waves at us before whipping her attention to Rex.

Rex throws his arms up. "Hey! Don't get mad at a man for taking a break and saying hello to his family!" He taps his thigh. "You can sit and chat if you want."

She pushes up her glasses before flipping him the bird.

Rex rises from his chair. "I'll see you guys when my boss lets me clock out." He throws his arm over her shoulders as they walk away.

"Are they a thing?" Chloe asks, her eyes on them.

Sierra shakes her head. "I wish they were. Rex is too chicken to pull the trigger."

Our Rex talk is interrupted by Maven and Molly storming in our direction, and I tense up, waiting for Molly to fall, break a leg, scrape a knee—something with how fast she's moving.

She makes it to us, safe and sound.

"We need ice cream money!" Maven shouts. "Pretty, pretty please!"

"And face-painting money!" Molly adds, sticking out her lower lip. "I want to get a unicorn face!"

"All right," Dallas groans. "You talked me into it."

He hands Maven money while I do the same with Molly as she jumps up and down in front of me.

They take off running, hand in hand.

That settles my heart.

Willow bumps Sierra's shoulder. "Forewarning: that paint is a pain in the ass to get off their face."

CHAPTER FORTY

Sierra

"WHERE ARE WE GOING?" I ask, rolling down the passenger window and sticking my head out like a little Chihuahua when Maliki turns onto a road that doesn't lead to Down Home.

"I have an idea," is his explanation as he continues driving.

I pull my head back into the car. "What kind of idea?"

"A good idea."

"I have an idea. How about you stop being vague?"

He chuckles and keeps his eyes on the road, not revealing said idea. I'm jabbering on about how I hate when he's vague and secretive, and I'm not a person who has patience when he pulls in the drive of an old farmhouse. It belonged to our town librarian before she passed a few months ago—in the library, not the house. Otherwise, I would be telling him to cut and run.

I don't do ghosts.

The home has been vacant since her death, and my mom mentioned it was recently listed for sale.

He shifts the car in park, cutting the engine. "I spoke with a realtor who found a few homes for us to view. If you're not a fan of this one, we can check out the others, but my vote is here."

His vote?

I cock my head to the side. "Your vote for what?"

He gestures toward the home. "Come on. Let's take a look."

We get out of the car at the same time and walk toward the front porch. It's a beautiful wraparound, begging for rocking chairs and children running around with lemonade in their hands.

I close my eyes, visualizing the scene.

"Tell me if you hate the house *or* the idea I'm about to pitch," he says before raising his hands as if he were staring through a camera lens. "You're an expert on beautifying older places without removing the authenticity of them. What do you think about buying and renovating it together?"

My heart dances in my chest.

This is the sweetest thing anyone has ever done for me.

He's mentioned moving from the apartment a few times, and as much as the idea thrills me, I've never pushed it since finding real estate here is difficult.

I clasp my hand around his forearm. "You have no idea how much I'd love that." I kiss his arm before catching his hand in mine and moving around the yard. "I could make this a home for us." I eyeball everything—from the foundation to the windows to the brick—taking mental notes of the makeover I'd give it.

Maliki leads me up to the porch and punches in the code on the padlock when we're finished looking outside.

I fall in love with it more when we walk into the foyer.

The bones of the home are beautiful, sturdy, and the ideas rushing through my brain ignite me. I continue my babbling—knocking down walls, changing windows, updating cabinets—while he laughs.

I lose his hold when we hit the fourth bedroom and whip around. "This can be Molly's bedroom. She can help me design it. I'll turn her into a little designer, just like me."

His lips smack into mine. "Does this mean it's a yes?"

I jump into his arms. "It's definitely a yes."

CHAPTER FORTY-ONE

Sierra

6 Months Later

"HAVE YOU SEEN MY TUTU? I can't find my tutu?" Molly yells from her bedroom.

"I'll check the laundry!" I shout.

I glance around the house in awe of my work as I walk through the kitchen and living room—as I've done so many times.

I love our new home.

We spent so many hours creating it into a place perfect for us … for our family.

Our home renovation gave me remodel jobs. As people saw it, they wanted to do the same in their homes. I'm remodeling two homes now, and I have a six-month waiting list.

I sift through the folded laundry. "Found it!" I hold it up and rush to her bedroom.

It's pink and ballerina-themed with a sparkling chandelier hanging from the ceiling.

"Do you have your bag?" I ask.

She nods and shoves the tutu into it when I hand it to her.

Jessa is picking her up for dance class. Our co-parenting has improved. We attend Molly's recitals and school functions without a glare sent in my direction. The new boyfriend is nice and definitely tames her.

Maliki and I kiss her good-bye, and she runs out to Jessa's waiting car.

I flop down on the couch and yawn. "Have I mentioned how comfy this thing is?"

One thing I was adamant on was a comfy couch. Growing up, we always had stiff, expensive furniture that felt like cardboard. Our sectional is pillow-topped, making you never want to get up.

Maliki chuckles and falls next to me. "You pick the best, babe."

I turn to rest my head on his lap and look up at him with a smirk. "Yes, I know this. Care to send any more compliments my way? I'll take them all."

He runs his hand through my hair—one of my favorite things he does—and I shut my eyes. "I'm so happy we're out of the pub apartment. I would've settled for a hard couch to have this peace with you. Plus, this home provides us with plenty of room for little ones."

My eyes fly open. "Little ones? Really? More than just Molly?"

He continues massaging my head. "If that's what you want. I know I do."

"Uh, I would have your baby right now."

His hand stops, moving to my face, and he cups my chin. "I'd make a baby with you right now."

He leans back when I rise to straddle him.

"Look at me, taming the wild bartender," I say, winding my arms around his neck.

He strokes my cheek. "Look at me, claiming the sexiest, smartest, most amazing woman in the world."

I place my hand over the one resting on my face. "I love you."

He kisses the tip of my nose. "I fucking love you."

"Now that the sweet stuff is out of the way, can we jump into the baby-making? I'm all for that, please and thank you."

He picks me up under my elbows and tosses me back onto the couch but stops, his lips tilting into a grin. "I forgot to show you what I found. You're going to love this."

I raise a brow. "Probably not as much as us having sex right now."

He tugs something out of his back pocket. "I was going through the rest of my office boxes and look at what I found."

He holds it up, and I see my young face.

"Oh my God, shut up!" It's my driver's license he confiscated when I snuck into his bar at eighteen.

"Damn, look at that sexy woman." He holds it out to inspect it. "I think we should frame it. We'll say it's the day Daddy met Mommy."

I grin. "I like that. Now, let's start trying."

KEEP UP WITH THE BLUE BEECH SERIES

All books can be read as standalones

Just A Fling
(Hudson and Stella's story)
Just Onc Night
(Dallas and Willow's story)
Just Exes
(Gage and Lauren's story)
Just Neighbors
(Kyle and Chloe's story)
Just Roommates
(Maliki and Sierra's story)
Just Friends
(Rex and Carolina's story)

Blue Beech Second Generation
Only Rivals
Only Coworkers

ALSO BY CHARITY FERRELL

BLUE BEECH SERIES

(each book can be read as a standalone)

Just A Fling

Just One Night

Just Exes

Just Neighbors

Just Roommates

Just Friends

TWISTED FOX SERIES

Stirred

Shaken

Straight Up

Chaser

Last Round

STANDALONES

Bad For You

Beneath Our Faults

Pop Rock

Pretty and Reckless

Revive Me

Wild Thoughts

RISKY DUET

Risky

Worth The Risk

ACKNOWLEDGMENTS

Thank you to everyone in the book community. I'm an introvert, but as I've started to open up and meet you, you've made me so comfortable and happy. I'm so thankful for the friendships and support you've given me.

Jill, you play *so* many roles in my life. Friend, the best assistant ever, and person who tells me to calm the hell down. I'm so thankful we found each other, and you're never getting rid of me.

Jovana, you're an editing genius, and are always there to answer any questions I have.

Mark, the other half, the person who deals with me, my dog baby daddy.

Zoe and Paris, my four-legged kids that can make any day brighter.

Lindee Robinson, your photo was perfect for the cover, and thank you for working with me.

AC Parker, you were the perfect Maliki.

ABOUT THE AUTHOR

Charity Ferrell is a Wall Street Journal and USA Today bestselling author. She resides in Indianapolis, Indiana with her boyfriend and two fur babies. Her passion is writing about broken people finding love while adding a dash of humor and heartbreak. Angst is her happy place.

When she's not writing, she's on a Starbucks run, shopping online, or spending time with her family.

www.charityferrell.com

Made in the USA
Columbia, SC
15 May 2022

60431931R00183